CW00485007

TIM WAGGONER

WE WILL RISE

This is a **FLAME TREE PRESS** book

Text copyright © 2022 Tim Waggoner

FLAME TREE PRESS
6 Melbray Mews, London, SW6 3NS, UK
flametreepress.com

US sales, distribution and warehouse:
Simon & Schuster
simonandschuster.biz

UK distribution and warehouse:
Marston Book Services Ltd
marston.co.uk

Publisher's Note: This is a work of fiction. Names, characters, places, and incidents are a product of the author's imagination. Locales and public names are sometimes used for atmospheric purposes. Any resemblance to actual people, living or dead, or to businesses, companies, events, institutions, or locales is completely coincidental.

Thanks to the Flame Tree Press team.

The cover is created by Flame Tree Studio with thanks to Nik Keevil and Shutterstock.com. The font families used are Avenir and Bembo.

Flame Tree Press is an imprint of Flame Tree Publishing Ltd

flametreepublishing.com

A copy of the CIP data for this book is available from the British Library and the Library of Congress.

HB ISBN: 978-1-78758-524-9
PB ISBN: 978-1-78758-522-5
ebook ISBN: 978-1-78758-526-3

Printed and bound in Great Britain by Clays Ltd, Elcograf S.p.A

TIM WAGGONER

WE WILL RISE

FLAME TREE PRESS
London & New York

This one's for you.
Whether you're new to my fiction or you've
been reading my stuff for a while now, know that
I'm grateful for each and every one of you.
Except that bastard Jerry.
He knows what he did.

From dust we came, to dust we returned,
and from dust we rise again.
The Monad

CHAPTER ONE

In Echo Springs, it started with Eddie Herrera.

Eddie worked third shift at Steiner Tire and Rubber. STR, as the town's residents referred to it, was the largest employer in Echo Springs, and had been since the 1950s. The company had been downsizing some in recent years, and Eddie – who was on the wrong side of forty – was grateful he still had a job. A lot of his coworkers had been laid off, and he kept wondering when his time would come. He had a family to support, and the thought of losing his job made him feel sick. So he did his damnedest not to think about it.

He was always exhausted by the time he got home in the morning, but despite how much he wanted to, he didn't fall into bed right away. He and Anna had two boys, ages six and eight, and he liked to see them off to school in the mornings. He often made breakfast for everyone, and today it had been waffles. Once the boys were on the bus and headed to school, Anna had taken his hand and led him to the bedroom. He was never too tired to spend time with his love. An hour later, Anna got dressed, gave him a quick kiss goodbye, and headed off to do the week's grocery shopping, while he hit the shower. He liked to wash the night's work off him before he slept, and standing under the water relaxed him, got him ready for sleep.

As he stepped under the warm-almost-hot spray, he sighed in contentment. His balls ached pleasantly, and he was sorry Anna had gone. It would've been nice to go for round two. Maybe if he was still awake when she got home....

Smiling, he squeezed body wash onto his hands and began rubbing it on his skin and hair. He still marveled that he was capable of enjoying water like this. For a large part of his life, he'd *loathed* water and had wanted as little to do with it as possible. But thanks to Anna's love, support, and understanding – not to mention a significant amount of therapy – not only could he tolerate being in water, he actually liked it. It was practically a goddamned miracle. In fact, he liked standing in the shower and feeling the warm spray caress his body so much that he often lost track of time and would remain in the shower until the water started to grow cold. He knew it was a waste of money – water wasn't free, after all – but he couldn't help himself. It just felt so damn good.

As he began scrubbing his hair, he started singing Queen's 'Bohemian Rhapsody'. He was an admittedly terrible singer, but he was alone in the house right now, so he could belt out tunes at whatever volume he wanted, without either Anna or the boys saying he sounded like a dying dog. After a couple lines, he noticed something smelled strange, and he broke off his song. He inhaled deeply through his nose and detected the fruit-mixed-with-menthol odor of his body wash. But there was a second smell beneath that, a rank scent of dead fish and rotting vegetation that he hadn't smelled for almost thirty years, but which he instantly recognized. His bowels turned to ice, his pulse galloped, and his stomach gave a queasy lurch, as if it were going to eject the waffles he'd eaten. It was a struggle, but he managed to keep his food down.

God, that *smell*....

Lake water. And not just any lake: White Stone Lake.

He had to get out of here – *now*. He didn't bother turning the water off, didn't even consider doing so. All he wanted was to get away from this horrible stench, grab a towel, and rub his skin raw until he got the stink off him. But the shower door wouldn't budge. It was a simple door – two overlapping panes of clear glass that ran along a metal track, the same as millions of others. It had no lock. Who the hell would need to lock themselves inside a shower? But no matter how hard he pulled, he couldn't move either pane, couldn't even make the glass shake. It was like the bottoms of the panes were embedded in concrete. While he fought with the door, the rancid lake water smell grew stronger, and the spray coming from the showerhead began to grow cold, the water turning thick and brackish. He heard a voice then, the words distorted and wavery, as if the speaker were underwater.

Hey, Eddie. Miss me?

The water was ice-cold now, but the chill that gripped Eddie's heart upon hearing his brother's voice was far colder. A memory came to him unbidden: a small boat in the middle of a large lake, a man sitting at the stern, fishing rod resting easily in his hands, his gaze fixed on the red tip of the bobber twenty feet away. Two young boys were also in the boat, one sitting in the middle, the other at the bow. They both had simple cane poles, and their bobbers floated only ten feet from the boat, if that.

Eddie – who at seven was the older brother by four years – hated sitting in the middle. He should be at the bow, not Randy. It was a much more awesome place to sit, and as the oldest, it should've been his place by right. But before they'd left the dock, Randy had whined and begged until Dad let him sit at the bow. As bad as giving up the bow seat was, being forced to fish with a cane pole was worse. He was big enough to use a rod and reel, but on shore Dad had taken him aside and explained that Randy wasn't old enough to use anything but a cane pole, and a small one at that.

He's not strong enough yet, not coordinated.

Eddie hadn't seen what any of this had to do with him, but then his father had added, *Randy will be jealous of you if you get to use a rod-and-reel and he doesn't. So I need you to use a cane pole too.*

Eddie had protested that he'd been allowed to use a rod-and-reel the last time he'd gone fishing with his dad.

It was just the two of us then, Dad had said. *Now Randy is with us, and I need you to step up and be a good big brother. Can you do that for me?*

Randy had wanted to ask Dad why *he* wasn't going to use a cane pole too. Wouldn't Randy get jealous of him as well? But he knew better than to backtalk his father. The man was kind and gentle – until you showed him any disrespect. Then he got mad. *Really* mad. So Eddie had nodded, reluctantly, and Dad had smiled and put one of his big hands on Eddie's shoulder.

Good boy.

The boys both wore puffy orange lifejackets, but their father didn't. *I'm a strong swimmer,* he'd explained. Eddie thought he was a good swimmer too, so why did he need a lifejacket? But he didn't argue that point either.

They'd been out on the water for what seemed like hours, and none of them had caught anything. Even more irritating, Randy kept casting his line too hard, and the worm – which Eddie had to slide onto the hook for him – would fly off every time. Whenever Randy pulled in his line to check the hook, which was often, Eddie had to bait it again. Randy also had a habit of humming tunelessly as he watched his bobber rising up and down with the motion of the water, and the sound was driving Eddie crazy. If Dad hadn't been there, he would've shouted for Randy to shut the hell up – and he would definitely say *hell* to underscore how angry he was. But all he could do now was glare at his little brother and grind his teeth. He was so irritated at his brother that when he noticed Randy fiddling with the buckles on his lifejacket, he didn't say anything about it, although as a *good big brother*, he knew he should have. But right then he didn't care if the little jerk fell into the water, sank, and never came back up. Eddie's life had been so much less complicated, so much *better*, before Randy's arrival.

So Eddie did his best to ignore his brother, and he didn't know anything was wrong until he felt the boat rock and heard a splash. Maybe Randy had gotten bored, tried to look over the side of the boat to see if he could spot any fish, and fell in. Or maybe he'd gotten a bite – or thought he had – stood up to try to pull his line in, lost his balance, and fell overboard. Whichever was the case, Randy was no longer seated in the bow. His cane pole floated on the lake's surface, and an instant later it was joined by Randy's lifejacket. Randy had messed with the buckles and straps so much that the jacket had slipped off of him in the water.

Eddie had heard that drowning people always rose to the surface three times before sinking for good, but Randy didn't come up even once. Dad jumped into the water immediately after Randy went overboard, and dove downward, searching for his younger son, but it was no use. Eddie's brother was gone. Later, a rescue crew would drag that part of the lake and recover Randy's body, so at least his family could bury him, but it wouldn't be much comfort.

Neither of Eddie's parents blamed him for Randy's death. At least, they never said so out loud. But Eddie had blamed himself, and although as the years passed he'd come to understand that what had happened had been a terrible accident and there was nothing he could've done to prevent it, he still blamed himself deep down. It was why he'd made sure the boys had started swimming lessons early on – so they wouldn't end up like poor Randy. Sometimes his guilt manifested in his dreams, and he'd be the one who fell into the lake and drowned instead of his brother, and as he sank down in the cold, dark depths, he'd hear – from a great distance – Randy laughing.

After that day, he'd never gone out onto the water in a boat again, had never gone swimming. When he took his boys to the pool, he always made sure to stay several feet from the edge. It was as if he feared that if he got too close, the water might surge forth, grab hold of him, and pull him in and drag him down and hold him under until he died the same way Randy had.

The brackish water blasting from the showerhead grew even colder, and the shock of it brought Eddie back to the present. Water pooled around his feet, the level rising fast, and he realized that the drain was clogged. He shouted for Anna, even though he knew she probably wasn't home yet, and when she didn't answer, he began pounding on the shower door with his fists. He knew that if he managed to break the glass, there was a good chance he'd be seriously cut, but right then he didn't care. He was in the grip of full-blown panic, and his body reacted on its own. He slammed his fists against the glass over and over, continually shouting Anna's name, his voice eventually devolving into wordless cries of despair. The shower door shook under the impact of his blows, but the glass didn't so much as crack. The water level in the shower had risen to his ankles by now, and frigid water continued blasting from the showerhead in an arctic torrent. His body shivered uncontrollably and his teeth chattered, and he wondered if the cold would kill him before the water rose high enough to drown him. He hoped it would. Any death would be better than drowning.

6 · TIM WAGGONER

Drowning's not so bad. Let me show you.

A pair of small hands gripped Eddie's ankles and with surprising strength yanked him downward. The shower floor seemed to melt away to nothing, and Eddie found himself descending into cold darkness. He gasped reflexively as he went down and drew water into his lungs. He coughed, inhaled, coughed again, took in more water. His lungs burned, became heavy, and his panic gave way to animalistic terror. He hadn't gone swimming since Randy's death, but his body remembered how, and it thrashed in the water, trying desperately to push itself toward air. But those small hands – a boy's hands, *Randy's* hands – were clamped tight around his ankles, and it was as if a great weight was dragging him downward, one so heavy that he could not fight it. Water roared in his ears, but despite this, he had no trouble hearing his brother's voice, the sound that of a boy, the words eerily adult.

Try to relax. Even if I let you go, it wouldn't matter. There's no surface here. No bottom, either. Just water in all directions, extending outward forever and ever. Once you get used to it, it's really quite peaceful.

Eddie couldn't make a sound. His mouth, throat, and lungs were filled with water, but he spoke to Randy in his mind.

Don't do this. Please! I have a wife and two sons....

He'd been descending deeper the entire time, but now he picked up speed, as if Randy was pulling him faster, eager to take him as far into the inky blackness as possible before he died.

I'm sorry, Eddie. But this is the way it has to be. Your time has come. Everybody's has. And there's nothing you or anyone else can do about it.

A pause, and then—

Who am I kidding? I'm not sorry. I fucking love this! You're just getting what you deserve, brother. And so will everyone else.

Eddie's lungs spasmed as they attempted vainly to draw in one final breath of air, and then they grew still. A darkness came for him then, one that was blacker than the water that surrounded him, the water that had become his entire universe. This darkness filled him, swept him away, and he was gone. And in his last seconds, did he feel some small measure of relief that it was over, that he'd finally repaid a debt to his brother that was long overdue?

Maybe.

*　　*　　*

When Anna came home, she carried in plastic bags filled with groceries, placed them on a kitchen counter, and began putting items away in cupboards and the refrigerator. She was surprised to hear the muffled sound of the running shower drifting down the hall from the master bedroom. Eddie didn't usually take showers this long. His back muscles must've really gotten jacked up at work last night, and he wanted to spend as much time as possible beneath the hot spray to ease the soreness. He was increasingly having trouble with his back as he got older, and although she'd gently urged – *not* nagged – him to see a doctor about it, he'd ignored her advice. She supposed she would have to be a bit more forceful, maybe even make an appointment for him and drag his ass there if she had to.

When the groceries were all put away, she headed to their bedroom. She went inside and decided that it might be a good idea to give Eddie a spoonful of sugar before she started in on his needing to see a doctor about his back. They'd already made love once this morning, but tired as Eddie might be, she knew he wouldn't turn down a repeat performance. She stepped out of her clothes and padded barefoot to the master bathroom. She opened the door, expecting to be met with a wave of hot air, but instead she shivered. It was goddamned cold in here! What the hell?

Eddie lay on the shower floor, curled into a fetal position, shower spray blasting his unmoving body, and even before she threw open the door, she knew her husband was dead.

CHAPTER TWO

The baby was crying, Mari was sure of it. The only problem was, there *was* no baby.

She stood at the kitchen stove cooking eggs in a pan – over easy, just the way her husband liked them – body frozen, listening. Eggs sizzled and popped, the stove fan whirred, Lewis opened and closed the fridge as he got creamer out for his coffee. And above all of this, the soft, mournful wail of a baby, upset that it was alone and not understanding why.

Not real, she told herself. *Not. Real.*

She took hold of a plastic spatula with a shaky hand, flipped the eggs, put the spatula back down on the counter. She reached up and switched the stove fan to high, hoping to block out the sound that didn't exist. It didn't help. The baby continued crying, even louder now as if it knew what she was doing and refused to be blocked out.

Not *it.*

Noelle.

Soft lips brushed the back of Mari's neck, and she spun around to see who it was. Lewis, mug in hand, stepped back, expression a mix of amusement and apology.

"Sorry, babe. Didn't mean to startle you."

Of course he didn't, but that didn't stop her snapping at him.

"Give a girl a warning next time."

"I *said* I was sorry."

She scrutinized her husband's face, searching for any sign that he heard the baby crying. She saw none, but maybe he was doing his best to ignore it, like she was. The only way to know for certain would be to ask, but if she did that and he *didn't* hear the baby, he'd think something was wrong with her, that she might need her medication adjusted, should return to therapy. She didn't want to deal with that right now, didn't want to face the possibility that she was losing it again, so she said nothing about the baby.

"The eggs will be done in a minute. Go sit at the table and I'll bring them to you."

Lewis was a tall Black man in his forties, stocky, with a round face and mustache. He wasn't what most people would call handsome, but she thought he was good looking in a big teddy-bear kind of way. He was dressed for work in a black polo shirt with the Car-Care logo stitched on the left side and jeans. He wore only white socks on his feet, though. His heavy work boots, stained with motor oil, were waiting for him in the garage. Mari wouldn't let him bring the filthy things into her house.

Lewis left the kitchen and entered the dining room. He liked to read the news on his phone and sip his coffee in the morning. Mari was a substitute elementary school teacher, and on the days she was called in to work, she left much earlier than Lewis, whose business didn't open until 10:00 a.m. He often skipped breakfast on those days, which was why, when the school didn't need her, she always made sure to make him a little something – eggs or pancakes – in the morning before he left. She wasn't a big breakfast eater, but she would usually have a little of whatever she served Lewis. One egg, a single pancake, and sometimes she wouldn't finish that. But she liked sitting with him at the table, sipping her own coffee, and watching him eat.

Today, however, she didn't intend to sit with him. The baby's cries had grown louder, and she knew she wouldn't be able to hide her distress from Lewis. If he thought something was wrong, he'd insist on her calling the doctor. She'd refuse – she was goddamned sick to death of doctors – and they'd end up in a shouting match and the morning would be ruined.

So when the eggs were finished, she slid them onto a plate, sprinkled a bit of salt and pepper on them, got a fork from the utensil drawer, and carried Lewis's breakfast into the dining room. She set it on the table before him and gave him a quick kiss on the side of the head. He had the Associated Press website on his phone. He liked the AP because it presented news in an absolutely neutral way. *I don't like being told what to think,* he'd say when explaining his choice of news outlet to people. And when he was reading, he became so absorbed that he barely noticed the world around him. When she left the room after serving him his eggs, he said nothing. If he noticed her go, he likely figured she was returning to the kitchen to get her own breakfast or maybe heading to the bathroom or something. He wouldn't notice if she didn't return right away, and even if he did, he would think nothing of it. He certainly wouldn't come looking for her. She hoped.

Mari was a Black woman in her late thirties – a few years younger than Lewis. A small woman, short and petite, and her long straight hair hung to the middle of her back. She was nearsighted, but while she had contacts, she hated wearing them, didn't like the thought of something artificial touching her eyes, so she wore her glasses much of the time. Besides, the glasses made her look more like a teacher. Although she hadn't been called to sub today, she'd dressed for work just in case. She had on a light blue sweater over a sleeveless black top, black slacks, and flats. No jewelry except for her wedding ring. She tended not to wear any around the house. She didn't see the point.

She passed through the kitchen. Normally she would've turned off the stove fan, but she let it keep running. She wanted its noise to mask any sounds she might make.

She and Lewis lived in a small ranch house in an upper middle-class neighborhood on the east side of Echo Springs, north of the river. They could've afforded a larger house, but this was enough for the two of them right now. They'd planned on moving to a bigger place once the baby—

She stopped that thought in its tracks. Whenever she thought about Noelle she cried, and if she started now, Lewis would be sure to realize something was wrong. She needed to keep her shit together, at least until he left for work. After that, she could cry all she wanted, all fucking day if she felt like it. It wouldn't be the first time.

She moved out of the kitchen and into the hallway that led to the bedrooms. The baby's (*Noelle's*) cries were louder now, and Mari's pulse thrummed hummingbird-fast in her throat. She felt disoriented, disconnected, as if she'd somehow stepped out of the physical world and into a dream. Her stomach roiled and she was glad she hadn't eaten anything yet and hadn't had her first cup of coffee, else it would've all come up now.

She passed the hall bathroom, her footfalls soundless on the thin carpeting. There were two bedrooms at the end of the hall, opposite one another. One was hers and Lewis's. The other....

Mari and Lewis had been married five years before deciding to start a family. She'd always found that phrase strange. Weren't a husband and wife already a family, albeit a small one? She'd shared this thought with Lewis once, and he'd grinned. *It's more socially acceptable than saying 'get knocked up'.*

A paragon of class, her man.

They stopped using birth control, but otherwise made no change in their sex life. Mari had read a number of articles that advised avoiding stress when trying to conceive. And working too hard at it – while fun – often proved stressful for a couple, especially if they didn't conceive right away. Still, Mari was hopeful, and she resigned her full-time teaching job at Echo Springs Elementary and started subbing to make it easier for her to stop working altogether when the baby came. Maybe more than one. Twins ran on her mother's side of the family.

A year went by, then two. Mari changed her mind about not focusing too much on trying to have a baby. She decided the problem was they weren't focusing hard enough. She visualized a child growing inside her, kept a journal in which she wrote to her baby, charted her most fertile days and only had sex with Lewis then. She talked him into getting the second bedroom – which up to that point they'd used as a home office – ready for a baby. They bought and assembled a crib, put in a changing table, laid in supplies of diapers, wet wipes, baby power, cream for a sore bottom, and stuffed animals. *Lots* of stuffed animals. They painted the walls ocean blue and then painted sea creatures – fish, squid, lobsters, sharks, whales, all happy and smiling.

Still no baby.

They visited a fertility doctor to make sure their respective equipment was in working order, which it was.

Sometimes it just goes like this, the doctor had said. *I know it's hard to keep being patient, but that's really the best advice I can give you. Often, once a couple has come to see me, they relax and end up becoming pregnant before I can treat them any further.* He'd smiled kindly. *Let's hope that happens with you.*

And it did.

Less than two weeks after seeing the specialist, Mari missed her period. She bought a home pregnancy test, peed on a plastic strip, and it confirmed she was pregnant. She'd been elated, as had Lewis, and they grew more excited every day after that. Mari had wanted desperately to tell all their friends and family the good news, but her obstetrician advised them to wait a few months.

Just in case, she'd said.

Logically, Mari had understood this precaution, but emotionally she hated it. She didn't believe in planning for failure, even as a contingency. She believed in remaining positive, that negative thinking produced a negative outcome. Still, she did as the doctor suggested, and a couple months later, when she found herself sitting on a toilet bowl filled with blood, she was glad she had.

That had been seven months ago, and she'd only recently started to feel something like her previous self. Her doctor said miscarriages weren't uncommon, that they were the body's way of dealing with a nonviable pregnancy before things got too far along. She hated that word. *Nonviable.* As if what she'd lost had been nothing more than a seed that had failed to take root. What she'd lost had been a *child*, goddamn it. And although the tissue her body had ejected was never examined by a doctor, she knew it would've continued growing into a beautiful little girl called Noelle, named after Mari's grandmother. She grieved her daughter's loss as intensely as if she'd been born, and that was something Lewis couldn't understand. He was sad, sure, but he was far from devastated. *He* hadn't fallen into a deep, dark, suicidal depression. *He* hadn't needed anti-depressants and anti-anxiety meds. *He* hadn't needed to see a psychiatrist. He loved her, she had no doubt about that, and she couldn't have made it through these last few months without his support. Even so, she was still ultimately alone in her grief.

How could it be otherwise? It was *her* body that had failed to provide a safe place for their daughter to grow, not his.

Lewis had wanted to try again, but if she wasn't willing to, for whatever reason, he was happy to adopt instead. He'd been adopted, and he was perfectly comfortable with their going this route. Mari had no objection to adopting, but regardless of which path they chose, she wasn't ready to let go of Noelle, not yet. Lewis said he understood, and while she very much doubted that, she was grateful for his patience.

But as hard as the last several months had been, she'd never experienced hallucinations like this. She'd had nightmares, sure, a shit-ton, but that was all. This sound, though, this wailing despair.... It was so *real*.

When she reached the baby's room – for that's how she still thought of it – she paused. In the first weeks after the miscarriage, she'd come here often. She'd go inside, sit in the rocking chair they'd bought at an antique store, one she'd imagined nursing Noelle in and holding her gently while she slept afterward. She'd rock slowly and gaze at the crib, empty now and empty forevermore. Sometimes she'd do this for hours, even coming here in the middle of the night when she couldn't sleep. Her psychiatrist had urged her to stay out of Noelle's room, said that by spending time there she was wallowing in her grief instead of working to come to terms with it. She'd taken the doctor's advice – reluctantly – and she hadn't entered Noelle's room since. If she went inside now, would she be taking a giant step backward in her recovery? Would it be better for her to turn around, go back to the dining room, and tell Lewis what she was experiencing? Maybe her psychiatrist could fit her in for an emergency session, during which she'd tell Mari that she was going to be fine, that an occasional hallucination was nothing to worry about, that she only needed a slight adjustment to her meds. Then again, the doctor might just as easily decide Mari needed to spend some quality time in a hospital psych ward. Regardless of what sort of treatment her psychiatrist would prescribe, Mari had to know what was behind this door. She had to see for herself what, if anything, was making this noise.

She reached out and took hold of the doorknob. When her fingers closed around the metal – which felt far colder than she'd expected –

the wailing stopped. It didn't dribble away to muffled sobs and hitching breaths. It cut out all at once, as if a switch had been thrown. Maybe the sound had only been in her head, and now that she was ready to confront the hallucination, it had dissipated like morning mist burned away by the first rays of the rising sun.

No, she thought. *Noelle stopped crying because she knows I'm here…knows Mommy's here.*

She opened the door, stepped inside, and slowly, softly, closed it behind her.

Although she knew what waited for her within, had sensed it with a mother's instinct, she still gasped when she saw that the cradle was no longer empty. Trembling, she stepped to the side of the crib, gripped the wooden rail with her hands, and leaned over to peer inside. A baby lay on the small mattress, a tiny thing in a white onesie covered with polka dots of various colors and sizes. Her arms and legs were bare, but a pair of adorable little socks covered her feet. Curly wisps of black hair clung to her head and she had the most gorgeous brown eyes. She gazed up at Mari with those eyes, and her tiny baby lips stretched into a smile and a happy gurgle escaped her mouth. Unrestrained joy filled Mari's heart, the sensation so powerful that for an instant she couldn't breathe.

She recognizes me! Praise God!

Wait. There was no blanket in the crib. It was early February, and while so far Ohio had enjoyed a mild winter, it was still cold out. Since this room wasn't in use, Lewis had closed the vents. Why waste money heating an empty room? Mari found it chilly in there, and she was fully dressed. Noelle must have been freezing.

She reached into the crib, took hold of her daughter, and lifted her. She stepped back from the crib and pressed Noelle against her chest to warm the child. The poor thing felt like a block of ice, and Mari hurried over to the dresser to get her a pair of warm cotton zip-up PJs. But halfway there, she stopped. She and Lewis hadn't bought any baby clothes. She'd wanted to wait to see how big the baby would be once she was born before buying any. She'd figured they could make do with blankets and onesies until they purchased some outfits. But after the miscarriage, there had been no point in buying baby clothes. Or baby blankets, for that matter. There was nothing in the room Mari could use to cover the baby.

The baby—

who shouldn't exist—

because she'd never been born.

But that was nonsense. Noelle was here, in her arms, exactly where she should be. And she was cold. So very cold.

Mari started toward the bedroom door, intending to carry Noelle to the linen closet in the hallway and find a blanket to warm her. But she only took a few steps before Noelle began squirming in her arms. The girl was stronger than Mari expected, far stronger than an infant should be, and for a horrifying moment, Mari feared she might lose hold of her and drop her. But Noelle grabbed her sweater with her tiny hands and clung tight. Then, moving with feral speed, Noelle crawled upward until she reached Mari's face. The baby continued holding on to Mari's sweater with her left hand as she stretched her right toward Mari's mouth. Tiny fingers clawed at her lips, their sharp little nails carving bloody furrows into the flesh. Mari was so startled that she let go of Noelle, but the child maintained her grip on the sweater and did not fall. She continued clawing at Mari's lips, her motions frantic, as if she were desperate for her mother to open her mouth. Noelle's features were contorted in an expression of anger, and fury blazed in her eyes.

Let me in!

Noelle's lips didn't move, but Mari heard her daughter's voice in her mind, tone shrill, words sharp.

I want to go home!

Noelle forced her tiny hand past Mari's lips and jammed her fingers into her mother's mouth. The baby's skin was soft and smooth, but cold as ice, so cold it burned Mari's tongue.

With a wordless cry of triumph, the baby hauled itself higher and shoved her hand further into Mari's mouth, across her tongue, reaching toward the back of her throat. Noelle's hand was slick with blood from Mari's wounded lips, and a metallic taste like pennies filled her mouth. That, plus the pressure of her daughter's hand made her gag. At first she was so stunned by what was happening that she couldn't think, but then Noelle's words – how could an infant speak? – replayed in her mind.

Let me in! I want to go home!

Mari was struck by a sudden wave of nausea that had nothing to do with the fact that her infant daughter was trying to ram her arm down her throat. She understood what Noelle was trying to do. What was the single greatest shock any human being could experience? Growing for nine months within the warm dark safety of Mother's womb, only to be cruelly evicted and thrust into a world of harsh bright light and cold unfeeling air. Noelle wanted nothing more to do with this world. She wanted to go home. And home was inside her mother.

With a cry of disgust, Mari grabbed hold of her daughter's tiny waist and pulled. Noelle's hand was yanked from her mouth, and the baby shrieked her frustration as Mari held her at arm's length. Noelle thrashed, kicked her legs, clawed at the air.

Bad Mommy! Bad, bad Mommy!

Mari felt a revulsion so deep, so strong, that it was close to blind, unreasoning hatred. She hurled Noelle away from her, no longer able to bear the feel of her daughter's cold, squirming body in her hands. The instant Noelle left her grasp she regretted her action, and she tried to catch hold of her child, wanted nothing more than to draw her back to her breast and tell her that she was sorry, and that she'd never do anything to hurt her ever again, so help her Jesus. But it was too late. Screaming now, as much in anger as fear, Noelle flew toward the crib. Her back struck the rail and she bounced off and fell. Mari ran forward, hoping to catch her before she hit the floor, but even as she started moving, she knew she wouldn't be fast enough. But then Noelle's screaming cut off, and the infant – mere inches from the floor – disappeared. One instant she was there, face crimson with fury, and then she was gone. Mari stared at the spot where Noelle should've landed, as if expecting the girl to reappear there. But she didn't.

Mari was relieved, but she also felt a crushing sense of loss. Her baby had come to her, if only for a moment, and now she was gone again. Mari trembled. She was losing her goddamned mind. She needed to talk to her psychiatrist, needed to check her ass into a hospital. Anyone who experienced a hallucination so vivid, so fucking *real*, had to have something seriously wrong with her.

She became aware of her lips stinging then, and she reached up to touch them. When she brought her fingers away and looked at them, she saw the tips were slick with blood from where Noelle had scratched her. The blood was real, and if that was the case....

Mari fell to her knees and sobbed.

CHAPTER THREE

Faizan Barakat *hated* Accounting 101. Not because of the math required – he found that relatively simple. What he hated was that the class started at 8:00 a.m. every Monday and Wednesday. That was what he got for putting off registering for classes until the last minute. The only open classes left were those scheduled at times no one wanted. And his only other M-W class was a Psych 102, and that met in the evenings, so every Monday and Wednesday he had to get up early, drive to class, come home, eat lunch and do homework for several hours – or more likely, play video games and mess around on YouTube – and then drive back to his college for his evening class and hope he managed to stay awake though it. He was currently a business major, but he wasn't really sure what he wanted to do with his life yet, so he ultimately might not need Accounting at all. He supposed he could always count it as an elective if he changed his mind later, though. Adkins State University was located a little over thirty miles from Echo Springs. Not a particularly arduous drive, but traveling back and forth more than once a day got old fast.

When he pulled into town just after 10:00 a.m., a warning message on his dashboard told him *Fuel Low*. He likely still had enough in the tank for another round trip, but he'd need to refuel after that anyway, so he figured he might as well do it now and be done with it. Besides, his glance at the weather forecast on his phone this morning had shown they were supposed to get a 'wintery mix' tonight, and if that was true, he wouldn't want to waste any time getting home this evening. The temperature was in the low forties now, but it was supposed to drop ten degrees by nighttime. That meant the roads might ice up, and the less time he had to spend on them, the better.

He pulled his yellow Ford Fiesta hatchback, which he'd dubbed the Rolling Banana, into the parking lot of a convenience store called Qwik-Mart. He drove up to one of the pumps, got out, filled the Rolling Banana's tank, then drove over and parked in one of the spaces in front of the store. He'd paid for his gas at the pump, but he felt like getting some junk food to nibble on while he was 'studying'. A couple Snickers, maybe a Hostess Fruit Pie too. Cherry was his favorite. He parked next to a rust-tinged pickup that had a Confederate flag painted on the tailgate along with a bumper sticker that said *Global Warming is a Hoax!*

Fantastic, he thought.

He stepped out of the car and shivered. He wore a black sweatshirt over a long-sleeved gray pullover and jeans, but it wasn't enough to insulate him from the cold air, and he hurried inside.

He hoped it would be warmer inside Qwik-Mart, but if anything, it was colder. Did they have the air-conditioning on? In *February*?

He stopped at this Qwik-Mart a lot on his way to and from school. It lay on the northeast side of Route 2, which was the road he took to reach the highway. The store was kind of on the scuzzy side – floor tile yellowed, windows cracked, and an ever-present odor of mildew in the air. And of course, the prices were higher than they'd be in a grocery. But despite all this it *was* convenient, which was the sole purpose of a place like this. So what if it wasn't pretty?

He recognized the guy working the register, a thin white man with blond hair and a sparse, patchy beard. He didn't know the guy beyond the fact his plastic name tag proclaimed him to be *Roy, Master of the Universe*. There was a small TV on a shelf behind the counter, and Roy was watching it, clearly fascinated by whatever was on. An electronic tone brayed as Faizan entered, alerting Roy to his presence. The man usually gave Faizan a nod whenever he came in, and he did so now. Faizan smiled, gave Roy a small nod in return, and headed for the coolers in the rear of the store. As soon as Faizan moved off, Roy returned his attention to the TV.

Faizan was jonesing for a Dr. Pepper, but when he saw a couple white guys – both in their thirties, one with shaggy brown hair, the other with a shaved head – he hesitated. Echo Springs was better than most small

Ohio towns Faizan had been in when it came to how people of color were treated, but it was far from perfect. His parents were from Lebanon, but he'd been born in America. Not that it mattered to some people. And not only was he clearly not white, he was a skinny guy of average height. Not exactly the most imposing presence. He might as well have a message tattooed on his forehead: *I'm different from you and I can't fight back. Harass me at will!*

Sometimes he wished he went to an out-of-state college, as his brother, Salman, and sister, Rida, had done. Both of them had graduated and gotten jobs in cities, and while they still encountered anti-Muslim prejudice from time to time, it was far less than what they'd experienced in Echo Springs. But he hadn't wanted to leave his mother alone, so he'd stayed at home and gone to Adkins U, despite her protestations. He didn't know what he was going to do once he graduated, though. He tried not to think about it too much.

He examined the two men more closely. They wore heavy winter coats unzipped over flannel shirts, jeans, and work boots covered with dried mud. What were the odds that the pickup with the Confederate flag belonged to one of them? They were talking as they looked over the drinks, and he listened in.

"It was the damnedest thing," Shaved-Head said. "That guy looked just like Mark."

"What?" Brown-Hair said. "You mean that guy on the sidewalk, the one we passed who was holding the cardboard sign?"

"Yeah, you see what was written on it?"

"No."

"*It's beginning.* Weird, huh?"

"I guess. It couldn't have been Mark, though. He's been dead almost two years now. Fucking heroin."

"I didn't say he *was* Mark. I said he *looked* like Mark."

Faizan considered turning and leaving. He had no reason to think these two men were racists, and he was well aware of the irony that he was prejudging them based on their appearance. And it wasn't as if he knew for certain that the pickup outside belonged to them. And even if it did, and even if they *were* racist, it didn't mean they'd do or say anything to him, beyond maybe giving him a pair of hostile stares. Surely he could handle that.

You have to be strong to make it in this world, boy. Have to be tough.

His father's words, repeated to Faizan so often that he'd never forget them. His father had made certain of that by following the words with a physical test of his son's toughness. A smack to the side of the head, a pinch on the back of the hand, a hard slap across the face, an arm twisted and pinned against his back...and later, when he was older, bruises, cuts, and burns.

Coward.

He heard this word in his father's voice, a taunting whisper in his ears. He'd already been cold, been fighting to keep from shivering, but now he trembled uncontrollably. That settled it. He was getting out of here – now. He turned to go, but as he did, a hand caught hold of his arm in a tight grip.

"What did you say?"

Faizan was yanked back around and found himself facing Brown-Hair. This close, he saw the man needed a shave, and his breath stank of coffee and cigarettes.

"I-I didn't say anything."

Faizan hated how meek he sounded, but he knew better than to match the man's belligerence. That would only lead to worse trouble.

Shaved-Head leaned in close to Faizan's face. His breath didn't smell any better than his friend's.

"You called him a coward. I heard it."

Faizan was sure he hadn't spoken, but there was no way he'd be able to convince these two of that.

"I was referring to myself. There's a girl I like. I...wanted to ask her for a date this morning, but I chickened out. I've been kicking myself ever since."

He hoped he sounded more convincing than he felt. His voice was shaky and nausea roiled in his stomach. He'd never been a good liar and his mother – who was very devout – would always say the same thing when she caught him in a lie.

You know what the Quran says. "And do not conceal testimony, for whoever conceals it – his heart is indeed sinful."

In this case, he hoped God would forgive him.

Brown-Hair's eyes narrowed as his gaze bore into Faizan. He then glanced at Shaved-Head, who shrugged. Finally, Brown-Hair's expression eased and he let go of Faizan's arm.

"Sorry, man. Nick and I have both been there, you know?"

"Yeah," Shaved-Head said. "Don't be so hard on yourself. You'll ask her when the time's right."

Brown-Hair gave him a pat on the shoulder, then the men grabbed a pair of Starbucks Double-Shots from the cooler and headed toward the register. When they were gone, Faizan released a sigh of relief. He'd gotten lucky. That could've gone a lot worse. His nerves jangling from adrenaline, he went over to the cooler where the Dr. Pepper was held. After what he'd just gone through, he figured he deserved an entire two liter instead of a twelve ounce.

He reached for the cooler door's handle, but he caught sight of his reflection in the glass and froze. Someone was standing behind him – and not just any someone. It was his father.

Asad Barakat looked exactly as Faizan remembered him: tall, broad-shouldered, full beard, severe features set in a disapproving scowl. He was dressed in an expensive gray suit and tie, the clothes he had been buried in. Faizan had helped his mother pick them out. It was the suit his father had liked to wear when making closing arguments in court. Asad had died of a sudden heart attack seven months previously, so seeing his reflection in the cooler door meant only one of two things. Either Faizan was looking at a ghost, or he was losing his mind. And he didn't believe in ghosts.

His father's reflection bared his teeth in what could only charitably be called a smile, and his eyes were cold as an arctic plain.

The way you debased yourself before those men was disgusting. I'm surprised you didn't get down on your hands and knees and lick the mud from their boots.

Asad's mouth didn't move, but Faizan heard his words clearly. They issued from within his own mind, and he could sense Asad's emotion, a deep disappointment bordering on loathing. He whirled around, expecting to see his father standing behind him, already flinching in anticipation of being struck. But no one was there. Relieved, he let out a short bark of a laugh. His brain was rotting away from all the sugar and chemical preservatives he ate. Maybe he should skip the Dr. Pepper and get a bottle of water instead. He turned back to the cooler, and there was his father, still standing behind his reflection.

I don't know how you can stand to look at yourself in the mirror, Asad said.

Faizan wanted to tell himself that this wasn't real, that he was experiencing some sort of mental breakdown caused by a lifetime of enduring his father's emotional and physical abuse. But no matter how much he wanted to, he couldn't deny the reality of what he saw. He *knew* it was real. But that didn't mean he had to engage with it.

He turned around and started walking away from the cooler. He expected to 'hear' his father demand that he come back and face him like a man, but Asad was silent, thank God. He almost looked back to see if his father followed him. He imagined Asad's reflection emerging from the glass, his transparent body assuming solidity and then coming after his son. Faizan didn't look back, though. Maybe his father was there, maybe he wasn't. Either way, right then he didn't want to know. He planned to leave the store without buying anything, get in the Rolling Banana and get the hell out of there – most likely never to return – but as he drew near the front register, he saw Brown-Hair and Shaved-Head standing there, talking with Roy. All three men were focused on the small TV behind the counter. Despite Faizan's desire to leave, curiosity got the better of him, and he slowed down and listened to see if he could catch what they were talking about. Had something important happened? Another mass shooting, maybe? There seemed to be a new one every few weeks in America. Or maybe a disaster of some kind? An earthquake or a plane crash?

"It's bullshit," Brown-Hair said.

"It's got to be some kind of hoax," Shaved-Head said. "No way it's real."

The skin on the back of Faizan's neck prickled. Something *was* going on in the world. He walked over to the three men and asked, "What's happening?"

All three of the men turned to look at him, but it was Roy who answered.

"Evidently, people are starting to see ghosts."

That word – *ghosts* – sent a chill rippling down Faizan's spine. He took a quick look back toward the coolers and was relieved to see no sign of his father. He faced Roy.

"You mean, like actual *ghost* ghosts?"

"It's bullshit," Brown-Hair repeated. "Some kind of publicity stunt."

"Probably advertising some movie or something," Shaved-Head added. "Viral marketing."

Brown-Hair nodded. "Right."

Faizan looked at the TV. Roy had turned the sound up, and he could hear the newscaster on the screen speaking.

"*...reports that people are experiencing, for lack of a better term, spiritual manifestations. What's more, many of them have what they claim is video evidence of these encounters which they've uploaded to the Internet.*"

The image on the screen changed to show a crowded street in what Faizan assumed was a city in some Asian country. Japan from the look of it. It was nighttime, but the lights from the buildings – business signs, advertisements – provided plenty of illumination to see by. People were running in wild-eyed terror from what looked like a mass of gray mist that floated in the air. Lines of electricity like miniature lightning coruscated across the mist's surface, and a dozen thrashing tendrils extruded from the main mass of the object. Faizan thought he saw a suggestion of faces within the mist – a dozen, maybe more – but he wasn't certain. The mist-thing floated down the street in pursuit of the people fleeing it, and when it got close enough, a tendril lashed out, grabbed hold of someone who hadn't been running fast enough, and hurled them away. People hit the sides of buildings, slammed into cars – both parked and moving – or landed on the street, all of them twisted, broken, bleeding. Sound accompanied the video, which Faizan assumed had been recorded by a witness with their phone. Screams of terror, cries of pain, moans of anguish. If this video was fake, it was exceptionally well done and convincing.

The newscaster came back on.

"There are dozens more videos like this one on the Net, maybe hundreds by now, all purporting to show different types of phenomena. I recently spoke with an expert on the occult from the University of Glasgow about these sightings, and here are some highlights of our conversation."

The screen cut to a pre-recorded segment in which the newscaster spoke with an academic type complete with glasses and a tweed jacket with leather elbow patches. Faizan wanted to hear what the expert had to say – and he thought the man's accent was cool – but just as he began to speak, a hand pressed against his back and shoved. *Hard.* The action took him completely by surprise, and he stumbled forward, fighting to keep his balance. He collided with Brown-Hair, who in turn was slammed against the counter's edge.

"I'm so sorry!" Faizan said. "Somebody pushed—" He turned to see who it was, but he saw no one and his words trailed off.

"What the hell, man?" Shaved-Head grabbed double fistfuls of Faizan's shirt and gave him a single rough shake.

Roy, who like the rest of them had been caught up in what was happening on television, turned to face Shaved-Head. He put out his hands, palms up, in an everybody-calm-the-fuck-down gesture.

"I know this guy. He's cool. I'm sure it was an accident that he—"

The impact with the counter had momentarily knocked the breath from Brown-Hair, but now he turned around and stepped toward Faizan, features contorted with anger. He ignored Roy and leaned his face close to Faizan's. Faizan reflexively tried to draw back but Shaved-Head held him too tight.

"Why the *fuck* did you do that?" he demanded.

Ordinarily, Faizan wouldn't have lied again so soon after his last untruth, but he hoped God would understand, given the circumstances.

"It's my shoes. They're new and I'm still getting used to them."

Kind of lame, but it was the best excuse he could come up with considering he was most likely seconds away from getting hit by one or both of these men.

Brown-Hair, Shaved-Head, and even Roy – who had to lean over the counter to do so – looked down at Faizan's worn, comfortable sneakers. He'd had them almost two years now, and while they'd served him well in that time, they were obviously not new.

The trio raised their heads, and Brown-Hair glanced at Shaved-Head.

"This muzzie thinks he's funny." He turned to Faizan. "You think we're *stupid*? You think we can't tell your shoes aren't *new*?"

Looks like I told one lie too many, Faizan thought. His mother had been right, as usual.

He intended to put those sneakers to good use and start running, but when he tried to lift his foot, it refused to obey him. It was as if something was holding his feet to the floor, a force of some kind, like weird localized extra-strong gravity.

Once more, he heard his father's voice in his mind.

Stand and face them, boy. Show me you know what it means to be a man.

Faizan didn't know what scared him more. The prospect of getting beaten up by these two men, or the fact that his dead father was somehow keeping him from fleeing. Right now, it was a toss-up.

He squeezed his eyes shut in anticipation of receiving the first blow. Would Brown-Hair strike him on the jaw or in the midsection first? But before the man could hit him, Roy said, "Dude, is that your pickup?"

Faizan opened his eyes. Roy, Shaved-Head, and Brown-Hair were all looking through Qwik-Mart's large front windows at the parking lot. At first, Faizan didn't see what had captured their attention. But then he saw a man was sitting behind the wheel of the pickup. At least, Faizan thought it was a man. Whoever – or whatever – it was, was blackened and charred, facial features reduced to dark smudges. The driver's-side window was down and tendrils of gray smoke curled from the cab and rose upward into the air. The horrible thing grasped the top of the steering wheel with black fingers that looked like lumps of charcoal.

"What the fuck is *that*?" Shaved-Head said. He still had hold of Faizan's shirt, but his grip loosened now, enough for Faizan to pull away and escape. But he was too transfixed by the sight of the apparition in the pickup to move.

Brown-Hair stared, face pale, gaze filled with confusion and disbelief.

"It's my brother," he said. "I think. He…died in a fire three years ago. Left a space heater on all night in his bedroom. The wiring was faulty and he was too drunk to wake up when it caught fire. Jesus, will you look at him?"

Faizan *was* looking, but he couldn't process what he saw. A burned man – a *dead* man – was sitting in the pickup, gazing at them with empty blackened sockets where his eyes had once been. Faizan recalled stories his grandmother had told him when he was a child, about evil spirits called *afreet*. That was what he was seeing now, and while the logical part of his mind wanted to deny it, a deeper, truer part of him recognized the creature for what it was.

There are more of us coming, Asad's voice whispered in his mind. *Many more. The fun's just starting.*

The pickup's engine rumbled to life, and Faizan wondered how the dead man had gotten hold of the vehicle's key. He supposed that if a spirit could find its way back from the realm of the dead, turning on a truck without a key would prove to be no great challenge. He recognized that he was dwelling on a mundanity. What did it matter how the creature had turned on the engine? Was he in some kind of shock? It seemed likely.

The burnt thing put the pickup in reverse and began to back out of the parking space.

"What the hell?" Brown-Hair shouted. "Phillip, don't you steal my truck, you bastard!"

Brown-Hair ran toward the door, shoved it open, and plunged outside. Shaved-Head hesitated a moment, but then he hurried after his friend.

Faizan and Roy watched as the ghost – Phillip – put the truck in drive and roared out of the parking lot and onto the street. Brown-Hair ran down the sidewalk in pursuit, shouting for his brother to get his "burnt ass back here!" Shaved-Head followed, running more slowly, as if he wasn't fully committing to chasing after Phillip but didn't know what else to do. Within moments the truck and the men were lost to sight.

Roy turned to Faizan then. There was a wild look in his eyes, and he gave Faizan a smile that didn't seem altogether sane.

"Fucking Mondays, huh?"

Faizan nodded his agreement.

CHAPTER FOUR

Oliver sat at the dining table, laptop open, staring at a sociology lesson on the screen.

He didn't have anything against homeschooling in theory, but some people – his parents, for example – did it to protect their children from what they viewed as an unhealthy environment. They considered public schools – especially high schools – as places filled with violence, drugs, psychological abuse, sexual temptation, and worst of all, godlessness.

The teenage years are fraught with peril, his father had once said. Oliver had wanted to tell his dad how ridiculous he sounded. Fraught with peril. That sounded like bad comic book dialogue, and Oliver wondered if Dad had read the phrase on some conservative Christian website and had memorized it for this occasion.

We're just thinking of what's best for you, his mother had added.

You mean what's best for yourselves, Oliver had replied

Neither of his parents had responded to that, which – as far as he was concerned – was an admission he was right.

Oliver's mother and father, who weren't trained teachers, used an online 'school' called Education for All, which supplied what they touted as a complete, accredited high school curriculum designed to meet standards in all fifty states. The lessons were self-paced, the homework mostly multiple-choice quizzes and tests graded automatically by the site's software. His parents received regular progress reports via email, but Oliver had no idea if they even opened those messages, let alone read them. Basically, his high school education consisted of him doing busy work on the computer while his parents went about their lives. Not only was it boring as hell, the material was so simplistic that he thought it was actually making him dumber. Whenever his parents weren't around, he watched anime – he was currently into *Attack on Titan* – but since he wasn't allowed to take the laptop to his room, he usually kept the Education for All website minimized so he could bring it up whenever Mom or Dad came to check on him. He didn't consider this goofing off. He wanted to be an animation artist, and he viewed watching anime as career preparation. His parents, however, would not see it like that.

Oliver was white, with a small, almost boyish body, and he kept his straight blond hair cut short. He wore jeans and T-shirts regardless of the temperature outside, and he went barefoot whenever possible. He had a large collection of anime shirts, and today's choice was *One Piece*, a favorite. He had a tendency to chew his nails, a habit he'd had since childhood that he'd been unable to break.

He minimized the Education for All page and had just started watching the next episode of *Attack on Titan* when he heard noise from the kitchen – footsteps, cupboards opening and closing, the coffeemaker being turned on…. He switched the computer screen back to the lesson he was supposed to be working on, and a few minutes later his mother entered the dining room, carrying a mug of fresh coffee.

"I thought you might like a little morning pick-me-up."

His mother had also brought in a coaster. She set it down on the table, then placed the mug atop it. It looked like his mother had added too much cream, as usual, and she'd probably put too much sugar in it as well. Still, he smiled and said thanks.

"What are you studying today, sweetie?"

His mother put her hand on his shoulder and leaned over to peer at the computer screen.

"It's a unit on income inequality in America," Oliver said.

His mother frowned. "That sounds political."

Oliver sighed.

Emily Patton was in her mid-forties, but she looked ten years younger. She was slender and taller than Oliver by almost a foot, and she had curly black hair, which he envied. She wore minimal makeup because she thought it wasn't 'seemly' for a woman to draw too much attention to herself. She worked as a manager at a pet store called Paws and Claws, but her shift today didn't start until three. She mostly worked afternoons so she could stay home with Oliver during the school week, although aside from occasionally asking what he was working on, she did nothing in the way of instruction, which suited Oliver fine. He preferred to be left alone to do his own thing. She wore a blue sweater over a white blouse, black slacks, and fuzzy slippers. She didn't like anyone wearing street shoes in her house.

"It's not political, Mom."

His mother leaned closer to the screen and squinted, as if this would enable her to analyze the information more deeply. "I don't know, Amanda. It sounds like a liberal talking point to me."

Oliver's body tensed and his mom – her hand still on his shoulder – felt his discomfort instantly. She jerked her hand away and straightened.

"I'm sorry! I didn't mean...." She forced a smile. "I'll let you get back to work. Enjoy your coffee."

She turned and practically fled the dining room.

Oliver sat stiffly in his chair for several moments, jaw clenched, hands bunched into fists. His mother hadn't meant anything, it had been only a verbal slip, but it still hurt. He couldn't help but take it as a comment, even if only a subconscious one, on how his mother felt about him being trans. He knew she was uncomfortable as hell – same for his father. His dad had his own business, Precision Paint, and worked fifty, sometimes sixty hours a week. Oliver sometimes wondered if his father worked so much so he could avoid being around his only child who he still thought of as his daughter.

His parents were enthusiastic and devoted members of Abundant Life Christian Worship Center, a megachurch located a couple miles outside town. Trans folk had become the latest boogeyman for conservative Christians, and to say his parents had mixed feelings about their son's gender identity was putting it mildly. Oliver had stopped going to church after being treated poorly by some of the congregation – not that he missed those small-minded, mean-spirited hypocrites – and he was grateful that his parents hadn't tried to force him to keep going. He figured they were probably relieved that they didn't have to deal with their son's presence in church – the quick glances, the long stares, the whispered voices, the outright criticism…. *You need to get that girl into some kind of program, get her mind straight, help her get right with God again.*

He had to give his parents credit, though. As difficult as it was for them, they were trying their best to understand and support their son in their own clumsy way. It was more understanding than a lot of trans kids got from their parents, especially when their parents were evangelicals.

Oliver drew in a deep breath, held it for several seconds, then released it slowly. He hadn't been to see a therapist – his parents didn't believe in them, thought true believers turned to God for help with their problems. But he'd read tons of Internet articles on how to deal with depression and anxiety, and he knew a number of techniques he could use to help release his negative feelings. He repeated this breathing pattern twice more, and when he was finished, he felt calmer, more relaxed. Just another year and a half until he graduated high school, then he could get the hell out of this town and move to someplace more cosmopolitan, not to mention more tolerant.

Someplace where there wouldn't be so many memories.

He decided he'd best return to work before his mind started down a path he did not want to travel today. *Back to* Titan, he thought. He minimized the sociology class window and brought up the video again. Except it didn't show people battling giant mutated humanoids. It displayed the photo of a girl. Delia.

His breath seized in his throat, and he felt suddenly sick. He recognized the picture, of course. It was Delia's sophomore yearbook photo, which he had copied from her memorial page on the funeral home's website and saved on the laptop. He hadn't opened it, though, so why the hell was it here?

He felt tears threatening, and while he knew the whole 'men don't express emotion' thing was bullshit, he still felt too girly when he let himself cry. But he couldn't stop the tears now, and he really didn't want to.

Delia had what Oliver thought of as regal features. She looked like a statue of some ancient Roman aristocrat, especially with her black hair, which was even curlier than his mother's. No, not curls. *Ringlets*, that was the right word. Her eyes were a bright, almost electric blue, and she had a smile so filled with joy it looked like she was on the verge of breaking out in happy laughter. It was that smile which had caught Oliver's attention when he first saw her one Sunday at church.

He hadn't told his parents he identified as male yet, hadn't told anyone. But he'd stopped wearing dresses to church and had cut his hair short. His parents didn't like these changes, but they'd adopted a 'this is a phase' stance, a phase they hoped their daughter would eventually grow out of. Delia sat in a pew with her parents directly across the aisle from where Oliver sat with his. During the service – which as usual was dull as hell – he kept sneaking glances at Delia, who *was* wearing a dress, a pretty blue one that made her eyes pop even more than they already did. Whenever Delia caught him looking at her, he turned away quickly, cheeks burning with embarrassment.

After the service was over, the congregation adjourned to the fellowship hall for a potluck lunch. When Delia got up from the table where she was sitting, Oliver got up as well. She headed over to one of the serving tables to get a cup of water, and Oliver – heart pounding like mad – joined her. Delia gave him one of her special smiles then, and he was a goner.

"Hi, I'm Delia. What's your name?" Her voice was soft but the tone confident, and there was a hint of amusement too, as if she was aware of how uncomfortable Oliver was and was enjoying it.

Without thinking, he gave her what he thought of as his real name. Not *Amanda*, but—

"Oliver."

Text messages and phone calls followed after that, leading to secret meetings during which they began to get physical. One July day when they were kissing in a secluded spot by the river, Delia got so enthusiastic she grabbed Oliver's crotch, only to not find what she expected.

"You're a girl," she said. She didn't, however, remove her hand from Oliver's crotch.

"I'm a boy," he said. "Right now my body just looks like a girl's."

Delia looked at him for a moment, and he thought, *This is it. It's all over.* But instead, Delia smiled.

"Okay."

She'd worn a T-shirt and shorts that day, and she peeled them off so fast it was almost like a magic trick. She got out of her underwear just as fast.

Oliver stared at her naked body, marveling at how perfect she was. She smiled again, only this time it had a naughty edge.

"Your turn."

Oliver suddenly felt self-conscious. He didn't like his body because it didn't reflect who he was on the inside. He wasn't ashamed of it, exactly, but he damn sure wasn't comfortable with the idea of letting anyone see him naked – especially Delia.

Delia, ever sensitive, seemed to understand what Oliver was feeling. "Let me help."

She stepped forward, kissed him slowly, lovingly, and then began disrobing him.

The rest of the summer passed like a dream. They continued meeting in their spot by the river, spending as much time together as they could without making their respective parents suspicious. Their moms and dads knew the 'girls' were 'friends', and because of this, Oliver and Delia felt safe enough. But Delia's father came to suspect there was more than friendship between them. Oliver never learned what it was for sure, but the church wasn't exactly tolerant of gay people and some – who Oliver assumed were closeted themselves – were downright obsessed with all things related to homosexuality. He and Delia were a straight couple, but there was no way for anyone to know that, and even if they were told, they wouldn't believe it. So Delia's father, concerned that his precious little girl might be – gasp! – a *lez-bee-an*, followed her to the river one day and saw what she did with her 'friend.' He didn't intervene then, but – as Oliver learned later – he confronted Delia when she got home. Oliver wondered what she'd said when her father accused her of being gay.

I'm not a lesbian, Daddy, although there would be nothing wrong with it if I was. Oliver is trans. He's a man.

If there was one group of people conservative Christians feared and loathed more than gays, it was trans folk. Delia's father went ballistic and decided not to spare the rod on his child. He grabbed a fireplace poker and by the time he was finished, his daughter lay on the floor, a broken, battered, bloody ruin. Her mother – who'd tried and failed to stop her husband – called 911, but when the EMTs arrived, it was too late. Delia was gone. That had been six months ago, and her father's trial was due to begin soon. Oliver prayed the sonofabitch would get the death penalty, but given how conservative Ohio was, Oliver wasn't going to get his hopes up.

He'd gone crazy with grief when he learned about Delia's death – and when he learned the reason why her father had killed her, he blamed himself. If he'd never approached her at church, never told her his name....

His parents did their best to console him over the loss of his 'friend', and Oliver – not seeing the point in hiding the truth anymore – told them who he really was. At first, they put his revelation down to grief and had him meet with their pastor. But after a few weeks, they'd come to, if not accept Oliver's identity, at least not argue with him about it, and they'd been doing their best to try to understand their son. Oliver thought their reaction would've been very different if Delia hadn't been murdered by her father. It was a powerful object lesson in what ignorance and hatred can lead to.

Oliver wished that he'd been the one to die instead of Delia, and he'd thought about suicide more than once, but thinking was all he'd done – so far. He wanted to live to honor Delia's memory, but sometimes it was so damn hard....

Tears streaming down his face, he reached toward the screen, gently touched his fingertips to the plastic surface, pulled them away.

"I love you, Delia. I always will."

I love you too.

The voice that whispered through Oliver's mind sounded so real that he looked around quickly to see if he was alone. He was. Delia was nothing but a memory now. Wiping away tears, he turned back to the computer screen—

—and saw Delia's head protruding from its plastic surface.

Oliver's breath caught in his throat and he gaped at his lost love. *I've lost my fucking mind.*

No, Delia said, lips unmoving, eyes twinkling with mischief. *You lost me. But I'm back now – and this time I'm not leaving. Ever.*

Then she smiled, and for the first time since her death, the grief that lay cold and heavy inside Oliver lifted. Delia's smile was a pure ray of sunlight slashing through the dark shell that had grown around his heart, and without pausing to consider the absurdity of his actions, he leaned forward and kissed her. He expected his lips to pass through the empty space where he only imagined her to be, to keep going until they touched the flat plastic of the laptop's screen. After all, she was only a hallucination, right? But his mouth touched hers, and while her flesh was cooler than he remembered, her lips remained as soft as ever. They kissed gently at first, as if neither of them was quite sure this was real, but then Delia's lips parted and the tip of her tongue emerged. Oliver responded, opening his own mouth, and Delia's tongue slid past his lips. He felt her probing, teasing, and if her tongue seemed longer now, the saliva coating it thicker, he didn't care. All that mattered was his love had returned to him.

"Oh my Lord!"

Oliver drew back from Delia with a start. He turned to see his mother standing in the dining room's doorway, staring at Delia's head with a look of absolute horror. Oliver had read stories in which a character was described as having the blood draining from their face in shock, but this was the first time he'd seen the effect occur in real life. It made his mother look unearthly, like a ghost. He recognized the irony of the thought and almost laughed.

"It's okay, Mom. It's just Delia."

Oliver knew the words coming out of his mouth were crazy. His dead girlfriend's head was sticking out of a fucking computer. How the hell could that be okay?

Without thinking, his mother used his deadname.

"Amanda, get away from that...that *thing*!"

Oliver looked at Delia, saw her beautiful features contort into an angry scowl. He looked back to his mother, his own anger rising.

"Don't talk about her like that!"

His mom's eyes – wide, fearful, disbelieving – remained fixed on Delia.

"That's not a *her*. It's a...a *demon*." Her voice became stronger then, louder, more confident. "'In later times some will abandon the faith and follow deceiving spirits and things taught by demons!'"

Oliver didn't recognize the quote, but from the way she declaimed it, as if she were standing behind a pulpit, he knew it was from scripture. Where else?

Delia's upper lip curled into a sneer. Her mouth still didn't move when she spoke.

I used to have to listen to that kind of shit from my father all the time. In fact, that was one of the things the bastard shouted at me while he was beating me to death. Here's another of his favorites: "If thine eye offend thee, pluck it out, and cast it from thee."

There was a forcefulness to Delia's words, a *push* that felt almost physical.

Mom's eyes widened further, more than seemed humanly possible, and her arms began to move with robotic stiffness. She reached toward her face, fingers curling into claws. She watched her hands draw closer, shaking her head as if to deny what was happening. Oliver didn't know how Delia was doing this, but he knew she was responsible. He turned to her.

"Stop it! Please!"

Delia didn't look at him. Her gaze was fixed on his mother, her lips stretched in a cruel smile.

Oliver jumped out of the dining chair so fast, he knocked it over. He ran to his mother, grabbed hold of her wrists, tried to pull her hands away from her face. Emily Patton was a thin, delicate woman, the kind that some people might have described as willowy. She didn't have much muscle on her, and her wrists were slender as a child's. Oliver should've had no trouble forcing her arms down, but whatever power had taken hold of her had imbued her with inhuman strength. Her wrists felt hard as marble, and no matter how hard Oliver tried, he couldn't slow the inexorable progression of her hands toward her eyes. Her fingers began clutching spasmodically then, as if they were hungry, multijointed creatures eager for the feast to come. Then, with a last violent surge like a pair of striking snakes, the fingers plunged into her eyes.

His mother screamed as blood gushed over her fingers, the digits scratching and digging frantically now. Crimson splattered Oliver's hands and face, and his scream joined his mother's. Her legs gave out and she slumped to the floor, pulling Oliver – he still had an iron grip on her wrists – down with her. Oliver continued trying to yank her hands away from the blood-covered mask that was her face, even though at this point, he knew it would do no good. And then whatever power had taken control of her dissipated, and she went limp. Her screams degenerated into weak sobs, and as she cried, Oliver – now in complete shock – wondered if her tear ducts could still function. He let go of her wrists, held his blood-slick hands out before him. They shook so hard they were almost blurs. Laughter filled the air then, a lovely, joyous sound that served as a bizarre counterpoint to the sight of his mother's eyeless face. He looked over his shoulder, expected to see Delia grinning in delight—

—but she was gone, the laptop screen once more displaying the two-dimensional image of her sophomore picture. And as Oliver watched, it winked at him.

CHAPTER FIVE

"I just don't know what to do, Karen."

Karen Gresham sat at the counter of the Sleepy Lizard Café, cup of black coffee in front of her, a burning cigarette resting in a tin ashtray at her elbow. You couldn't smoke in Ohio bars and restaurants, but Karen owned the goddamn place, and she'd do *whatever* the fuck she liked *whenever* she liked, and her customers could do the same. And if anyone complained, they knew where the door was.

A man in his late forties sat on her left. Leon Davis was a skinny guy, only a couple inches over five feet, with a mustache so thin it was practically invisible. He worked as a guard for Nightwatch Security, and he'd gotten off work only a few hours earlier. He still wore his faux cop uniform – white shirt, blue tie and pants, blue jacket with the NW logo over the left breast – and he carried a 9mm pistol holstered on his hip. Karen knew that some people weren't comfortable seeing someone with a gun in her place, but she didn't give a shit. As far as she was concerned, the Second Amendment was absolute, and anyone with a permit could carry a weapon in her café. And if they didn't have one? Don't ask, don't tell, baby.

Karen reached up to adjust the volume on the hearing aid in her right ear. Leon was a soft-spoken man, and she sometimes had trouble hearing him – especially when he was depressed.

"I'm sorry my advice didn't work out for you," Karen said, fighting to keep from smiling as she spoke. She wasn't sorry in the slightest, was in fact enjoying herself enormously.

Leon let out a bitter bark of a laugh. "That's an understatement! I thought Renee was going to rip my goddamn balls off."

A plate of blueberry pancakes sat in front of him, with a side of link sausages. He got the same thing every day, but this morning, he hadn't touched his food. He'd poured syrup on the pancakes, but he'd sat here talking for so long, the spongy things had absorbed the thick liquid, making them look brown and soggy. Karen didn't give a shit whether he ate them or not, just so long as he paid for them.

Karen was in her late sixties, about the same height as Leon, but significantly heavier. She dyed her short hair blond, or at least tried to, but the color always came out too faint, a washed-out neutral shade closer to gray than blond. She wore jeans half a size too small, along with a black microfleece jacket with the Zephyr Air logo printed on the left side of the chest. Her husband, Bennie, had worked as an airline pilot for almost thirty years before his heart popped like a blood-filled balloon. She always told people he'd died during a flight, but he'd really died at home, on the toilet, straining to take a shit.

Leon had been coming into the Lizard for…Christ, almost ten years now. And in that time he'd had more girlfriends than Karen could remember. Attracting women wasn't his problem, although she didn't know what the skanks saw in the man. His problem was *keeping* them. The longest relationship she'd ever known him to have lasted a little over two months. Of course, he might've had more success at love if he didn't keep asking her for a 'woman's perspective' on relationships. Karen had decided years ago it would be fun to see how fast she could sabotage his attempts at finding a fuck buddy. Her personal best so far was three days.

Last week, Leon had confessed to her that he'd slept with his latest girlfriend – a hairdresser named Renee – for the first time, and from the way she'd reacted afterward, she'd been less than impressed. He'd managed to wrangle another date from her, and he asked Karen what she thought he could do in bed to wow her. Karen hadn't hesitated.

Anal, she'd said. *It's every woman's secret fantasy. Even if they say they don't like it, they're lying. And what they* really *like is when a guy doesn't ask them if they want to do it. They just want him to get back there and get to it, the faster and harder the better. And forget that shit about lube. No one likes that stuff. Too messy.*

She'd thought not even Leon would be dumb enough to take that advice, but here he was, telling her he had, and Karen was having a fantastic morning listening to his story and pretending to sympathize.

"I did just what you said, but she started squawking before I could get in there. Slapped me, too. Hard."

He rubbed his cheek as if it still hurt. Karen hoped so.

Leon looked at her, and the pain in his eyes made her feel wet. "Do you think she's a lesbian or something?"

Karen smiled and patted his hand. "I'm sure that's it, hon."

She picked up her cigarette and took a long, satisfying drag. Christ, it was good to be alive.

The café was only half full right now, but it was always like this when breakfast had ended and lunch hadn't begun. She recognized most of the customers, all regulars who came here at least three days a week and often more. Retired men who sat around drinking too much coffee and arguing about how to solve all the world's problems. Harried mothers of toddlers who looked like they'd rather be alone at a bar chugging wine than watching their snot-nosed offspring scrawling on the backs of placemats with crayons. Truckers and delivery drivers taking a break from the road. Single middle-aged men like Leon who worked second or third shift and wanted to be anywhere, do anything except go home. No homeless who'd come in to get out of the cold, though. This was a place of business, not a fucking charity. Any of those losers came in here, Karen ran them out before they had a chance to sit their smelly asses down. A few of the customers were smoking, but not as many as she might've expected. What was the point in being free if you didn't exercise your freedom?

Fucking cowards.

Karen used to work here every morning from open to close, six days a week. The café was closed on Sundays, not because she was religious but because she needed at least one day away from the goddamn place. She was retired now, mostly. She still came in most days and hung around for several hours, keeping an eye on things and playing her games with customers like Leon. Manipulating others was her greatest joy in life, and she'd be damned if she'd give it up just because she was getting old. Sandra Pope – her bitch sister Erika's daughter – was manager now, earning money while she worked her way through grad school one course at a time. Sandra was behind the counter today while Jimmy Griffith and Lester

Armstrong manned the grill. Diane Ellis and Holly Douglas were waiting on tables. Diane was an old workhorse like Karen, while Holly was a sweet young thing barely out of high school. They were all right, too. Everyone she employed at the Lizard was at least adequate at their work – not that she'd ever let them know that. The moment you started praising your workers, they started asking for raises. Greedy fuckers.

Sandra delivered a BLT and fries to Kyle Warner, a mailman who spent more time eating in here than he did making deliveries, and then she walked over to where Karen was sitting.

"Aunt Karen, do you think we could turn the heat down a bit? It's getting pretty steamy in here." She drew the back of a hand across her forehead as if to emphasize her point.

It *was* hot in here. In the winter, Karen always kept the temperature at seventy-five degrees. She got cold easily these days, but that wasn't her main reason for keeping it so warm. Warm people were *uncomfortable* people, and uncomfortable people became grumpy people, who in turn became foul-tempered people. And the longer they sat and simmered in their own juices, the worse they got. They'd start bickering, minor disputes escalating into full-fledged arguments. Hell, just before Christmas a couple bikers had gotten into an honest-to-fuck fistfight. It had been glorious. She'd experimented with different thermostat settings over the years. Too low and nothing happened, too high and people left early, if they even sat down at all. She'd long ago discovered that seventy-five degrees was the perfect temperature, and from the first of November to the first of April, that's where she kept it, and to hell with the extra money it cost her. The entertainment was worth it.

"The temperature is fine where it's at, sweetie."

Karen had long ago learned that people would accept just about anything you said if you spoke in a soft, calm voice and added the word *hon* or *sweetie* at the end. In her mind, these words were the equivalent of *you fucking moron*, as in, *The temperature is fine where it's at, you fucking moron.*

Sandra sighed softly, but she smiled and nodded. That sigh, and the weary disappointment and frustration contained within, was like Mozart to Karen's ears.

Sandra was in her early thirties, and she looked a lot like her mother. Karen was Sandra's identical twin, and when they'd been kids, Karen had tormented her ceaselessly. She'd been so cruel to her sister, in fact, that the woman still bore physical scars of Karen's attentions. And, of course, she bore far less obvious ones. Karen honestly wasn't sure what had possessed Erika to allow Sandra to come work for her. She knew better than to think the memories of the abuse she'd visited upon her sister had faded over the years. She'd done too good a job for that to happen. She thought maybe Erika had deluded herself into thinking Karen had changed, grown softer, mellower as she'd aged. Or maybe she planned for Sandra to take over the café somewhere down the road, taking it away from Karen in some kind of half-assed revenge. As if Karen gave two shits about this place. She could always find somewhere else to torment people. Hell, she could cause a *lot* of misery in a nursing home. It might be the perfect retirement place for her. Almost make it worth being dumped in one of those shitholes to rot.

Sandra looked like she was going to say something else, but then another of the regulars at the counter raised a hand to get her attention, and she went off to see to him. Karen had never had children – no way in hell would she have gone through that pain for anything – but she often wondered what it would've been like if she'd had. The idea of having a small child to do with as she pleased was intriguing, but ultimately unsatisfying. Mentally torturing them would be too easy. She preferred to fuck with adults' minds. They had the strength to resist, to fight back, and that's where the real fun was.

God, how she missed Bennie.... He'd given as good as he got, and their marriage had been an ongoing game of who could hurt who the most, usually on an emotional level, but their battles sometimes became physical, too. They'd had such a good time. Leave it to that goddamn bastard to die on her and get the last laugh. She didn't believe in an afterlife, but if there was one, she was looking forward to picking up with Bennie where they'd left off. They could bicker and snipe and name-call and hit and scratch and bite for all eternity. It would be bliss.

"What do you think I should do next?" Leon asked.

Karen had almost forgotten about him. *Learn to be happy jacking off,* she thought. Aloud, she said, "To hell with her. She was never right for you anyway. You need somebody who'll put your needs before her own. Someone who'll really care for you the way you deserve." She didn't think there was anyone in the world like that. Everyone, no matter how good they seemed, was always out for themselves. Some were just more honest about it than others. Still, she didn't want Leon to get *too* discouraged. She wanted him to have just enough hope so that he'd find someone else to date, and then she could give him more shitty advice and watch as another potential relationship crashed and burned.

Life was good.

She was about to give Leon a few more bullshit platitudes when a hand gripped the back of her head. It shoved violently, and her forehead slammed against the counter. White light exploded in her vision, followed instantly by pain. She straightened, dizzy and suddenly nauseated. *What the fuck?* She turned around, the action intensifying her vertigo, causing her to grip the edge of the countertop to steady herself. She was ready to unload on the asshole who'd done that to her…but no one was there. Everyone in the café was staring at her, and she felt exposed. Vulnerable. It was not a feeling she was used to.

"Are you all right?" Leon asked.

She turned to face him, moving slowly, but before she could answer, Sandra – who'd rushed over to see to her aunt – said, "What happened? Did you faint or something?"

By or something, *she probably means,* Did you have a stroke?

"Some motherfucker pushed me!"

Normally, Karen was careful to watch her language in public. A few *damns* or *hells* here and there, no problem. But anything worse made it more difficult to maintain her façade as a good-natured, caring, and helpful woman. But right then she was too angry to worry about how people saw her.

Sandra and Leon exchanged a glance.

"No one was there, Aunt Karen."

Leon nodded. "That's right. I'd have seen them."

Both kept their tones neutral, the way you would if you thought you were talking to a crazy person. Fury blazed inside Karen, her anger momentarily making her forget about the pain throbbing in her skull.

"Are you fucking *kidding* me? Do you think I smashed my head onto the counter for shits and giggles?"

Both Karen and Leon looked startled, and they drew back as if she'd slapped them. Despite how angry she was, Karen found their reactions highly satisfying.

You're such a cunt.

"Who the fuck said that?"

She spun around, wincing at the pain in her head. The café's customers were still staring at her, and some of them looked afraid, as if they thought she'd lost her goddamn mind.

Maybe you have. It's not like you had all that much to lose in the first place.

The voice was a buzzing in her ear, and she realized then that it was coming from her hearing aid. She recognized the voice, too. She hadn't heard it for years, but she knew it as well as her own. It was Bennie.

Christ, how hard *had* she hit her head? Did she have a goddamn concussion or something? Maybe she should ask Sandra to take her to the hospital to get checked out.

She realized then that not all of the customers were looking at her. Several were looking at their phones, holding them up so that their dining companions could see the screen display, everyone talking in hushed, worried tones. Something was happening. Something *big*. It reminded her of the morning of 9/11, when people struggled to process what had seemed like an impossible event, like something out of a goddamn movie. There was the same feeling of tension in the air, of disbelief, of *fear*, and despite her throbbing head, she took a moment to drink it in. They were like animals that had caught the first faint scent of smoke somewhere in the forest. Alert and on guard, but unsure exactly why.

Through the Lizard's front window, Karen watched as a pickup flew into the parking lot. The truck was moving so fast, she thought it was going to crash into the cars parked right in front of the café, but at the last instant the driver hit the brakes and spun the wheel, and the vehicle came to a stop perpendicular to the row of cars. The driver's-side door opened, and a burnt and blackened thing stepped out. It was shaped like a human, but it had no discernable features, and coils of smoke rose from its charred body.

That's Philip. New friend of mine. Died in a fire. He's here to do me a favor.

Karen watched in mounting disbelief as 'Philip', moving with awkward, jerky motions, stepped up to the café's window. He stood there a moment, looking in, although how he could see anything without eyes, she didn't know. And then with a sudden violent motion he slammed his blackened hands to the glass.

Every flammable object in the café ignited simultaneously – tables, chairs, curtains, menus, even goddamn napkins. But that wasn't all. People's clothing caught fire too, along with their hair. They began screaming and flailing around, waving their arms and pounding their heads in vain attempts to stifle the flames. People jumped up from their tables and rushed to the door in a panicked mass, fighting to be the first to get outside. But there were too many to fit through all at once, and all they managed to do was block the exit so that none of them could get out. They were packed so tightly together that the flames rising from their bodies merged into a single larger conflagration, and their screams became a crescendo of agony. The smell of burning flesh filled the air, and Karen thought it smelled like roasting pork.

Thanks, man, Bennie said. *See you later!*

Philip raised a charred hand in farewell, then walked back to his truck with spastic, wobbly steps. He got in the vehicle, slammed the door shut, and then roared out of the lot and onto the street.

He's headed to the fire station now. Man, those guys are in for one hell of a surprise!

Karen turned away from the window. She saw that Leon had fallen off his seat and lay thrashing on the floor. He rolled back and forth to try to extinguish the flames eating away at him, but they refused to go out. Behind the counter, Sandra had grabbed a pitcher of water and dumped it on her head. The flames eating her hair went out for a moment, but then they flickered back to life, flaring brighter and stronger than before. Her scream was like an ice pick in Karen's ear, and without thinking, she reached up to lower the volume on her hearing aid. Better.

In the kitchen, the natural gas stoves exploded and the cooks screamed as they died. Smoke began filling the air, making everything look hazy and gray, and Karen started coughing. Only then did she realize that the flames had not touched her. She could feel their heat all around her, and her skin hurt, as if someone were pressing hot metal against her, but she was not burning.

You think I'd let my best girl get barbecued to death? I don't want you to miss out on all the fun that's coming.

Despite how low her hearing aid's volume was set, she had no trouble making out Bennie's voice. A cold hand took hers, but she saw no one there. Still, she let it pull her off her seat and begin leading her toward the back of the café, where the restrooms – and more importantly, the rear exit – were. She coughed as she went, struggling to draw in enough oxygen to breathe, but she wasn't afraid that she was going to die. She knew Bennie wouldn't let her. That would be too kind.

This is going to be a great day, Karen. The best! Unfortunately, it's also going to be the last.

Bennie continued guiding her toward the back door, the screams and sobs of the dying accompanying them all the way.

CHAPTER SIX

Jerome Gallagher was pretending to reshelve books in the True Crime section, but he'd really come here because he wanted to look at *it* again. He'd grabbed a stack of books that had been dropped through the overnight return slot by patrons since closing last night, but he hadn't so much as glanced at what sections they belonged to. They were just an excuse, props, camouflage. As soon as he reached True Crime, he deposited them on an empty part of a shelf, then – with a quick glance around to make sure no one was looking – he reached for a hardcover that he referred to, if only in his mind, as *The Book*. He pulled it away from the lesser volumes it was forced to share space with, and slowly, reverently, lovingly examined the cover.

He'd viewed it hundreds, maybe thousands of times, but he always paused to look at the cover before opening *The Book*. The color scheme was a garish blood-red that, while lacking in subtlety, certainly was eye-catching. The title was printed in large black capital letters: *THE SKINTAKER*. At the bottom of the cover, also in black, but smaller, was the author's name: Ella Lambert. Between the title and the author's name was the silhouette of a man's head and shoulders, the only features visible a pair of white eyes without pupils. The image was simple, almost cartoonish, he supposed, but chilling nonetheless. Directly beneath the title, in letters even smaller than the author's name, was the subtitle: *A True Story of Murder in the Midwest*. Jerome thought the subtitle was bland, dull, lifeless. It was his least favorite part of *The Book*. He supposed some might look upon its restraint as laudable, and granted, some readers might find the alliteration of *Murder* and *Midwest* appealing. But it could use a little more zing. *The Hunt for the Echo Springs Killer* – a bit of a rhyme in that one – or *Death, Blood, and Madness*. Something along those lines.

Then again, he was a librarian, not an author or publisher. What did he know?

He'd read this book countless times. Not this particular copy, of course. He had his own well-worn copy at home. By this point, he was so familiar with the text that he could practically recite it from memory, like a character from the end of Bradbury's *Fahrenheit 451*.

Jerome brushed the tips of his fingers across the cover and then began speaking softly, quoting a passage from Bradbury's book.

"'Books were only one type of receptacle where we stored a lot of things we were afraid we might forget. There is nothing magical in them at all. The magic is only in what books say, how they stitched the patches of the universe together into one garment for us.'"

There was only one section of *The Book* he was interested in this morning, the only section he turned to again and again – the series of black-and-white photos printed in the middle. He opened *The Book* and turned to them. The first was a picture of a little boy sitting cross-legged on a white platform against a blue background and smiling at the camera. It was a generic professional shot, the kind of thing you'd get from a mall photographer, entirely lacking in personality or artistry. Yet, given what Jerome knew about the boy, the image was, in its way, chilling. Below the photo were the words *Randall Beck, age four*. He turned the page. This one displayed a pair of photos of Randall as a teenager, one above the other. In the first, he was dressed in a high school band uniform and holding a trumpet. This was Randall the way Jerome remembered him. He'd been in the band, too, and he'd also played trumpet. Randall had been two years older than Jerome, and while they hadn't exactly been friends, Randall had treated him well enough, even if Randall did call him names sometimes. The second was from the end of Randall's senior year, but it wasn't a school photo – it was a mug shot. This was his favorite picture of Randall. Shaggy blond hair, narrow face, thin unsmiling lips, dead eyes. Those eyes fascinated him. They looked almost painted on, like a doll's eyes, nothing beneath their flat surface. They were almost alien, and whenever Jerome looked at the photo, he wondered what thoughts – if any – had been going through Randall's mind when the picture was taken. Had he known then that he'd become the closest thing to a celebrity Echo Springs would ever have? A local legend, albeit an extremely dark one? There was no way to know, of course, but that didn't stop Jerome from speculating. The next page was the one he really wanted to look at, but he never turned to it first, always looked at the ones before it in order to prolong his anticipation. It was almost a type of foreplay, he supposed. Gratification delayed was always the sweetest.

He turned the page.

Three photos, three girls, side by side. These were school pictures, and the girls were dressed nicely, hair perfect, makeup on, all smiling. They'd all been in band, and Jerome had known each of them. Becky Marshall played the clarinet, Tami Phelps played the flute, and Linh Choi had been captain of the color guard. Becky was a pretty blonde with long hair who looked more like the stereotype of a cheerleader than a band geek. Tami was thin and delicate, with short, straight brown hair, and while Linh's features were somewhat sharp, her broad smile exuded an energy and confidence that Jerome thought made her the most attractive of the three. Even after all this time, it was still so strange to look at these pictures and know the girls in them would all be dead within three months. It was like being able to look into the future.

Linh's smile widened.

Jerome was so startled he almost dropped *The Book*. He stared at Linh's picture, but her smile was once more frozen in time.

He knew that he was a bit obsessive when it came to the subject of Randall and his three victims, but he'd thought his…*hobby* was, for the most part, innocuous, harmless, benign. But if he was starting to see things that weren't there – that weren't even *possible* – then maybe it was a sign that he needed to take a break. He should put *The Book* back on the shelf and start reshelving the returns for real. But he didn't. Instead, he turned to the next page.

This was a photo of the first crime scene, where Tami's body had been discovered. Her nude body lay facedown on the north bank of the Iden River. There was no blood on her – the water had washed it all away – but knife wounds covered her shoulders, back, butt, and legs. And while you couldn't tell from this photo, Jerome knew the damage was even more severe on her front side, and her face had been cut entirely off. The police would never find it, and Randall refused to tell them where it was. Some people, Jerome among them, thought he'd eaten it. Becky and Linh had been found the same way – naked, stabbed, and faceless – and it had been this latter detail that had earned Randall his *nom du meurtre*: The Skintaker. The image of Tami's ravaged and waterlogged body was the only crime-scene photo in *The Book*, and Jerome had no idea how the author had managed to get hold of it. Presumably, the author had paid someone in the Echo Springs PD for the picture, but she refused to divulge the identity of her source. The news of *The Book*'s publication had already stirred up the citizenry of Echo Springs, but when it was released and people saw the photo of Tami's body, they went nuts. Tami's parents had been devastated when they learned about the photo, and the residents of Echo Springs demanded that the publisher pull *The Book* from print. All of this publicity only helped sales, and it made *The Skintaker* a modest bestseller. In the end, all the town council could do was ban *The Book* from Echo Springs's library system, and after a couple years, the ban was overturned, and anyone sixteen and older who wanted to check out *The Skintaker* had been able to do so ever since. Jerome had been pleased with the decision. As a librarian, he didn't believe in the restriction of information for any reason, and he thought *The Book*, in an admittedly lurid way, was a tribute to the memories of Lihn, Becky, and Tami.

Jerome had tried many times over the years to understand what it was that drew him to *The Book* so strongly, but he had no real answers, only guesses. Part of it was his proximity to both killer and victims. He'd known them all, had even had a crush on Lihn – not that he'd ever told her. He hadn't been friends with any of them, but they'd all gotten along well enough, although Becky *could* be snappy with him at times, usually just before a performance when she was nervous and freaking out. And while Lihn was the girl he'd liked the most, he'd been a teenage boy, which meant he'd been sexually attracted to all three of them. Hell, back then he'd been attracted to the entire female gender, it seemed. All he'd had to do was look at a girl, and his dick would harden instantly. But another part of his attraction to this story, perhaps the biggest part, was that he'd detected no sign whatsoever of Randall being the kind of twisted personality that could do such awful things. Randall hadn't been sullen and withdrawn, and he hadn't erupted in sudden, unexpected displays of anger and aggression. He was well liked at school, got good grades, performed well in band, and had plans to go to college and study electrical engineering. There was nothing about his home life to indicate that he was a killer in the making. His parents weren't divorced and by all accounts they loved each other and worked hard to give their son a good life. It was as if he'd woken up one morning and thought to himself, *I'd like to kill someone today. And to make it extra special, I think I'll cut off her fucking face and eat it, too.*

There had been one slight indication of what was to come, though. One night in fall after a home football game, everyone had been trudging across the parking lot back to the band room, when Randall, without any obvious reason, began singing 'Bad to the Bone' very loudly. He quit when he got halfway through and started laughing, as if he'd just heard the most hilarious joke in the world. There'd been a manic edge to his laughter, and Jerome – like a lot of other kids – had wondered if Randall had taken some kind of drug during the game. Then again, it wasn't uncommon for band members to end up punch-drunk at the end of a long day, so Jerome had dismissed Randall's impromptu solo concert as nothing more than a bit of post-game silliness. But now, almost thirty-five years later, he wondered if Randall hadn't been trying to tell them all something that night, and they'd been too stupid to listen.

Becky was found dead a week later, Linh two weeks after that, and Tami only three days after Linh. The coroner would later determine that Tami had died before Linh, but Linh's body had washed ashore first. Randall might well have gotten away with the murders. Throwing bodies into the river was an effective way to get rid of any forensic evidence that might have clung to them, and since Randall hadn't raped them pre- or post-mortem – *I wanted to keep them pure,* he'd later explain – there wasn't any biological evidence to tie him to the girls' deaths. But less than twenty-four hours after Tami's body was discovered, Randall walked into a police station and confessed. Why he'd chosen to do this, he never said. He was eighteen, so he was charged as an adult. He was found guilty and received the death penalty, but after only a couple years in prison, he got into a fight with a much bigger, much tougher inmate and was killed. Most of Echo Springs's residents were elated that Randall was dead, although a number of them thought he'd gotten off too easy in the end.

Jerome turned back to the page with the girls' school photos.

As he often did, he wondered what their lives would be like today if they'd lived. What careers they'd have, what their families would be like – assuming they chose to have any – what unfulfilled dreams, hopes, aspirations…. Jerome had been far too shy to speak to Linh back in high school, but if she was alive today and single and he asked her out, would she say yes? And if she did, would they kiss at the end of the night, maybe – if he was extremely fortunate – end up in bed together? If so, what would her skin feel like? He closed his eyes, imagined running his hand across the length of her unclothed thigh…flesh discolored, cold, swollen, and wet. He then imagined touching her face, or rather, where her face had been. Imagined his fingertips touching raw, red exposed muscle, feeling the bone beneath…. Imagined leaning down to kiss her lipless mouth, pressing his own lips to her teeth…. He was many years removed from being a teenager, but his cock stiffened rapidly, becoming so hard it was painful.

His eyes flew open. He slammed *The Book* shut and quickly replaced it on the shelf.

You're a fucking pervert, you know that? But that's okay. I like perverts.

Ashamed that someone had caught him being aroused by a book about a trio of hideous murders, he turned around, ready to offer some sort of excuse. But whatever he might have said died in his throat when he found himself looking at Randall Beck.

He was leaning against a shelf, arms crossed, an amused smile on his face, dead doll eyes fixed on Jerome. He looked exactly like his mug shot photo: eighteen, shaggy blond hair, wearing a Sonic Youth T-shirt, jeans, and a pair of old sneakers. It was ridiculous, given that this was surely another hallucination, like seeing Lihn's photo wink at him, but Jerome felt suddenly self-conscious. He was fifty-one with a receding hairline, a double chin, and a few pounds too many around the waistline. His curly hair was still red…well, reddish. The color was darker than it had been when he was in high school, almost sandy brown now. He sported a mustache too, so full it qualified for walrus status. He wore a dark blue turtleneck, matching slacks, and black sneakers that mimicked dress shoes but which were a hell of lot easier on his feet. He must look so *old* to Randall. Broken down, worn out, used up.

"You're not real," Jerome said, half statement, half question.

Real enough. Randall's mouth didn't move when he spoke, which was weird and spooky, but kind of cool too.

Jerome kept his voice low so none of the library's patrons or his colleagues would hear him.

"Are you a…."

Ghost? Not really, but that word's good enough for now. Do you know what today is, Jerky?

Jerry Jerk-Off was the nickname Randall had given Jerome in high school, although eventually he'd shortened it to just *Jerky*. Jerome had almost forgotten the name, which he found surprising given how much he'd hated it.

Jerome remembered the question Randall had asked, and he shook his head.

It's Homecoming. Across the whole goddamn world, Jerky. Gonna be a hell of a party. Literally. Wanna be my plus one?

"I don't understand."

Someone sitting at a reading table close by shushed him, but whoever it was, Jerome ignored them. He couldn't take his eyes off Randall.

Do you know why you're really obsessed with me?

Jerome wanted to protest, wanted to say that it was the girls that he was most interested in, young lives with so much promise, like beautiful flowers cut before they could fully blossom.

Randall snorted as if he could read Jerome's thoughts.

He's a ghost, a spirit, a specter, so maybe he can, Jerome thought.

You're obsessed with me because you're jealous. You want to know what it's like to be *me, to kill without mercy, hesitation, or regret. You want to feel strong, single-minded, driven…. And you really, really want to fuck some dead girls. I gotta say, that's pretty damn disgusting even for me. I never fucked Becky, Tami, or Linh. For me, taking a life was greater ecstasy than mere sex could ever be. But to each his own, I suppose.*

Randall waved his hand in a languid gesture, and an invisible force took hold of Jerome. It yanked him off his feet, and hurled him toward the bookshelf behind him. He'd been standing only a few inches from the books and should've struck them immediately, but it seemed he flew through the air for a long time, spinning and tumbling. There was a momentary flash of red, and then he was falling. He hit hard, rolled, came to a stop and lay on his side, breathing heavily, body hurting all over. What the hell had just....

He became aware of sound then, a loud, constant *sssshhhhh* like a vast amount of flowing water. He pressed his hands to the ground, felt grass beneath his fingers and palms. Except it couldn't be grass. Grass was green. This stuff, whatever it was, was gray. He pushed himself into a sitting position and found himself looking at a river. And not just any river – the Iden. Except the water, normally a greenish blue, was now slate gray. The sky was a light gray, the clouds that drifted within it pure white. The buildings on the other side of the river were all various shades of black, gray, and white. Jerome started to panic, and he looked at his hands, turning them palms up as he examined them. They were gray, too. Light gray, like the sky.

Something had thrown him toward the books on the shelf...no, not books. *The Book.* That flash of red he'd seen, that had been the cover as he passed through it. Somehow he was inside *The Book*, more specifically, within one of the black-and-white photographs printed in the middle. He rose to his feet, lightheaded and trembly, and he gazed out upon the river. As he watched, its slate-gray darkened, became almost black, and he saw objects bobbing on the surface, only a few at first, but then more appeared, and more after that, until the Iden was choked with them. It took him a moment to realize what they were, and when he did, his gut squirmed.

They were bodies. Hundreds of them, naked, mutilated, faceless. All girls, all *young* girls.... And that wasn't water they were floating in. The black stuff was *blood*, but in black and white.

Ever read the Bible?

Jerome jumped and quickly turned to see Randall – who was also in black and white – standing next to him, looking at the mass of dead bodies floating by. He went on without waiting for Jerome to answer, spreading his arms wide as if to take in the entire river and its contents.

All this I will give you if you will bow down and worship me.

As if in response to Randall's words, bodies began washing up onto the riverbank. Four, ten, twenty, more....

Jerome's mouth was dry, and he felt his penis grow swollen and hot.

Go on, Randall said, *knock yourself out. We've got a little time before things back in the real world really get going. Why not start the Homecoming off with a bang?* He gave Jerome a wicked smile. *Literally.*

"This isn't real," Jerome said. "It *can't* be. It's a delusion, a fantasy...."

But if that was true, then whatever he did here would be just a fantasy too. All in his mind.

Sure, Randall said. *Let's go with that for now.*

Jerome, hands trembling so hard he could barely make them work, began to unbuckle his belt.

CHAPTER SEVEN

"It was a demon!" the woman shrieked. "A demon made me do it!"

Her face was a mask of blood, and there were two cavernous holes where her eyes had been. She sat on the floor of her dining room, body rocking back and forth, while her daughter – *No, son,* Julie Nguyen reminded herself; he'd introduced himself as Oliver – stood off to the side, staring at his mother with a blank expression. *He's in shock,* Julie thought, but for some reason that didn't seem right. It was more like he wasn't sure what to feel, so his face remained blank. For some reason, he held a closed laptop tucked beneath one arm, its plastic casing slick with blood.

Julie and her partner, Nick Stoler, had been dispatched after Oliver called 911. The fire station where they worked was located close by, and it had taken them only a few minutes to arrive, which was good for the woman – *Emily,* Julie remembered – because if it had taken them much longer to get here, she might've bled out given the severity of her injuries. Julie and Nick knelt on either side of Emily, and Julie could feel blood soaking through the knees of her uniform pants. Julie wasn't squeamish – you couldn't be and survive as an EMT – and she was used to getting bodily fluids of one kind or another on her clothes while she was working. And it wasn't like she was a rookie. She'd been an EMT for nearly seven years, and during that time she'd seen the aftermaths of shootings, stabbings, messy suicides, and horrific traffic accidents. But she'd never seen anything like this. There was blood everywhere – on the woman's face, hands, and clothes, on the floor all around her, on Oliver's hands and clothes, as well as on the laptop he held. It was like Emily's goddamn eyes had exploded and shot blood all over the place.

Speaking of her eyes, they lay on the floor – bloody gobbets with lengths of optic nerve still attached. Blood splatter marred a nearby wall, and Julie imagined Emily hurling the eyes away from her after she'd pulled them out, as if she wanted to get the things as far away from her as possible.

"Please try to remain still, ma'am," Nick said.

The woman – Emily – paid him no mind and continued rocking back and forth, back and forth. He gave Julie a look that said, *You ready?* and she nodded. He moved behind Emily and took hold of her shoulders with his gloved hands in order to keep her steady so Julie could work. Emily shrieked again – a wordless cry of fury this time – and tried to twist out of Nick's grip. Nick was a big guy and a weightlifter, and Emily was short and thin, but the woman was a fighter. She flung herself backward, and in the process smashed her head into Nick's face. His nose broke with a sickening *crunch*, and blood gushed onto the back of Emily's head and ran down Nick's face.

"Fuck!" he shouted. "Fuck-fuck-*fuck*!"

Oliver took a step forward, as if she – *he* – was afraid Nick might harm his mother in retaliation for injuring him. Julie wasn't worried about that. She'd worked with Nick for a long time, and she'd never once seen him lose his cool and handle a patient roughly. She was, however, worried that Emily would hurt herself further if she continued to resist them like this. When she and Nick had entered the house, she'd carried the duffle bag containing medical supplies, and he'd carried the backboard. It was the latter they needed now. Working together, she and Nick forced Emily onto the backboard and got her strapped down. In between bouts of screaming, the woman babbled about a demon coming out of a computer screen, but once they had her secured, they could finally get to work.

Emily's wounds were still bleeding, so Julie pulled some gauze and bandages from the duffle bag. She handed some to Nick, they each took an eye, and began packing gauze into the ruined sockets. Nick's bent and swollen nose was still bleeding, but he ignored it, his attention focused entirely on his patient. Emily whimpered as they worked, but she didn't scream. That was a relief. Without looking away from her work, Julie asked Oliver to tell them what had happened.

"She gouged her eyes out. I don't know why. I tried to stop her, but I couldn't. She just kept *digging*...."

The boy's voice sounded faint and dreamy, like he was having trouble believing this was real. Julie knew just how he felt. Most eye injuries were puncture wounds, and up to this point the worst she'd encountered was a toddler who'd somehow ended up with a ballpoint pen jammed into the corner of his eye. But *this*…. Unlike what you saw in movies and TV shows, pulling out eyes wasn't easy. You had to really work at it, had to keep *digging*, like Oliver had said, but Emily had managed it. The optic nerves were connected directly to the brain's frontal lobe, and detaching them forcibly had likely given Emily significant brain damage. While it was possible Emily had gouged out her eyes because she thought she'd seen some kind of demon, it was also possible that her mad ravings were the result of injury to her frontal lobe. She might be mentally ill *and* have physical damage to her brain. Christ, this poor woman….

When both sockets were packed, Julie and Nick wrapped white bandages around Emily's head to keep the gauze firmly in place. Once that was accomplished, it was time to take her outside, put her in the back of Julie and Nick's medic, and hurry to the hospital. Although Julie didn't think there was much any doctor could do for the woman now. But before they could leave, they had one last detail to attend to.

Julie looked at Oliver. "How old are you?"

Oliver frowned as if suddenly suspicious, and he gripped the laptop harder. "Why?"

Nick answered, his broken nose making him sound as if he had a severe cold.

"Because if you're a minor, we can't leave you alone. We'll need you to come with us. You can ride in the back with your mother."

Oliver didn't answer right away. His lips moved silently, as if he was speaking to himself. It was weird, but Julie told herself that the kid had probably been traumatized. Hell, anyone would be after watching their mother tear her eyes from her head. For a brief moment, Oliver glanced down at the laptop he was holding, almost as if he were consulting it, and Julie thought of how Emily had ranted about how the demon that had forced her to mutilate herself had emerged from a computer screen. This laptop was the only computer in the room.

Julie wasn't superstitious. She believed there was no world other than this one, which was why it was so important for her to save every life she could. This existence was all there was, and once someone was gone, they were never coming back. Still, seeing Oliver gripping the laptop tight while mumbling to himself struck her as more than a little creepy.

"I turned eighteen last month," he said.

Julie exchanged a skeptical glance with Nick. *If this kid's eighteen,* she thought, *then I'm Awkwafina.*

Before she could call Oliver's bluff, he went on.

"I called my dad right after I called 911. He should be here soon."

Good enough, Julie thought. She gave Nick a nod, put the canvas bag on top of Emily's legs, and together they lifted her up, Julie at the front of the backboard, Nick at the rear. Once they got Emily into the back of the transport, one of them would return to collect her eyes, putting them into a plastic bag with a cold pack. Julie doubted there was anything a surgeon could do to reattach the eyes, but she was an EMT, not a doctor. If there was a chance, no matter how slim, that Emily could get her eyes back, Julie would retrieve them, even if they most likely would be disposed of at the hospital.

Julie and Nick carried Emily out of the dining room, Oliver following behind, still carrying the laptop. They went through the kitchen, then into a hallway, and then to the foyer. There was a large, framed painting of Jesus hanging on the wall here, hand raised in a benediction, a heart with a small flame rising from it floating in the air over his chest. He was a very white-looking Jesus, brown hair and beard so light they almost looked blond. Julie had barely noticed the painting on the way in, so focused had she been on reaching Emily, but now it caught her attention. He had a kind expression but sorrowful eyes, and although Julie didn't believe in the man's divinity – or for that matter, his existence at all – she assumed Emily did, considering the way she'd ranted about a demon forcing her to gouge out her eyes. It was a shame she couldn't see the painting on their way out. Maybe it would've given her some measure of comfort.

As was standard procedure, she and Nick had left the door open when they'd entered the house so their exit would be unimpeded. As they carried

Emily outside, the cold air hit Julie like a slap in the face, and she was grateful for the sensation. This had been a bad run so far, and the bracing winter air helped calm her a bit. She needed to stay focused until they got Emily to the hospital. After that, she could fall apart all she wanted. Nick had backed their transport medic into the driveway when they'd arrived, and they'd left the rear doors open and placed a wheeled stretcher on the ground so it would be ready when they brought Emily out. All they had to do was carry Emily to the stretcher, put the backboard on it, secure it, roll the stretcher into the transport, then get moving. Easy enough. She'd done it hundreds of times.

Except this time there was a problem.

The way to the transport was blocked by a small crowd of people – perhaps a dozen in all – men and women, young and old, a few children and toddlers, even a couple babies. They stood – or in the case of the babies sat or held themselves up on hands and knees – packed close together, forming a living wall. They glared at Julie, eyes burning with hate, and their loathing struck her with almost physical force. There was something wrong about them. For one thing, none of them were dressed for the weather. Both she and Nick wore heavy jackets, but none of the people blocking the transport had on coats. Some wore button-up shirts, blouses, and jeans, while others wore T-shirts and sweats. Some were dressed in nightgowns and pajamas, while others wore only underwear. A couple were completely naked. But regardless of how they were clothed – or not – none of them seemed to be bothered by the cold. No one was shivering, and no one hugged their arms close to their bodies for warmth. But as weird as that was, it wasn't the worst thing about them. Most of these people were injured in one way or another, some severely. Arms and legs bent at unnatural angles, broken ends of bone jutting out. Limbs missing entirely, stumps ragged and bloody. Flesh marred by cuts and puncture wounds, contusions and burns. Skin dotted by petechial hemorrhaging, faces purple, tongues black and swollen, eyes bulging. Great gaping wounds on abdomens, organs protruding, loops of intestine hanging out, spilling onto the ground. And so much blood that it looked as if they'd all been drenched by a storm of thick crimson rain.

As awful as all this was – and it was fucking *horrifying* – it became worse when Julie realized that she recognized a number of these faces. The skinny old man with the massive head wound was Ed Clayton. He'd shot himself after learning that he had Alzheimer's and had died on the way to the hospital. The little girl whose head lolled loosely on her neck was Bonnie Reese. She'd been struck by a driver while crossing an intersection on her bike. She'd been alive when Julie and Nick got to her, but they'd been unable to stabilize her for transport, and she'd died before they could get her onto the medic. The heavy middle-aged woman with the badly dyed hair was Geraldine Rowe. It had been snowing the night she'd had a massive heart attack, and the roads had been a bitch to drive on. Nick had been forced to go slowly, and by the time they reached Geraldine's house, she was dead. The man whose chewed-up left arm hung limply at his side was Bill Dawson. He'd been clearing brush on his property with an old chainsaw after having one too many beers, and he'd ended up nearly cutting off his arm. He'd bled out in the ER. Perhaps worst of all was a two-year-old girl named Jasmine Hart. Her father was a drug addict who used to 'rent' his daughter to anyone to do with as they pleased for the princely sum of twenty dollars. The girl was naked, and her crotch looked like raw hamburger. She'd died on the way to the hospital, crying and whimpering in pain.

Julie didn't remember all their names, of course, but she remembered most, and she recalled the various conditions that had led to their deaths. These were the people who haunted her nightmares, the ones that she'd been unable to save – all of them.

"Are you seeing this?" Nick asked in a quiet voice.

Julie looked back over her shoulder at her partner. "Are *you*?"

He nodded, unable to take his eyes off the apparitions that blocked the path to the medic. Julie looked to Oliver then. He stood in the doorway of his home, clutching his laptop in one arm while stroking its surface with his other hand, as if he was petting it. His gaze was also fixed on the assembled…. What the hell were they? Ghosts? They seemed too solid, too *real* to be spirits. Julie thought then that at least Emily would be spared the sight of these things. A small mercy, perhaps, but a mercy nonetheless.

YOU FAILED US....

None of their mouths moved, yet they spoke with a single thunderous voice. The sound stabbed into Julie's ears like ice picks, and she winced. Emily might no longer have eyes, but she had no trouble hearing the phantoms' combined voice, and she let out an ear-splitting scream. Julie was so startled by the sound that she almost dropped her end of the backboard.

She wanted to deny the ghosts' accusation, to tell them that in each of their cases, she'd done the best she could at the time. But while that had been true, it hadn't been enough. Every time she lost someone, she'd replay the run in her mind over and over, examining every step she'd taken, every decision she'd made, trying to determine what she could've done differently to ensure a better outcome. One way or another, she'd failed all of them, and she couldn't deny it.

"Leave them alone!" Oliver shouted. He stepped out of the doorway and onto the lawn. "They need to take my mom to the hospital!"

Oliver sounded scared, but not as scared as Julie might've expected him to be. Brave kid.

The ghosts glanced at him, their heads moving in unison as if they were some kind of conglomerate life-form. They then turned as one to fix their gazes on his mother.

She should join us. You all should join us.

The ghosts started coming toward them, using whatever form of locomotion their broken bodies permitted – walking, shuffling, limping, crawling....

Julie's first impulse was to start running and hope Nick followed her lead. She wasn't thinking about herself – although she sure as shit didn't want any of those ghoulish creatures touching her – but she didn't want to add Emily to their roster. She and Nick had to protect their patient. That was the job, after all. But where could they go? The ghosts had left the driveway and entered the yard, and now they spread out with the clear intention of blocking access to the sidewalk. If Julie was on her own, she would've tried to run past them. She assumed that those with intact legs could pursue her, but she felt confident she could outrun them. She ran every day to keep in shape, and she thought she'd have a decent chance of escaping. But she wasn't on her own. She had Nick and together the two of them had Emily. No way could they move fast enough carrying her. And what about Oliver? Julie couldn't just abandon him to these *things*. They couldn't go forward, which meant there was only one direction they could go.

"Back in the house!" Julie shouted. "Quick, before—"

The advancing ghosts did nothing obvious, but the front door slammed violently shut, and she heard the soft *snicks* of locks engaging.

"—something happens," she finished.

"We have to put her down," Nick said. "We need our hands free."

To do what? Julie thought. *Wave goodbye to each other?* Even if these people weren't…whatever they were, there were too many for the three of them to fight physically. Julie had taken some self-defense classes, but she'd never been in an actual combat situation. It was her job to help people, not hurt them, and even though she didn't think these ghosts qualified as people any longer, she still wasn't sure she could bring herself to harm them. They had to do something, though, so together she and Nick gently lowered Emily to the ground.

"They're going to kill us," Oliver said. "Make us like them." He looked down at his laptop, scowled, and rapped a knuckle against its surface. "No, that will *not* be nice!"

Julie had no idea why the kid was talking to his computer, and right then she really didn't care. She and Nick took up defensive positions in front of Emily, although what they were going to do to protect the woman, she had no idea. Give the ghosts a stern talking to? *Just because all of you died horrible deaths, it's no reason to hurt this poor lady. She's already gouged out her damn eyes this morning. Isn't that enough pain for one day?*

As if the ghosts had read her mind, they said, *There can never be too much pain.*

They smiled.

Julie thought she might piss herself there and then, but she caught a flash of movement off to her right. She turned in that direction and saw a man jogging on the sidewalk. Like the ghosts, he wasn't dressed for the weather – My Chemical Romance T-shirt, shorts, socks, and running shoes. He was Asian, somewhere in his thirties, lean, in good shape. She thought she recognized him, but she couldn't…. Then it hit her like a hammer blow to the gut. It was Brian. Her brother.

When Brian reached the sidewalk in front of Oliver's house, he veered into the yard and continued jogging toward Julie and the others. He looked good. No, scratch that. He looked goddamn *great* – especially for a dead man. He'd died three years ago, while he'd been out running. He was much more into the activity than she was, but he was the type who always threw himself a hundred percent into everything he did. He'd graduated near the top of his class in med school, and had landed a residency at an excellent hospital in Cleveland. His health was top notch save for one little thing: he was extremely allergic to bee stings. He always carried an epinephrine auto-injector with him wherever he went – except for one summer day when he'd decided it would be pleasant to run in a park that had trees, a large pond, and flowers. *Lots* of flowers. Julie didn't know why Brian had left the injector behind. Had he simply forgotten it? He hadn't been stung since he was a boy, and although he'd nearly died then, three decades had passed since. Had he relaxed his guard too much, figured that the odds of him getting stung as an adult were so low that it wasn't necessary to drag an injector with him everywhere he went? The odds of him getting stung were a hundred percent on that day, though. A bee got him on the back of the neck, just one little sting, but that was all it took. He was found and rushed to a hospital, but he'd died there less than an hour later of anaphylactic shock. It had been a goddamn stupid way to die, and one that might've been easily prevented if he hadn't left his fucking medicine behind. Brian had such a bright career ahead of him – he'd intended to become a neurologist – and he could've helped so many people. Julie had been close to her big brother growing up, and his loss had devastated her. But now here he was, as the old song went, 'looking better than a body had a right to'. Especially a *dead* body, one that had been cremated, its ashes scattered in Lake Erie.

The group of dead patients turned toward Brian as he drew near, and they bared their teeth at him like a pack of snarling wolves.

She's ours! they said.

Brian responded, mouth unmoving, and Julie realized she'd been hearing the ghosts' thoughts in her mind all along.

She's my sister.

Brian came to a stop when he was within ten feet of the dead patients. He raised his arms, held out his hands, and the flesh of his palms burst open, releasing twin blasts of small objects that looked like...thorns.

Not thorns, Julie thought. *Bee stingers....*

The storm of stingers Brian had unleashed struck the ghosts and embedded in their undead flesh. They cried out with their thought-voices and raised their arms to protect their faces. *How can ghosts feel physical pain?* Julie wondered.

Brian continued blasting stingers at the ghosts, moving closer as he did so, but he spared Julie a quick smile.

Because they're getting hit with ghost *stingers,* he said, as if it was obvious.

Feeling as if her sanity was teetering on the brink, she nodded, as if what her brother had said made sense.

The patients were covered with stingers now, and their flesh – or whatever substance encased their bodies – was beginning to blacken and swell. Their forms seemed less solid than they had only moments earlier, and as Julie watched they began to fade, becoming increasingly transparent and insubstantial until they were gone. The stingers that had missed them and fallen to the lawn disappeared as well.

The flesh on Brian's palms closed over, and then he gave her a little wave, as if to say, *See you,* turned, and started running again. He ran down the driveway past the medic, got back on the sidewalk, and continued running until he was lost to sight.

The three of them – Julie, Nick, and Oliver – stared in the direction Brian had taken. Emily lay on the backboard, quiet, as if she too were struggling to process what had just taken place.

"What the fuck was *that*?" Nick asked.

"I have no idea," Julie said. "Come on. We need to get this woman to the hospital."

She hoped Nick wouldn't argue with her. She wanted— no, she *needed* to return to some semblance of normalcy, to do something, *anything* so she wouldn't have to think about what had happened. Because if she didn't distract herself, if she continued thinking about those vengeful patients and her dead brother – who was now filled with bee stingers – she thought there was an excellent chance that she was going to scream.

"Yeah," Nick said. "Sure."

Together they bent down, picked up the backboard, and continued carrying Emily toward the medic. Once they got her onto the wheeled stretcher and secured the backboard to it, they put the stretcher into the medic. Nick jogged to the driver's side, and Julie climbed into the back and prepared to close the rear doors. Before she did, she gave Oliver one last look. The kid stood in front of the house, holding the laptop screen up. It looked like he was talking to someone, and Julie wondered if he was Skyping. If so, it was kind of odd. Wouldn't it be easier to just call someone on the phone, even if you wanted to video chat with them?

Then something emerged from the screen. A hand, followed by a wrist, and then a forearm. The hand reached for Oliver's cheek and gently caressed it. Oliver closed his eyes and smiled.

CHAPTER EIGHT

Mari returned to the kitchen, feeling as if she were walking through a dream. She tore a sheet of paper towel off the roll on the counter, wadded it, then pressed it to her bleeding lips. She did this automatically, her mind too filled with images of what had happened in Noelle's room to have space for any other thoughts.

I want to go home!

She walked into the dining room. Lewis still sat at the table, empty plate pushed aside, staring at his phone screen. She walked to the other side of the table, slid out the chair opposite his, and sat. She said nothing, thought nothing. Her lips throbbed but the pain barely registered. She kept the paper towel pressed tight against the wound and looked at her husband, her expression blank. Lewis didn't look up from his phone.

"The whole world's lost its goddamn mind," he said.

His words held no meaning for her. He continued speaking, still not looking at her.

"Reports are coming in from...well, from *everywhere*. People are seeing visions, I guess you could call them. No one knows what they are. People claim they're being visited by the ghosts of dead family and friends, but these ghosts are *pissed*. They're hurting people, even killing them. I thought it was some kind of hoax at first. But I've checked a half dozen different news sites – reputable ones – and they all say the same thing. It's fucking *insane*."

"I saw a ghost," Mari said softly, voice partially muffled by the paper towel. "At least, I think that's what it was."

That got Lewis's attention. He looked up from his phone and frowned when he saw Mari was pressing the paper towel to her lips.

"Are you okay? What happened?"

Mari's mind was slowly starting to clear, and she understood that Lewis was asking about the injury to her lip. But before she could answer, he said, "What do you mean you saw a ghost?"

"I heard a baby crying, so I went down to Noelle's room. She was there, Lewis. In her crib. The room was cold, so I picked her up to warm her. She...she wanted...." Mari lowered the paper towel from her bleeding lips. "She did this to me."

He leaned forward, as if to examine her lips more closely. He opened his mouth, and she thought he might say something like *What the hell are you talking about?* or *Did you have a stroke or something?* But she wasn't the sort of person given to fanciful thinking, and Lewis knew this. Plus, he'd read all those news reports.

"Show me," he said.

A jolt of fear burned away the last of Mari's mental fog.

"I don't think that's a good idea," she said.

She didn't want to go back into that room, not for any reason. And if Lewis went inside, would he even see Noelle? *He* hadn't heard her crying. *He* hadn't been the one she wanted. She hadn't wanted to crawl inside *him.* Would Noelle reveal herself to him at all?

"Why isn't it a good idea?" he pressed.

"She's angry, Lewis. So very angry."

He fell silent then. She sensed that he was appraising her, and she could guess what he was thinking: that losing Noelle had finally driven her over the edge. Suddenly she *did* want to return to Noelle's room. For the first couple months after Mari's miscarriage, Lewis had been supportive and understanding, but the longer her grief had gone on, the more he began to become impatient. *Yes, it was a tragedy, but these things happen. It sucks and it sucks hard, but you have to get over it, have to move on.*

Get over it.

Move on.

People who offered this empty advice had never experienced true grief, the soul-deep sorrow that sat at the center of your being like a ravenous black hole, threatening to pull you in and devour you. And it hadn't only been Lewis urging her to *move on.* Her mother, her sister, her best friend at work.... All of them had told her the same thing. They all had children, but none had *lost* a child, not like she had. None of them understood the *pain*. But Lewis had been – *was* – Noelle's father. If there was anyone who should understand, it was him.

She was no longer afraid. She was angry – just like her daughter.

She rose from her seat, came around the dining table, grabbed Lewis's hand, and pulled him to a standing position. She did not do this gently.

"You want me to show you? Then let's go."

Without waiting for him to reply, she turned and began pulling him after her. She led him out of the dining room, through the kitchen, and down the hall to Noelle's room. Once there, she let go of Lewis's hand and gestured toward the closed door.

"After you," she said.

She was aware that the way she was acting wasn't making a good case for her sanity, but she didn't care. She needed Lewis to *see*, needed him to *understand*, but no way in hell was she going to go inside first.

He looked to the door, then back to her. He pointed to her lips. "She did that." Not a question.

"Yes."

"But...even if she *is* in there, she's just a baby, right? She wouldn't be strong enough or coordinated enough to hurt anyone."

"Whatever she is, she's *not* a baby."

Lewis looked at the door again, and she could feel his resolve wavering. He might still be unsure about her story, but it wasn't as if it existed in a vacuum. He'd read those news articles. It galled her to think that he put more stock in accounts posted by random reporters than he did his own wife's experience, but she supposed she'd feel the same if their roles had been reversed. She thought he might change his mind, decide that it wasn't worth taking the risk to go into their daughter's room. He'd return to the dining room to get his phone and do more research on what was happening, maybe go into the living room and put on a cable news channel to see what they were saying. When Lewis was uncertain about something – or when he was anxious or afraid – his way of coping was to gather as much data as possible. It gave him a feeling of control, made a problem seem smaller, less intimidating.

But he surprised her. He took hold of the knob, turned it, and pushed the door open.

Cold air – far more frigid than it had been only a few moments earlier – blasted into them. It carried a foul odor with it, a scent of infection and rotting meat that made Mari gag. She grabbed hold of Lewis's arm and tried to pull him away. She no longer cared if he believed her about Noelle. Let him think she had completely lost her mind if he wanted. It had been a mistake to come back here, and they needed to leave *now*, while they still could.

"Close the door!" she shouted. "Let's go!"

She pulled harder on his arm, but Lewis resisted. He shrugged her off, then stepped into the room.

"Sweet Jesus…" he whispered.

Don't do it, she told herself. *Don't follow him.* But he was her husband. She couldn't let him face the thing their daughter had become alone. She went inside.

The room itself looked the same as the last time she'd been here – crib, dresser, curtains, sea animals painted on the walls – but now it was filled with crisscrossing lengths of some sort of rubbery tubing, twisted into a corkscrew shape and threaded with thin blue lines. No, not lines. *Veins.* It was an umbilical cord, an impossibly long one that stretched back and forth across the room like some hideous version of a spider's web. It was anchored to the walls, ceiling, and floor at various points by some kind of thick greenish-yellow substance that looked like pus. Now she knew where the horrible stink was coming from.

Noelle crouched at the center of this web, the cord – which her father had never gotten to cut – protruding from her small belly. The flesh around it was red and swollen, and blood and pus leaked around the edges. The cord was infected, Mari realized, all the way through, from one end to the other. She had a crazy thought then: were she and Lewis looking at the ghost of Noelle's *actual* umbilical cord, the one that had tethered child to mother for the short time she'd grown within Mari's womb? Noelle had been so small when the miscarriage occurred, and her cord would've been equally as tiny. But whatever was taking place in their home – and evidently across the entire world – wasn't bound by logic or natural laws, at least none known to Mari.

Noelle's eyes fixed on Lewis, and she cried out with her thought-voice. *Daddy!*

Lewis shook his head, raised his hands as if to ward her off, took a step backward. "You're not our daughter! You're some kind of fucking monster!"

Noelle's features scrunched tight in fury and she blasted a new thought at them. *BAD DADDY!*

As if in resonance with Noelle's anger, the umbilical cord web began to quiver. Sections of the cord lengthened, bowed outward, stretched toward Lewis like spiral-shaped serpents. Coils swiftly looped around his arms, legs, neck, and torso. They drew tight, pulling his arms out to his sides and lifting him several inches off the floor. He turned his head to look at Mari, tried to speak, but all that came out of his mouth was a strangled gurgle.

Mari tried to go to him, but the lengths of cord in front of her drew closer to each other, becoming a thick tangle, and no matter how hard she pushed against their hard, slick surfaces, she couldn't budge them. All she could do was watch as Noelle lifted Lewis higher into the air. Noelle scuttled forward, moving through her web with inhuman speed until she was nearly nose to nose with her father.

Noelle stood on one section of the cord, holding on to another with both of her tiny doll hands as she regarded Lewis, her features still contorted in anger. The skin of her abdomen around where the cord protruded was swollen, and pus oozed from the edges of her belly button. Keeping her brown eyes fixed solely on Lewis's, she reached down with her right hand, grasped the cord, and gave it a quick, hard shake. Vibrations rippled along the cord, up and down, back and forth, until they reached the coils that had ensnared Lewis. They tightened, pulled, and Lewis tried to scream, but no sound came out. The coils then yanked Lewis in multiple directions, and his body came apart with horrible wet tearing sounds. Blood sprayed the air, and Mari screamed as Noelle clapped and giggled in delight. Warm drops struck Mari's face and hands, splattered her clothes, and she thought, *I'm wearing my husband's blood.*

The coils continued to grip the pieces of Lewis's body, blood running from their ragged ends, pattering to the floor like crimson water. The expression on Noelle's face was no longer one of dark joy at watching her father come apart like a shoddily made toy. Now she looked hopeful. She let go of the umbilical cord, stretched her hands toward Mari, said, *Mommy?* in a plaintive, almost pleading tone. Mari knew what she wanted. Noelle was asking her to come pick her up, hold her close, open her mouth and let her go *home*....

"Fuck you!" Mari screamed.

She turned and ran out of the room as a mass of umbilical coils shot toward her. She reached the hallway and increased her speed, and the coils struck the door to the master bedroom with a loud, wet *thump*, barely missing her. She tried not to think about what her daughter had become, what she'd done to poor, sweet Lewis. She concentrated on putting one foot in front of the other, on moving forward and not looking back. A loud squishing-sliding sound came from behind her as something big, heavy, and wet dragged itself across the floor. Noelle was coming. Mari did her best to shut out the awful sound and keep running.

She ran into the living room, past the couch where she and Lewis would sit and snuggle as they binge-watched TV shows on their large flat-screen TV. She almost broke down crying at the realization she would never sit next to her best friend and lover ever again, never hold him, never kiss him. But she shoved those thoughts from her mind. There would be time to mourn Lewis later – assuming she survived the next few minutes.

The inside entrance to the garage was located on the other side of the living room. They hung their various keys – car keys, house keys, keys to the backyard shed – on hooks mounted next to the door. Both she and Lewis had a bad habit of losing track of their keys if they put them anywhere else, and for once she was grateful for their mutual forgetfulness. As she headed for the door, she snatched the keys to the Honda Odyssey minivan they'd bought when she'd first learned that she'd become pregnant. Now, instead of ferrying Noelle around in her car seat, Mari would use the vehicle to escape her daughter. *How's that for irony?* she thought, and let out a wild, half-crazed laugh.

She threw open the door to the garage, closed it behind her, and hit the wall switch to activate the garage door opener. The royal-blue van was the only vehicle in the garage. Lewis's pickup had magnetic Car-Care signs on each side, and he always parked it in the driveway. *Free advertising,* he always said. She ran to the van as the garage door ratcheted open, got in, closed and locked the door behind her. The van had keyless ignition, which was good. As badly as her hands were shaking, she didn't think she'd be able to work a physical key. She put her foot on the brake, pushed the ignition button, and the van's engine came to life. She latched her seatbelt, the habit so ingrained that she didn't realize she did so, put the vehicle in reverse, and waited for the garage door to open all the way.

Come on, come on....

The door to the house burst open and a tangled mass of umbilical cord spilled out onto the garage's concrete floor. Noelle was perched on top, riding the mass as if it was some kind of grotesque steed. She glared at Mari, and her daughter's enmity smashed into her as waves of pure hatred.

Bad Mommy, bad Mommy, bad Mommy!

Each of the soundless words pierced her mind like a cold, sharp blade, and Mari cried out in pain. She didn't look to see if the garage door was all the way up, didn't care if it was. She jammed her foot down on the accelerator and the van lurched backward. The vehicle's roof clipped the bottom edge of the garage door, but it kept going, and Mari might've cheered if she hadn't seen the white flash of Lewis's pickup in her rearview mirror. She was on a direct course to hit the goddamn thing. How many times had she told Lewis to pull over all the way to the side of the driveway when he parked so she would have enough room to get the van out easily? This time he'd practically parked in the middle of the fucking driveway. If he hadn't already been dead, she'd have killed him. She let out a sound that was a combination of a laugh and a sob, and then yanked the van's steering wheel to the right and hoped she'd miss the pickup.

She struck the side of the garage as she pulled out and sideswiped Lewis's pickup, but she made it. She veered partway onto the lawn as she continued backing up, and she pulled the steering wheel to the left to correct her course. Her eyes were focused on her rearview so she didn't see Noelle coming at her. There was a wet *smack* as the mass of umbilical cord struck the van's windshield, and she reflexively screamed. The van juddered as it backed over the curb and into the street, and Mari hit the brake, bringing the vehicle to a sudden stop. The windshield, along with both the driver's-side and passenger windows, was completely obscured by coils of umbilical cord. Mari's instincts told her to drive, to get away, but how could she if she couldn't see?

The coils covering the middle of the windshield parted to allow Noelle's head to slide through in a hideous parody of birth. The creature that was her daughter pressed her face to the glass, small eyes blazing with white-hot fury. *Bad Mommy!* she said again, and then the driver's-side window exploded.

A length of intestine slithered inside the van, looped around Mari's neck, and pulled tight. She let go of the steering wheel, reached up with both hands, and clawed at the cord, trying to pull it away from her throat, but without success. The surface was too slick to get a proper handhold, and her fingers kept sliding off. The cord continued to tighten, and Mari began having trouble drawing in breath. Sparkles of light danced in her vision, and through them she saw Noelle, face still pressed to the windshield, grinning with her toothless mouth.

Not today, you little bitch!

Mari took her foot off the brake and jammed it down on the accelerator.

The van jumped forward, swerved to the right, and kept going. Mari was still trying to loosen the cord wrapped around her throat, so she wasn't steering as the vehicle moved down the street – not that it mattered since she couldn't see a goddamn thing. Darkness began gliding in from the edges of her vision, indicating that she was on the verge of unconsciousness, and she knew if she passed out, she'd never wake again.

And when you're asleep, I'll crawl back inside you, Mommy. Then we'll be together forever and ever....

There was a loud *crump* as the van struck something – another car from the sound of it – and Mari lurched forward and back as the vehicle came to a halt. Noelle and the mass of umbilical coils flew off of the windshield and landed on the trunk of a silver Camry that belonged to one of their neighbors across the street. Noelle may have been dislodged, but the loop of umbilical cord around Mari's neck remained tight as ever, and her vision had gone almost completely black now. Mari was a teacher, and when she and Lewis had been trying to get pregnant, she'd read everything she could find on fetal development and childbirth. One of the things she'd read was that in the days before people cut umbilical cords, they bit through them in order to detach the baby from the placenta. At the time, Mari had been disgusted by the thought, but now it seemed like her only hope. She fumbled around with her hands until she found a section of cord that wasn't wrapped around her neck. She took hold of it with both hands, pulled it to her face, opened her mouth, slid the cord between her teeth, and bit down as hard as she could. Mari had tried octopus tentacles at a seafood restaurant once, and the hard, rubbery texture of the cord was similar. She bore down harder with her jaws, and just when she thought her teeth wouldn't be able to break through, she felt a *pop* and her mouth was filled with thick, foul-tasting fluid. She thought of the greenish-yellow pus she'd seen oozing from the site where the cord was attached to Noelle's tummy, and she gagged.

Noelle's psychic wail of pain blasted through Mari's mind, and she felt the two ends of the cord slither out of her mouth. The loop around her neck loosened, lifted over her head, and retracted out the window. Her vision began to clear, and while it was blurry, she could see Noelle lying on the Camry's trunk, some sections of the umbilical cord resting on top of her while others hung over the edges of the car. Noelle's eyes were squeezed shut, her mouth was open in a silent cry, and tears gushed down her cheeks. Mari didn't feel an ounce of pity for her.

She turned her head, spit pus onto the passenger seat, then put the van into reverse. She backed up, put the vehicle in drive, and floored the accelerator. As she roared past Noelle, she stuck out her right arm and gave her the middle finger. She continued down the street, not having any destination in mind, only wanting to put distance between herself and the thing that had killed her husband and had tried to kill her. She heard Noelle's thought-voice then, faint and growing fainter.

I hate you, Mommy...I hate you....

"The feeling's mutual, kid," she said, and kept driving.

CHAPTER NINE

As soon as Faizan left Qwik-Mart, he called his mother. He didn't exactly believe the world was under attack by hordes of angry ghosts, but he didn't *dis*believe it, either. Not after what he'd experienced.

Stand and face them, boy. Show me you know what it means to be a man.

He shuddered at the memory of his ghost-father's voice. At least, he *hoped* it was a memory. He looked around quickly, certain he'd see his father's semi-transparent figure sitting in the passenger seat next to him or in the back. But he was alone.

His mother didn't answer, but that didn't necessarily mean anything bad had happened to her. She worked as an officer manager for a dental practice called Smiles, Inc., and she was very disciplined about not checking her phone until lunchtime. Why couldn't his mom be a social-media obsessed slacker like everyone else and check her phone every few minutes? The call went to voicemail, and he started to leave a message, but he couldn't think of what to say. *Hey, Mom! Dad's ghost harassed me at Qwik-Mart a few minutes ago, and I'm calling to make sure he hasn't started haunting you too. Love ya!*

He disconnected. He tried Salman and Rida, but neither of them answered. His siblings were most likely at work as well, but this time he left short messages telling them to call or text him as soon as possible. He told himself that his mom, brother, and sister were all right. And even if they were experiencing some kind of spirit visitations, what real harm could ghosts do? His dad's ghost had mostly taunted him which, while no fun, hadn't actually hurt him. Yeah, he'd shoved Faizan into one of the rednecks, almost getting him beat up, but it wasn't as if his dad had done anything directly harmful. Ghosts could scare you, maybe move a few objects around here and there, but otherwise they couldn't *really* hurt you, right? He thought then of the video footage he'd seen on the TV in the convenience store – the strange mist-creature grabbing people with its tendrils and throwing them around like rag dolls, leaving their broken, bloody bodies in its wake.

Then again, maybe these ghosts were a little bit more dangerous than the sheet-wearing variety or mischievous poltergeists.

He'd been driving on automatic pilot as he made his calls, and without really thinking about it, he'd started heading home. Rida and Salman lived too far away for him to check on them physically – not unless he wanted to hop on a plane and fly for several hours – but he could be at Smiles, Inc.'s office in less than fifteen minutes. He turned around in the parking lot of a Taco Bungalow and began heading back the way he'd come. His nerves jangled like he'd mainlined a triple espresso, and while he normally drove the speed limit, or close to it, he accelerated until he was going ten miles an hour over. He'd have gone even faster if it wasn't for the other cars on the road. He didn't usually have the car radio on while he drove, preferring instead to listen to podcasts on his phone. But he turned on the radio now and flipped through the channels until he found NPR. He listened to a reporter – who sounded as if she was trying really hard not to come across as scared as she felt – discuss what some people were evidently beginning to call The Event. She said the same basic things as the reporter he'd listened to on the Qwik-Mart's television, only she consulted different experts. He learned nothing new, other than the situation was worsening. Thousands of attacks had been reported worldwide – most of them fatal. All kinds of video evidence had been uploaded to the Internet, and despite all the experts' breathless theorizing about what was happening, no one really had a clue.

"How in the hell are police and military supposed to stop them?" one pundit asked. *"Shoot them? Bomb them? That won't work – the damn things are already dead!"*

As Faizan drove, the voices on the radio faded into the background, and his attention became focused on what was happening outside the Rolling Banana. He passed a fire station that was, ironically enough, engulfed in flames. A number of bodies lay on the ground outside the station, blazing like miniature pyres. The dark smoke that billowed up from the burning building was shaped like a large human figure, twenty, maybe thirty feet high, arms raised to the sky, head thrown back as if laughing. An afreet indeed.

In the parking lot of a FoodSaver, he saw people running toward their cars pursued by insectile metal creatures that looked as if they'd been formed from shopping carts. One of the creatures leaped toward an elderly woman who couldn't run very fast. It sailed through the air like a grasshopper and landed on her, the impact knocking her to the asphalt. It plunged praying-mantis-like claws into her back and began digging into her flesh with furious motions, tearing her to shreds. In the center of the lot, a naked woman whose image cut in and out like a bad signal swung her arms about, as if she were conducting an orchestra. Faizan looked away quickly, unable to watch.

He passed a library and saw people fleeing into the parking lot in terror as a tidal wave of blood surged out of the building's front entrance, carrying with it what looked like dozens of dead, unclothed women – some of their bodies intact, some reduced to pieces. Faizan feared the blood tide would reach the street, and he tromped on the Banana's accelerator, hoping to outrun it. He almost made it, but the leading edge of the blood wave rolled in front of him, bodies and all. He tried to swerve around the mess, but there was a paramedic vehicle racing toward him in the opposite lane, lights on and siren blaring. He didn't want to hit it, but he wasn't going to pull over and give it room to pass, either. Not only couldn't he afford the delay – he had to get to his mother, had to make sure she was safe – he wasn't going to just sit there and let the full force of the blood wave slam into his car. Instead of slowing, he accelerated even more, gripping the steering wheel tight as the Banana rolled over several bodies, the vehicle bouncing and shaking. He sent up a quick prayer for forgiveness for further mutilating the bodies, and to ask that the Banana didn't break a tire rod or even an axle in the process. He thought the car might start to lose traction on the road's blood-slick surface, causing him to spin out and crash, but while he did hydroplane several feet, he managed to keep the Banana under control, and then he was past the blood slick and on dry road again.

He looked in his rearview to check if the EMTs had made it past the blood tide, and he was glad to see they had. He didn't envy them. He imagined Echo Springs's emergency services were getting a real workout right now, and it was only going to get worse. No way the town had enough police, fire, and EMTs to handle an all-out attack like this. But that was a matter for the mayor, the city council, or whoever ran the day-to-day operations of Echo Springs to worry about. His only concern was his mother.

He drove on, doing his best not to be distracted by the horrible vignettes playing out all around him and failing miserably.

★   ★   ★

When Faizan reached Smiles, Inc., he was relieved to see the building looked normal enough. No smoke demon hovering above the roof, no blood tsunami pouring from the entrance. There was an open space next to his mother's car – a white Honda Civic – and he parked the Rolling Banana in it. He got out and quickly scanned the parking lot to make sure the surrounding area was safe. Within the space of a half hour, he'd become as paranoid as if he was living in a war zone. He supposed in a way that's exactly what Echo Springs had become. Everything looked safe enough, at least as far as he could tell, and he started walking toward the building.

Smiles, Inc. was housed in a nondescript one-story brown-brick structure with rectangular windows and a black-shingled roof. On the outer wall next to the main entrance was a sign with the practice's name, below which was a cartoon image of an anthropomorphic tooth – wide eyes, big smile, stick arms emerging from the sides, one white-gloved hand holding a large red toothbrush. Faizan had always hated the cartoon mascot, which he'd dubbed Tommy Toothy when he'd been younger. Not only had he found it creepy, it had raised uncomfortable questions in his young mind. How could a tooth have its own mouth filled with smaller teeth? And did each of those teeth have their own eyes and smile? And if so, did *their* teeth have mouths, and did *those* teeth have mouths? Did the progression continue onward tooth after tooth for infinity? He'd asked his mother about it once, but his father had overheard and had told him to stop being foolish. *It's just a picture,* he'd said. And then, as if it had been an afterthought, his father had smacked him on the back of the head – giving Faizan another reason to dislike Tommy Toothy.

Smiles, Inc. shared the same parking lot as a daycare called Time for Tots. Its building was separate from Smiles's, but it looked exactly the same, except for its sign – shaped like a large blue balloon with the business's name spelled out in red letters – and a small courtyard with playground equipment enclosed by a wrought-iron fence. None of the kids were out playing right now, which Faizan was relieved to see. It would be best if the teachers kept them inside today, he thought, although he wasn't sure that *inside* was any safer than *outside* at the moment.

He entered Smiles, Inc. and found the waiting area empty. He'd never been in the place and not seen at least a few people sitting in chairs, flipping through old magazines or staring at their phones. He told himself that this wasn't necessarily a sign that something was wrong here. If people were dealing with ghostly manifestations, whether at home or at work, the last thing they'd worry about is keeping their dental appointments. They might be glued to their television or computer screens, watching news reports and wondering if the world had gone mad. But when he walked over to the reception counter, no one was there. In fact, the entire front office area was deserted. His mother's desk was visible from where he stood and her chair was empty. His mother rarely left her desk when she was at work and often ate lunch there. But there was no sign of her now.

This was not good.

"Hello?" Faizan called out. "Anyone here?"

No answer.

Up to this point, he'd been nervous, but now he was becoming scared. A wooden door separated the waiting area from the rest of the practice, and while patients usually didn't go in and out on their own, it wasn't kept locked. He went to the door, opened it, and stepped through.

Dentists' offices have a particular blend of smells and sounds: the minty scent of the gritty toothpaste hygienists use to clean patients' teeth, the sharp astringent odor of Novocaine, the whirring whine of dental drills, the gurgling of suction tubes, the bland tones of easy-listening pop music playing over the sound system, the voices of staff talking to patients as they worked. The smells were all present, but the only sound was the music coming through speakers set into the ceiling. Otherwise, it was silent.

Definitely not good.

You're a coward.

Faizan froze upon hearing his father's voice. He didn't want to turn around, didn't want to *see*, but he couldn't stop himself. Asad Barakat was no longer a reflection in the glass of a cooler door. He was as three-dimensional, as real, as Faizan himself.

Faizan felt a strong urge to reach out and poke his father's arm with an index finger to prove he was solid. He also experienced an equally strong urge to keep his hands to himself. He wanted to maintain the possibility – however small – that his father was a hallucination. Plus, what if his father's condition, whatever it was, was contagious? By touching his father, he might get some kind of ghost disease. Or maybe he'd just flat out die.

Asad sneered. *You're pathetic.*

"At least I'm still breathing," Faizan said. He was shocked to hear these words come out of his mouth. In his entire life, he'd never talked back to his father. If he had, it would've earned him a strike across the mouth. And now that his dad was a ghost, he could theoretically do much worse to him. But Faizan didn't care. He'd been relieved when his father had died; he had finally been free of the man's endless criticism and cruelty. He *liked* being free, and he wasn't about to give that up easily.

Faizan steeled himself for his father's reprisal, but the man surprised him by only smiling coldly.

Living is a disease. Death is the cure.

His words made Faizan shiver, but he hadn't come here for a philosophical debate with a dead man.

"Is Mom here? Do you know what's happened to her? Did you *do* something to her?"

Asad's mouth remained closed as he laughed with his thought-voice.

Not yet.

Faizan didn't know if his father was telling the truth, and he didn't really care.

"If you're not going to help, what good are you?"

Faizan turned away and started walking. The staff had to be around here somewhere. All he had to do was find them. He didn't look back to see if his father followed him – either he would or he wouldn't. All Faizan cared about was that the man didn't interfere with his search. For all of Faizan's life, his father had been his own personal boogeyman, an afreet if there ever was one. But now that Asad had become the real thing, or something close to it, Faizan was no longer afraid of him. Wary, yes. Mistrustful, of course. But afraid? No. Asad had been a worse monster in life that he could ever be in death.

Faizan began exploring Smiles, Inc., checking examining rooms, offices, supply closets, restrooms, all without any luck. He called out for his mother several times, but he received no response, not from her or anyone else. It was as if the entire staff and their patients had simply vanished. Could that be what had happened? Had a ghost appeared and taken them away to a hidden dimension of some sort?

More likely it snapped its fingers and they crumbled to dust. You saw that movie, right?

His father sounded as if he was right behind Faizan, but Faizan refused to acknowledge him. He had a few more rooms to check, and so he continued with his search. In the last examining room at the end of a hallway, right before one of the emergency exits, Faizan at last found someone. The person sat in a dental chair, tilted back almost horizontal, as if in preparation for being worked on, blue paper bib fastened around the neck. A flat-screen TV mounted on the wall near the ceiling was displaying a slideshow of dental health facts. *Did you know that by maintaining healthy gums, you reduce the chances of developing bad breath, dental decay, and many harmful diseases?*

Faizan took in all these details at a glance, but for some reason his mind initially refused to focus on the patient lying back in the dental chair. But now he took a good look at him – or her, or it – and he understood why his brain hadn't wanted to deal with the patient at first. The being possessed the rough shape and dimensions of a human, but its body was made entirely from teeth, thousands of them, jammed together and jutting outward, as if glued that way. Incisors, canines, bicuspids, molars. Some white as snow, others stained yellow or brown from years of tobacco use and coffee drinking. Some were clean and healthy, while others were so encrusted with plaque it looked like it would take a sandblaster to get it all off. Some were diseased, a sickly gray or rotting black, and while some were fully intact, others were chipped, cracked, or broken.... Bits of food were lodged between the teeth – threads of meat, chunks of vegetable matter, other substances unidentifiable – and the stink wafting off the creature was truly stomach turning. The thing had no facial features – no eyes, ears, or nose – with the exception of a gaping orifice that served as a mouth.

Go on, Asad urged. *Take a look.*

Faizan didn't want to go anywhere near the monstrous thing reclining in the dental chair, but then a small movement in the creature's mouth caught his eye, and he found himself slowly moving toward it, breathing through his mouth to avoid the stench. He had a suspicion of what he'd see when he got there – and it made sense in a bizarre way – but he wasn't prepared for the reality of it. Inside the creature's mouth, in place of where teeth would be for a human, were miniature people, each embedded in the thing's jaws up to the waist. They were moving, waving their arms and shouting to get his attention. Their voices were so faint he could barely hear them, let alone make out what they were saying.

Ever wonder what happens to all those teeth dentists remove? Asad said. *You're looking at it. Of course, holding all these teeth together is the spirit of a woman named Amy Stokes. She absolutely* hated *going to the dentist, and she did so only when it was an emergency. Right before she died, she had seven teeth pulled here, at Smiles, Inc. She's returned for some rather poetic revenge.*

A dental light was mounted on the ceiling above the chair. Faizan reached up to grab one of the handles on the side and pulled the light closer to the creature's mouth. Holding his breath because of the thing's stink, he leaned over and peered inside. The mouth of an adult human held thirty-two teeth. He didn't do a count, but it looked like around that many tiny people were stuck into the creature's tooth sockets. They were all dressed

— some in medical smocks, some in street clothes, a few in white lab coats which marked them as dentists. His mother was there, on the right side near the front of the mouth.

Technically, that's the position of the right mandibular first bicuspid, Asad said.

Faizan didn't look at his father as he replied, "You're a lawyer. Since when did you become a dentist?"

You learn a lot of things when you're dead.

Asad said this in a flat, toneless voice that made Faizan shudder.

"Mom? Can you hear me? Are you okay? Sorry, that's a dumb question. Of course you're not okay. You're stuck inside the mouth of a tooth monster."

Inaya Barakat was in her late fifties, a thin, pretty woman with black hair, dressed in a blue smock and matching hijab. Even though she was the practice's office manager, she preferred to dress the way most of the other staff did. *Makes me feel more like one of the team,* she'd once told Faizan.

Inaya cupped her hands to the sides of her mouth to amplify her mouse-squeak voice. She shouted, "Run! Get out of here!"

Isn't that just like your mother? Asad said. *Always putting you before herself.* He leaned forward, glared at her, then added, *Always weak.*

Asad had been an even worse monster to Inaya than he had been to Faizan, and now he was a giant compared to her. She shrank back from the hatred blazing in her dead husband's eyes. Faizan wanted to stretch a finger toward his mother, to reassure her with physical contact, however strange the situation might be. But he was afraid he might hurt her, so great was the difference in their sizes, and he held back. He turned to his father.

"Did you do this?" he demanded.

No, this is solely the work of our friend Amy the Tooth Fairy here. Although I have to say I admire the creativity employed, and I'm extremely interested to see how this all plays out.

Faizan frowned. "What do you mean?"

You want to free your mother, don't you? There's only one way.

Asad gestured toward a stainless-steel tray on a nearby dental cart upon which a number of tools rested. They weren't normal dental equipment, though. They were *actual* tools, the kinds of things you'd find in someone's garage or backyard shed, and they were all old and rusty: pliers (both needle-nose and slip joint), a hammer and several chisels (all different sizes), and a full set of kitchen knives, from a small peeling knife to a full-sized butcher's knife.

Faizan shook his head. "No. No, no, no...."

Asad shrugged. *I don't make the rules here. She does.* He nodded toward the tooth creature. *To free your mother – or free any of them, for that matter – you'll have to do a bit of primitive dentistry. Who knows? By the time you're finished, you may have found yourself a new career. Being a dentist isn't exactly a high-status position, but it's better than floundering around aimlessly, which is what you've been doing ever since you graduated from high school.*

Only Faizan's father could deliver terrifying news – *You'll have to do a bit of primitive dentistry* – while at the same time letting his youngest child know what a disappointment he'd been. One thing about Asad Barakat: he was a *good* multitasker.

Faizan looked into the tooth creature's mouth once more. All the people trapped there were trying to communicate with him now, shouting, waving their hands, weeping. He had difficulty making out specific words in the mass of sound, but near as he could tell, there were three basic messages: *Help us, Escape while you still can,* and *Bow down before our ivory lord and master.* Faizan would never bow to an afreet, and while escape *was* a tempting prospect, he couldn't leave his mother like this. What would happen to her then? Would the Tooth Fairy kill her, maybe close its mouth and grind its jaws together, until everyone trapped in its mouth was reduced to smears of bloody jelly? Or would the creature leave and head off to cause havoc elsewhere, carrying its human 'dentures' along for the ride?

Inaya had no one else to help her. Faizan was her only hope, and he wasn't going to abandon her.

With a trembling hand, he reached for a pair of pliers.

CHAPTER TEN

Oliver watched the EMTs depart with his mother. He held the laptop open, and Delia — hand reaching through the screen — stroked his face. At the moment, though, her touch didn't register on his consciousness. Images and sounds of his mother tearing out her eyes swirled in his mind: fingers jammed into her eye sockets, blood running down her face, the horrible wet *squelches* as she tried to get a grip on her eyeballs, her high-pitched shrieks of agony as she kept digging and digging....

It's over now, Delia said. *It's just me and you — the way it should be.*

Oliver remained outside until he could no longer hear the EMT vehicle's siren, then he went back into the house. He was still in shock after what had happened to his mother, and it didn't occur to him to close the door. He returned to the dining room and stared at the blood on the floor. There was such a large amount of it. Oliver found it hard to believe a single human body had that much blood in it.

People have about a gallon and a half in them, Delia said. *It doesn't sound like a lot...until someone springs a leak.*

Oliver saw two bloody gobbets of flesh lying amidst the blood, and he realized the EMTs had forgotten to take his mother's eyes with them. He put the laptop on the dining table, went into the kitchen, washed his hands thoroughly, then got a plastic storage bag from one of the drawers. He filled it with ice from the freezer, walked back to the dining room, and squatted next to the eyes. He hesitated a moment before reaching down to pick one up. It felt slippery, and with the optic nerve trailing out behind it, it looked like the remains of some kind of small sea creature. He put it in the bag, picked up the other eye and dropped it in, then he sealed the bag. He returned to the kitchen, put the bag in the refrigerator, and then washed his hands again. He took his time now, used lots of soap and rubbed until his hands felt raw. He dried them with several paper towels, then used the same towels to wipe the blood smears from the refrigerator's handle. He tossed the bloodstained towels into the trash, and then headed back to the dining room. The entire time he'd performed these tasks, his mind had been blessedly blank, but now he knew he had to confront Delia.

He'd left the laptop open, but Delia had withdrawn her arm, and now she was an image on the screen, as if she was video chatting with him. Except instead of having a room behind her as a backdrop, there was only a roiling gray mist that seemed almost alive.

Delia gave him a pouty face. *Don't look so angry, love. I might've gone a little overboard with your mom, but it had to be done. She wanted to keep us apart, and I won't allow that. We've been separated too long already, you and me. I can't lose you again.*

Oliver's mother had struggled to understand and accept her son, but she'd tried. She loved him, and she hadn't deserved what Delia had done to her.

"Why not go after your father?" Oliver said, angry. "He's the *real* reason we were separated."

Delia smiled. *I paid a visit to him in his cell before coming to see you. I made him slam his head against the bars until his skull cracked open like a rotten egg. It didn't take long.*

When Delia had first appeared on Oliver's computer screen and he had heard her thought-voice and known it was really her, he'd been so overwhelmed with joy that he hadn't questioned her return. But now, after what Delia had done to Oliver's mother, he was no longer certain this was Delia, at least not *his* Delia.

Being brutally murdered by your own father tends to change a girl's perspective, Delia said.

Oliver supposed it would.

His phone was in his pocket, and when he received a text alert, he took out the device and looked at the screen. It was a message from his dad. A short one, just three words.

Be there soon.

Who's that? Delia asked.

Oliver slipped the phone back into his pocket. "No one important."

Delia gave him a skeptical look, but she didn't say anything more about it.

Take me down to the basement.

Oliver was unsure he'd heard her right.

"What for?"

If you love me, you'll do this for me.

Delia's gaze bore into him, and he felt suddenly lightheaded. He was angry with her about something, but for the life of him, he couldn't remember what it was. He mentally shrugged. Well, if he couldn't remember, that meant it had to be no big deal, right? He picked up the laptop and walked out of the dining room. A distant corner of his mind tried to get him to look at the blood spread across the floor one more time so he would *remember*, but he didn't listen to it.

★　　★　　★

The Patton family's basement was tidier than most. A washer and dryer, along with a table for folding clothes, rested in one corner. The furnace and water heater were located down there too, and while the Pattons used their basement for storage, like so many people did, there was no cluttered assemblage of odds and ends. Metal shelves held rows of plastic containers with neatly handwritten labels that said such things as *Christmas Decorations, Winter Clothes,* and *Tax Records* (the latter arranged by year, of course). There was no dust or cobwebs. Oliver's mother believed a house should be clean from top to bottom. *Like a person's spirit,* she'd once told him. The basement was unfinished, stone walls and concrete floor. Oliver had lived in this house all his life, and during that time, his father had continually promised that he'd get around to finishing the basement 'one day'. So far, that day had yet to arrive.

Put me on the table.

Oliver did as Delia ordered.

Step back.

Oliver complied.

Things happened fast then. Delia's hands thrust through the laptop screen. She gripped the edge of the table and began to pull herself out of the computer. The water heater and the furnace tore open, light and liquid flowing outward. Blades of grass forced their way through the concrete floor, and the walls and ceilings began to pull away, rapidly withdrawing into the distance. The light from the furnace coalesced into an orange ball and rose upward, growing in size as it went. The water streaming from the heater expanded as well, became longer, broader, deeper. Trees exploded through the floor and stretched toward what was now a blue sky. The orange ball took up residence in that blue, and it was soon joined by white-cotton clouds that drifted in from the sides. Oliver experienced a dizzying, lurching sensation, as if the entire universe tilted to the side for an instant, and when it righted, he found himself standing on the bank of the Iden River, in his and Delia's special spot.

Oliver slowly turned in a circle, marveling at the transformation that had befallen his family's basement. He could smell the river, hear its rushing waters, feel the warmth of summer sunlight and the cooling touch of a breeze. Some signs of the basement remained, though. The washer and dryer were gone, but the folding table with the laptop on it was still there. The wooden stairs that led to the house's ground floor were still visible, although now they stopped in the middle of the air, connected to nothing.

Delia's hand slipped into his, and he turned to her and grinned.

"This is *awesome*."

Delia smiled. "I take pride in my work."

Delia spoke aloud now, but Oliver didn't question it. She had emerged from the laptop, a solid being of flesh and blood once more. Why wouldn't she talk normally?

She leaned close to Oliver until her lips brushed his, the brief contact sending an electric jolt through his body.

"I can do more than talk," she whispered. "A *lot* more."

Oliver pulled her close and kissed her.

★   ★   ★

Grady Patton drove his silver Ford F-150, the Precision Paint logo – with the T in *Paint* designed to resemble a golden cross – displayed on both sides, faster than he'd ever driven in his life. He believed in obeying all earthly laws, as scripture dictated. *Let every person be subject to the governing authorities. For there is no authority except from God, and those that exist have been instituted by God. Therefore whoever resists the authorities resists what God has appointed, and those who resist will incur judgment.* But this was an emergency, so if he was going to incur judgment for speeding, so be it. He thought God would understand.

Grady, however, could not understand what was happening. It was like a nightmare, one you couldn't wake from. He'd been working at the Sheltons' house this morning, painting the upstairs bedrooms. He'd worn white coveralls – what he thought of as the housepainter's traditional uniform – only this pair was a bit small on him. *Must've grabbed an old pair,* he'd thought. He'd put on some weight recently.... Okay, he'd been putting on weight for a while now, but he'd been too stubborn to get rid of his smaller coveralls. *I'm going to start exercising soon,* he'd told Emily last week. *Start jogging or something. Then I'll fit into my old clothes again, you'll see.*

Alex and Jenny Shelton went to the same church as Grady and Emily. Grady received a good portion of his business from fellow worshippers, and if he hadn't been a believer himself, he might've pretended to be one just for the networking. There was good money in being a Christian sometimes. He'd just gotten started painting when Jenny, who was a stay-at-home mother to two toddler-age children, had gotten a call from Alex. He had no idea what Jenny's husband had told her, but when the call was finished, she scooped up the kids, ran to the garage, and raced down the street in her SUV as if pursued by the Devil himself – all without saying a single word to Grady.

Grady hadn't been quite sure what to do. Should he continue working? It didn't feel right to remain in the house without Jenny here, especially since she hadn't given him express permission to do so. On the other hand, he remembered what it had been like when Ama— when *Oliver* had been little. Sometimes he and Emily had been so busy helping with homework and driving to soccer practices that they didn't know what day it was.

Jenny had probably just been stressed and had forgotten to talk to him before she left. That's all. He decided to continue working, and less than five minutes later, he received a call of his own.

Dad, it's Mom. She...hurt herself. Bad. I called 911. They're on their way. Get here as soon as you can, okay?

He'd tried to get more information from Oliver, but his son had hung up without saying another word. Grady had found that almost as disturbing as Oliver's message. His boy hadn't sounded right. His voice had been flat, emotionless, as if he'd been traumatized. Just what in God's name had happened to Emily?

Please, Lord, give her the strength she'll need to get through this.

Whatever had happened to his wife, he knew it was God's will. He believed that God didn't give people more than they could handle, even if it didn't seem that way to them at the time. It had been that way when Oliver had come out to Emily and him. At first they didn't accept what he'd told them, had argued that God had made him female and that was the way he should stay. Oliver hadn't yelled at them, hadn't accused them of being small-minded and bigoted. Instead, he asked, *How do you know that God didn't make me trans? How do you know he doesn't use trans people to teach others how to be more tolerant and loving?*

Neither he nor Emily had been able to answer that. So they'd prayed for patience and understanding and had done their best to accept their son *as* their son. It hadn't been easy, and both Grady and Emily still struggled at times, but they loved Oliver, and they both believed true love should be unconditional. God had been helping him and Emily with Oliver, and he'd help the three of them get through whatever this new challenge was. Grady believed that. He *had* to, otherwise his fear for his wife would overwhelm him, and he wouldn't be able to function.

The Sheltons lived on the southwest side of the river, while Grady and his family lived on the northeast side. Normally, it would've taken him fifteen minutes or less to travel from one house to the other during this time of day, but even though he sped when he could, he was often forced to slow down – and even come to a complete stop – because of the traffic. People were driving like lunatics today. They flew past him at highway speeds, wove in and out of traffic like race car drivers, ran red lights, slammed on the brakes in the middle of the street for no apparent reason. He witnessed half a dozen accidents during his journey, and he avoided getting into at least that many. The left side of his pickup did get sideswiped by a Volkswagen Beetle at one point, but the impact was little more than a love tap, and it didn't slow him down. He looked at the driver as she passed, ready to shout some very un-Christian-like words at her, and he caught a flash of a skeletal thing with a too-wide screaming mouth behind the wheel. But before he could get a second look, the Beetle had sped past. That wasn't the only strange thing he saw. When he drove across the river, the bridge swayed as if in the grip of violent storm winds, but the air was still. And when he glanced down at the water, for an instant it looked blood-red, and he thought he saw people floating in it. No, not people. *Bodies.* It reminded him of one of the Old Testament plagues that had struck Egypt, and he shuddered.

He saw a number of emergency vehicles – police cruisers, fire trucks, EMT vehicles – racing toward one disaster or another. *Has the whole world gone mad?* Then he remembered Oliver's call. *Maybe so.*

He reached his home twenty-four minutes after speaking with Oliver. He'd tried calling back several times during his trip, but Oliver hadn't answered. Grady hoped that wasn't a bad sign, but feared that it was. There were no vehicles in his driveway – no police, no EMTs. Had they not arrived yet or were they still on their way? Or were they so tied up with everything else that was happening across town that they weren't going to be coming at all? If so, he'd drive Emily to the hospital himself. Assuming she was still alive. He scolded himself for thinking like that, for not having faith, but he couldn't help it. He parked in the driveway, turned off the pickup's engine, threw upon the driver's-side door, jumped out, and started running as soon as his feet hit the ground.

The front door was open, and his first thought was that someone had broken in. Was that what had happened to Emily? Had someone tried to rob their home and hurt her in the process? Had they tried to rape her or even kill her? As he ran inside, he called both Emily's and Oliver's names, but he received no replies. He continued calling their names as he raced through the house, checking the bedrooms, the bathrooms, the living room, the kitchen, and finally the dining room. When he saw the blood on the floor – so *much* of it! – the shock hit him hard and his legs almost gave out on him. He grabbed the side of the doorway to steady himself. Now he screamed their names.

"Emily! Oliver!"

Had they both gone with the EMTs? If so, maybe they were at the hospital already. He should try to call Oliver again, and if he still couldn't reach his son, then he could call the hospital and check if Emily had been admitted. The hospital was on the southeast side of the river, but he could use the east bridge this time and be there within ten minutes, unless the traffic had gotten even more insane, then who knew how long it might take?

He reached for his pants pocket, only to realize he'd left his phone on the front seat of his pickup. "Damn it!" he swore, and he didn't feel a second's guilt about using foul language. They didn't have a landline – who did anymore? – so he was going to have to go back outside and....

The entrance to the basement was located in the sunroom, which was on the other side of the dining room, and the door was clearly visible from where he stood. Light filtered through the spaces between the door and the frame, much brighter than it should be. The basement lights weren't strong enough to produce that much illumination. So where was it coming from? Could Emily and Oliver be down there? Had they for some unknown reason sought shelter in the basement? It didn't make sense that they would, but he needed to check to make certain they weren't there.

He walked through the dining room, careful to avoid stepping in any of the blood, then tried the basement door. It was unlocked, but he paused, hand gripping the knob, and he realized that part of him didn't want to enter the basement, was in fact shouting at him to let go of the knob, turn around, and get the hell out of the house as fast as he could.

"Get behind me, Satan," he said softly, and opened the door.

★   ★   ★

Oliver sighed in contentment. It had been a long time since he and Delia had been together, but it was just as good as he remembered. Better, even. There had been an almost desperate need to reconnect after their separation, and this had added both urgency and intensity to their lovemaking. They now lay side by side on the riverbank, naked bodies warmed by the summer sun, skin slick with sweat after their exertions, scents mingling to create a thick heady musk that smelled like fine wine to Oliver. He inhaled, drinking it in.

He ran his fingers lightly over one of Delia's breasts. She closed her eyes, let out a soft *mmmmm* of pleasure.

"I could stay like this for eternity," he said.

She opened her eyes and looked at him. "Funny you should say that...."

Before Oliver could ask her what she meant, he heard the heavy *clomp-clomp-clomp* of boots on wood. His father was coming down the basement stairs, in the air behind him a rectangular space that displayed a view of the Pattons' sunroom. As Grady descended, he gazed upon Oliver and Delia's special place – grass, trees, river, sky, clouds, sun – with an expression of utter astonishment. He was so mesmerized by what he was seeing that he didn't seem to notice both Oliver and Delia were naked.

Oliver stood, then reached down to take Delia's hand and help her to her feet. As embarrassed as Oliver was at the thought of his dad seeing him naked, Grady was his father. He didn't want Delia to feel ashamed, though, so he stepped in front of her. She let out a soft laugh.

"Thanks," she said, "but modesty's one of the first things to go when you die."

She stepped out from behind him, took his hand, and stood at his side. He was proud to be with Delia like this, out in the open, bold as hell, with nothing to hide.

Grady stopped on the bottom stair, reluctant to set foot on the grass, as if he didn't trust it to be real. But then he stepped forward, officially entering the world Delia had created in his basement. His gaze turned toward them, and he saw – really *saw* – them for the first time since beginning to descend the stairs.

"Oliver? Why are you—" He broke off, eyes widening. "*Delia?* Is that you?"

It appeared nudity was less shocking to Grady than seeing someone returned from the dead. Oliver was surprised. As uptight as his parents were, he'd have figured it would be the other way around.

"Hello, Mr. Patton," Delia said, smiling sweetly. "It's good to see you. Unfortunately, that's something Mrs. Patton will never be able to say again."

Grady frowned in confusion. "What's she talking about, Oliver? What happened to your mother?"

"She...." Oliver trailed off. What *had* happened to her? He was having trouble remembering. He looked to Delia but she didn't take her eyes off his father. Grady was no longer looking at them, though. He was looking past them, at the river.

"I saw that before," he said. "On my way here."

Oliver turned to see what he was talking about and saw the river had become a surging torrent of blood. Dead bodies floated in the current, naked women, not all of them intact. The smell of the blood river was horrific, and Oliver's gut cramped with sudden nausea.

"Sorry about that," Delia said. "We have difficulty with boundaries, and sometimes things get a little mixed up. It's an interesting effect, though, don't you think? Very dramatic."

"You're doing this," Grady said.

Oliver and Delia turned. Grady was coming toward them, his gaze fixed on Delia.

"I know what you are," he said.

Delia sighed, and when she spoke, she sounded bored.

"You think I'm a demon. Your wife accused me of being one too – right after I made her tear her eyes out of her head."

Oliver remembered now. The blood, the screaming, the awful wet sounds of his mother's fingers clawing at her own flesh.... Delia had done something to make him forget these things, or maybe he'd been so grateful to have her back that he'd forced himself to forget. Either way, he remembered now. He released Delia's hand, then stepped away from her. Delia gave him a disappointed look.

"And we were having *such* a good time."

"Get away from my son," Grady said. He'd come within five feet of them, and his hands were balled into fists. Oliver had never seen his father commit an act of violence before, wouldn't have thought him capable of such a thing, but from the look in his eyes, Oliver knew he'd hit Delia if he thought he had to.

"I have to say, you're a lot more tolerant than my father was," Delia said. "Listen to you, using Oliver's right name and everything." Her expression hardened and her voice grew cold. "But I've been beaten to death once already, and I'll never let anyone else lay their hands on me – *ever*. And speaking of hands...."

Delia did nothing outwardly – made no gesture, spoke no command – but the blood river behind them exploded as a large shape emerged: a giant blood-slick hand, formed from the dead bodies of women, intertwined and holding on to each other. The hand shot toward Grady, closed its fingers around him, lifted him off the ground, and then retreated back into the blood river, submerging once more and pulling him under with it. It all happened within the space of a few seconds. One instant Oliver's father was standing with them on the riverbank, the next he was gone.

Oliver stared at the spot where his father had disappeared. He waited to see if Grady's head would break the surface, if he had somehow escaped from the monstrous hand's grasp. But the water continued flowing undisturbed.

Delia stepped close to him, put an arm around his waist.

"Sorry you had to see that, love. But there's no one to come between us now. It's just you and me." Her lips pulled back from her teeth in a cold smile. "Forever."

She tightened her grip around his waist, and pulled him close to her as he began to cry.

CHAPTER ELEVEN

Karen sat in the passenger seat of her red Ford Explorer while Bennie – who'd manifested in physical form – drove. Whenever they'd gone anywhere together, he'd always insisted on doing the driving, and evidently death hadn't changed that about him. *I'm a pilot,* he used to say. *Car or airplane, I'm in charge.* He looked the same as he had when he'd been alive: early seventies, paunchy and jowly. He wore his navy-blue pilot's uniform, complete with hat, and despite his age – he was ten years older than her – and his less-than-athletic build, she thought the wrinkled bastard cut a dashing figure.

She smoked a cigarette and looked out the window as they traveled, enjoying the chaos she saw: people driving like maniacs, running from homes and stores in blind panic, screaming in yards, on sidewalks, in the street, many of them covered in blood....

The Homecoming is going beautifully so far, don't you think? Bennie asked.

"It's wonderful," Karen said, and she meant it. She turned to look at Bennie. "Is that what this is? A Homecoming?"

Sure. What else would you call it?

She turned back to the window. In the parking lot of a pharmacy, all the light poles had become rubbery and sinuous, and they were attacking people like giant serpents, encircling them in metal coils and squeezing them to death. Just down the street, the asphalt in the road was fissured with huge cracks from which tendrils of glowing green vapor emerged. Whatever the vapor touched – vehicles, people – began to age rapidly and soon fell away to dust. Bennie drove through the mist without incident.

Friends of mine, he said by way of explanation.

Karen smiled in contentment. She'd never imagined she'd get to witness other people's pain on such a large scale, and it was marvelous. It was the end of the world, and she felt fine. *Fine as wine,* she thought.

"We going anywhere in particular or just taking in the sights?" she asked.

I've got a special surprise for you, Bennie said, grinning. *Who would you like to see suffer more than anyone else?*

There were a *lot* of people she'd like to see hurt, but only one name was at the top of the list.

"Erika."

That's right. We're going to pay your sister a visit at work. She's having a terrible day, but then, so is everyone else on the planet.

"Not me," Karen said.

No, not you, Bennie agreed, then added, *Not yet, anyway.*

She gave him a sideways glance, but didn't say anything. She knew he'd love to see her in torment, just as she'd love the same if their roles were reversed. She'd been raised Catholic but hadn't been to church in decades, not even for Christmas or Easter services. She wasn't especially religious, and up to today, she hadn't believed in an afterlife of any sort. But her views on that issue had evolved considerably since Bennie had appeared and his ghost-friend had burned down her café.

"So…were you roasting in hell or what?" she asked.

Bennie laughed. *You wish! Being dead is actually pretty quiet – except when it's not. Like today.*

His answer bored her. If he didn't have any tales of terrible pain to tell her, she wasn't interested. She continued looking out the window, enjoying other people's suffering, and wondering what they'd find when they reached Erika's workplace. Whatever it was, she hoped it would be awful in the extreme. The bitch deserved nothing less.

Karen and Erika might have been identical twins, but from the very beginning, their lives had been different. Erika had been born five minutes before Karen, technically making her the older sister. And while Erika's birth had been an easy one, Karen's umbilical cord had been wrapped around her neck, almost killing her. Things only got worse after that. Erika had a sweet, kind disposition, and was clearly their parents' favorite. Karen was always grouchy and irritable. Erika slept through the night almost from the moment they came home. Karen didn't get a full night's sleep until she was a teenager. Erika drank her formula – and eventually ate her baby food – without complaint. Karen was such a picky eater that some days she barely ate at all, and when she did eat, she was just as likely to throw it up as not. Erika liked to play games and got along well with other children. Karen was bossy and argumentative and often got into fights with other kids – fights which unvaryingly ended up with those kids getting hurt, sometimes severely. Erika was smart. She enjoyed learning and she did it fast. Karen wasn't exactly dumb, but she was nowhere near as bright as her sister, and because of this, learning was torture for her – especially when their parents compared her to Erika, which they did. A lot. *Why can't you be more like your sister?* they'd ask. Translation: *We might actually love you, you miserable thing, if you were smart like Erika.*

Erika had been popular in high school. She'd excelled in every subject she studied, and she'd caught the eye of Tyler Pope, one of the varsity football players. They'd fallen in love, gone to the same college – where again, Erika had excelled in her studies – gotten married after graduation, and eventually Erika had given birth to Sandra. In college, Erika had double majored in early childhood education and business, and when Sandra entered first grade, Erika had started her own daycare-slash-preschool called Time for Tots – which as far as Karen was concerned was a fucking stupid name. But the school had been a success (naturally), and even though her sister was now old enough to retire, she continued working because she loved being around kids. *They keep me young,* she'd once said, a sentiment that made Karen want to gag.

There was nothing intrinsically special about being a twin – twins were just nature's clones – but people still viewed twins in a quasi-mystical fashion. They were supposed to be so close that they could practically read one another's thoughts, so in sync that when one hurt, the other felt it, so devoted to each other that even a spouse couldn't be as close to them as their other sibling. That was all bullshit, at least when it came to Karen and Erika, but they did embody one popular myth about twins: that one was always good while the other was always bad. Karen had sensed this expectation from the time she was a toddler – it was, after all, their parents' attitude toward them, conscious or not – and she'd embraced her destined role, tormenting her sister at every opportunity. She'd continued the torture throughout their childhood and into adolescence – pinching, biting, kicking, and hitting Erika, shoving her off playground equipment, twisting her arm behind her back, feeding her brownies with laxatives in them, tying her to her bed when she was asleep, taking pictures of her when she was showering and showing them to everyone at school, writing lies about her sexual habits on bathroom stalls, and the ultimate – pretending to be her and sleeping with Tyler Pope. He'd turned out to be a lame fuck, which had been a disappointment, but when she'd told Erika it had devastated her – which after all was the point, so mission accomplished.

She'd gone too far that time, though. Throughout their lives, Erika had never told their parents about her sister's hatred of her, nor about the pain and humiliation she'd suffered at her hands. But after that, she'd started standing up for herself. *You do one thing more to me – just one – and I'll kick your fucking ass.* Karen had been tempted to test her on this, but she could tell from Erika's voice and the look in her eyes that she was serious. Erika never told Tyler that Karen had screwed him. Karen had considered telling him herself many times over the years, but she'd always decided against it. Better to let the threat of her telling him continue to hang over Erika's head.

After Erika left for college, they didn't see much of each other. Holidays, weddings, and funerals, mostly. The usual times when estranged family members managed to stomach one another for short periods. She'd been surprised – actually, shocked – when Sandra had applied for a job at the Sleepy Lizard. She'd barely known the girl as she was growing up, and she'd suspected that Erika had purposely kept the girl away from her all those years. Which, although she resented it, was probably a good idea. After all, look what had happened to Sandra – burned to death along with everyone else in the café. Karen didn't feel one way or the other about her demise. Everyone died eventually, and for most people the sooner that day came the better, as far as Karen was concerned. She was, however, looking forward to breaking the news of Sandra's death to Erika. The look on her face was going to be *delicious*!

Time for Tots shared a parking lot with a dental practice called Smiles, Inc. Bennie pulled into the lot and drove past the ugliest yellow car Karen had ever seen. It was such an eyesore that she actually admired whoever had the guts to drive the fucking thing in public. Bennie pulled into an empty space in front of Erika's school, parked, and cut the engine.

"How bad is it going to be in there?" Karen asked.

Bennie's grin stretched wider than it should have.

Even worse than you hope.

★　　★　　★

"You don't want to do this," Erika said.

Don't be silly. Of course I do.

Erika's body was pressed tight against a wall in one of the classrooms, pinned by an invisible force, and no matter how hard she strained, she couldn't free herself. She was director of the school and spent most of her working hours on administrative duties, although she'd also taught when she'd been younger, and she still liked to help out in classes whenever she could. This was Connie Brooks's classroom, but Connie, unfortunately, was very much dead. She lay atop her desk, although she was no longer recognizable as Connie, not even recognizable as human. Kathleen Bishop had decided to show the children what a human body looked like when it was turned inside out, and Connie had not survived the demonstration. She was now a mass of bones and organs through which pieces of cloth protruded. Connie had still been wearing her clothes when Kathleen had rearranged her. Surprisingly, there'd been very little blood spilled, and Erika thought that was one small thing to be grateful for. The children had been traumatized enough as it was.

The children, ranging in ages from three to five, sat on the carpet in front of Connie's desk, arranged in two semicircles, one behind the other. Most were crying – some silently, some loudly – but several sat motionless, faces blank, as if they'd gone somewhere deep inside themselves and might never return. None of the children made a move to get up and run away, but Erika was certain that was Kathleen's doing. Just as the woman was keeping her pinned to the wall, she was keeping the kids' butts glued to the floor. No one was leaving until she wanted them to.

Kathleen stood in front of the desk, facing the children. She was a thin, frail-looking woman in her seventies dressed in a hospital gown. Her eyes had receded far into the sockets, the flesh around them dark and parchment thin. Her cheekbones were sharp and prominent, and her liver-spotted scalp was bare, revealing a long crescent-shaped scar that stretched from her forehead and down to her ear. Her hands were twisted into arthritic claws, nails long and jagged, and Erika thought no one had ever looked more the part of a storybook wicked witch.

Now, which of you little dumplings would like to volunteer to be first?

Kathleen didn't move her mouth when she spoke, but all of them heard her words nevertheless. The children continued to cry – or in some cases, stare without expression – but none of them answered her. Kathleen's almost nonexistent lips pursed in displeasure.

If no one volunteers, I'm going to have to choose someone myself. Is that what you want? She gestured at the mass of meat that had once been Connie. *No one volunteered to be a visual aid in my last demonstration, so I selected your teacher. It didn't turn out very well for* her *now, did it? Volunteers get to live. Those who stay quiet and refuse to participate in class die. Now, which is it going to be, hmmmmm?*

"I volunteer," Erika said. "Use me."

Kathleen turned toward her and gave her a toothless bleeding-gum smile.

I appreciate your willingness, Erika, but I'd much rather you watch. This is all for your benefit, you know.

Kathleen had once been a teacher at Time for Tots. Erika had hired her ten years ago because one of her other teachers quit unexpectedly to have a baby, and she was desperate to replace her ASAP. During Kathleen's interview, she'd come across as a deeply caring person, one with a passion for teaching young children, especially two- and three-year-olds – who were the hardest ages to manage, Erika thought. Kathleen had the right qualifications and experience, so Erika hired her immediately upon the conclusion of her interview. But she'd done so with a certain amount of trepidation. Kathleen hadn't done or said anything specific to give her pause, but Erika's instincts – honed through years of surviving her abusive and sadistic twin – told her to keep an eye on the woman, and so she did.

Everything seemed to go fine for the first year. Erika received the occasional complaint from parents that Kathleen was speaking more harshly than necessary to their children, but Erika herself had never seen any evidence of this. She spoke with Kathleen about the matter, and Kathleen promised she'd be careful to watch her tone and word choice more closely in the future.

As much as I love the little ones, the older I get, the more I have to work at being patient with them, she'd said.

They can be a handful, Erika had agreed.

The complaints increased throughout Kathleen's second year, however, and now they included accusations that she physically handled the children roughly at times. Erika had been so disturbed by these reports that she installed a pair of hidden cameras in Kathleen's classroom one weekend. The cameras would allow her to monitor what occurred in real time as well as record those events, and she could watch the live feed on her office computer with the door closed. That Monday, as soon as classes began, Erika was sitting at her desk, watching Kathleen teach. Ten minutes later, she summoned Kathleen to her office, asking another of the teachers to cover her classroom, and ten minutes after *that,* she fired Kathleen. Everything the parents had complained about – the verbal and physical abuse – was true, and she had proof. Confronted with that proof, Kathleen had no choice but to accept her dismissal, although she hadn't been happy about it.

Goddamn spying bitch, she'd said. *This is the shittiest school I've ever worked at, and all of you are a bunch of dumb cunts. I hope your vagina rots from the inside out and your tits deflate like leftover party balloons.* And then, thankfully, she'd left.

Erika didn't hear anything more about Kathleen until six months later, when another of the staff said she'd been visiting her father in the hospital when she'd run into Kathleen. *She'd just undergone an operation for a brain tumor. From what she said, it sounded like a pretty big one, too.*

Erika had wondered if the tumor had been responsible for Kathleen's conduct in the classroom. If so, she felt awful about firing the woman, but she couldn't allow her to continue teaching, not with the way she'd treated the children. A month after that, Erika heard that Kathleen had died. She said a silent prayer for the woman, then went on with her life.

Then this morning, Kathleen's goddamn ghost – or whatever she was – appeared in her old classroom, which was now Connie's, and told Connie to call Erika to the room. Connie, terrified, had done so using the wall intercom, and when Erika arrived, Kathleen gestured with one of her claw hands, and she found herself flying through the air and then stuck to a wall. Then Kathleen had turned to Connie and the kids and said, *Who wants to help me with a little demonstration?*

Kathleen looked away from Erika now and faced the children once more.

All right, you little shits – which one of you wants to die first?

"How about the girl with the curly red hair?"

Erika was startled by this voice, but of course she recognized it. She knew it as well as her own because it basically *was* her own.

Karen stood just inside the classroom, her husband next to her. On any other day, this latter detail would've disturbed Erika greatly since Bennie had died several years ago. But given that she was currently being held captive by a ghost herself, Bennie's presence wasn't all that miraculous.

Kathleen looked at Karen, eyes narrowing within their dark hollows, then she turned to Bennie.

Happy Homecoming, she said.

Same to you, Kathleen, he replied.

Karen frowned. "You two know each other?"

Bennie and Kathleen answered at the same time.

The dead are one.

"Wow," Karen said, "like *that's* not creepy." She looked at Erika and grinned. "Hey, sis. Long time, no see. I'd ask you to drop by the café sometime, but unfortunately, it burned to the fucking ground this morning. It's nothing more than a heap of ashes by now." She paused, then her eyes turned cold as she added, "Just like everyone who was inside."

Erika and Karen were polar opposites when it came to temperament and personality, but they were still twins, and Erika understood exactly what her sister was telling her – Sandra was dead.

The news was like a knife in her heart, but she told herself that she couldn't think about it now. The children were in danger, and she had to do what she could to protect them.

"You got here just in time," she said. "Kathleen was about to give the kids a demonstration. Like that one." She nodded toward the desk and Connie's inside-out corpse. "I volunteered to be her helper. Wouldn't you like to see that? Isn't that what you came for?"

She felt certain it was. Whether Karen had been led here by Bennie or her own instincts, the only reason she would've come is if it provided her an opportunity to see her hated twin suffer.

Karen looked her over from head to toe and back again.

"You look awful chummy with that wall," she said. "Why don't you walk over here and give your old sis a hug?"

Erika glared at her. "You know I can't."

"I do. And unless I miss my guess, this ugly dead bitch—" Karen nodded at Kathleen, "—is here to cause you a shitload of misery. What did you do to piss her off?" She held up a hand before Erika could answer. "Wait. Don't tell me. I don't really give a damn about the details. But I would *love* to see what she has in mind for you." She turned to Kathleen. "Please, go ahead."

Kathleen stared at her a moment before slowly grinning.

The red-headed child, you said?

Karen nodded.

The little girl in question started bawling her eyes out. Her name was Rayna Hammons, and her parents had been bringing her here since she was an infant, first for daycare, then when she was old enough, for classes. She was bright and inquisitive and filled with enough energy for three children. And now Kathleen shuffled over to stand directly in front of her. Rayna tried to stand, but couldn't. Erika tried to pull herself free from the wall, but couldn't. Both could only watch as Kathleen touched a twisted, swollen index finger to the top of Rayna's head.

Today, you little fuck-monkeys, I want to introduce you to a concept called a chain reaction.

Rayna exploded.

Blood sprayed the air as chunks of meat and bone flew outward, splattering Kathleen, the other children, Karen and Bennie, before striking Erika. A small bit of Rayna's skull, red hair still attached, caught in her mouth. She immediately spit it out, was about to shout at Kathleen to stop it, when the child that had been sitting next to Rayna – a little boy named Carver Shipley – also exploded, with similarly messy results. Then one after another, the children burst apart as if they'd swallowed grenades. By the end, the remaining children were shrieking in absolute terror, but they were soon silenced. When it was over, the classroom ceiling, walls, floor were covered with bone shards, fragments of organs, shreds of skin and blood, seemingly gallons of the stuff. Kathleen, Karen, and Bennie dripped with gore, as did Erika.

And that class, Kathleen said, *was a prime example of a chain reaction.*

Karen and Bennie laughed. Erika shrieked in both rage and sorrow.

While I'm at it, I should take care of the rest of the staff and children, Kathleen said. *Just to be tidy.*

More wet explosions, dozens of them, more screams, then silence.

Karen wiped a bloody gobbet of meat from her right cheek before addressing Kathleen.

"I know you came here to torture Erika, but she is *my* sister. Would you mind?"

Kathleen fixed Erika with a hate-filled gaze. *Be my guest.*

Smiling, taking her time, Karen walked over to the wall where Erika was trapped. When she reached her sister, she stopped and gently wiped blood away from her throat. She then flicked the worst of it off her hands and onto the floor.

"You know, if I didn't love you at least a little, I'd let you live with the memory of what you just saw," Karen said.

"No, you wouldn't," Erika said.

Karen smiled. "You're right."

Then slowly, almost gently, she placed her hands around her twin's throat and began to squeeze.

CHAPTER TWELVE

Jerome stood on the riverbank, naked body slick with blood, balls pulsating, aching, throbbing. He'd come so many times he'd lost count, one orgasm after another, with barely a pause between. He'd pull one body out of the blood river at a time, fuck it, toss it back in, then look for another. He'd lost track of how many corpses he'd violated. Ten? Twenty? More? It was like he was an inexhaustible well of sexual energy, and he'd never felt more alive. Obviously this place – wherever it was, exactly – operated by its own set of rules, and biological limitations didn't apply here. He was profoundly grateful for this. His throat and mouth were dry as sand, and he wondered if it was possible to die of dehydration by ejaculating too much. Much more of this, and he might find out. Still, what a way to go.

He was watching dead women float by, trying to decide which one he wanted to fuck next, when he saw the body of a man dressed in blood-soaked coveralls pass in front of him. The man lay facedown in the water, and Jerome assumed his coveralls had been white before he'd ended up in the river.

Forget about him, Randall said. *He doesn't have anything to do with us.*

Jerome wondered about the man's identity as he watched the current carry him away. He knew the man wasn't in *The Book.* Randall's victims had all been women.

He glanced at Randall. The teenager stood several yards away, arms crossed over his chest, smiling. He supposed Randall had been watching him this entire time, but he'd been so caught up in his orgy of necrophilia that he hadn't been fully aware of his surroundings, Randall included. Normally the idea of someone watching him fuck – not that he ever *did* fuck back in the real world – would've made him feel self-conscious and violated. But he was surprised to find that he didn't mind Randall watching him. It wasn't as if he got a sexual thrill out of it. Okay, maybe he did, a little. Mostly it was because the experience bonded them on a deep level. They were both men unafraid to act outside the bounds of so-called civilized society in order to fulfill their truest selves. They were strong, defiant, they took what they wanted when they wanted, and no one could stop them.

Easy enough to be like that inside your own private little universe, Randall said. *But it's an entirely different matter when your actions have lasting consequences. Can you remain strong and defiant then?*

An invisible hand grabbed hold of Jerome, yanked him off the ground, and bore him skyward. Vertigo seized him as he picked up speed, and the world around him blurred into nothingness. He passed through a red barrier – the cover of *The Book*, he remembered – then with a last dizzying lurch, he found himself standing before a set of bookshelves once more. He looked down at himself, saw he was clothed, his skin clean of blood.

Randall stood in the aisle next to Jerome, arms still crossed over his chest.

Afraid you'd end up naked and bloody in the middle of the library, Jerky? he asked. *That would be a shitty thing to do to a friend, wouldn't it? Funny, but shitty.*

Jerome looked around to see if anyone was looking at him, but no one was. He wondered if what he'd experienced on the bank of the blood river had been a hallucination, a kind of vivid waking dream.

How do your nuts feel?

"Like a pair of lead bowling balls," Jerome answered.

Then you know it was real. Balls never lie.

Jerome smiled. "Wisdom for the ages."

I meant what I said. It's easy to transgress when there's no chance of getting caught, when there's no price to pay. But can you do it in the real world? That's the question.

"What are you trying to say?"

Follow me, Jerky. Bring The Book.

Randall dropped his arms to his sides, turned, and started walking. Jerome hesitated a moment before pulling *The Book* off the shelf, tucking it under one arm, and following. Randall led him out of the stacks and toward the main reference desk. On the way, Jerome noticed that many of the early-morning patrons were looking at their phones. He'd never understand why people would go to a library only to sit around and stare at those goddamn things. Something was different today, though. There was an atmosphere of confusion, worry, even fear. Some people were texting rapidly, others were talking in hushed tones to someone on the other end, and some stopped whatever they were doing and rushed toward the exit. Something was happening – something *big*. He could sense it.

Things are really starting to heat up now, Randall said.

Jerome recalled something Randall had said before they'd entered *The Book.*

It's Homecoming. Across the whole goddamn world, Jerky. Gonna be a hell of a party.

Is that what was happening? This Homecoming, whatever that was?

If Randall heard Jerome's thoughts this time, he chose not to respond to them. Instead, he continued toward the reference desk and the woman seated behind it – Alexandra Valenti. She was in her early thirties, short, with a cute round face and beautiful auburn hair that reached down to the base of her spine. She wore a turquoise sweatshirt with a picture of an open book on the front above the word *Lover.* Jerome had seen her wear this sweatshirt before, knew it was meant to communicate *Book Lover,* a perfectly normal sentiment for a librarian to display. But the word *Lover* conjured other associations for him. She was typing on her computer as they approached and didn't look up from her work at first. Randall stopped several feet from her desk, and Jerome stopped next to him. Together, they watched her work.

She preferred to be called *Alex,* and Jerome honored this wish, although in his mind he always used her full name. *Alexandra* sounded so much more sophisticated, mysterious, alluring…. She'd transferred here from a branch on the south side of town two years ago, and he'd immediately been struck by her resemblance to one of Randall's victims: Tami Phelps. Alexandra's hair was the same shade of brown as Tami's, and while the girl had been thinner, they shared a similar facial structure. And if Alexandra's brown eyes were compared to a close-up photo of Tami's, you wouldn't be able to tell the difference. All of this was more than enough to capture Jerome's interest, but when he learned that Alexandra was actually one of Tami's *cousins* – thanks to one of their more gossipy co-workers – his interest became an obsession. Alexandra was fifteen years younger than him, and they hadn't attended high school at the same time, otherwise he might've known she was related to Tami. He made any excuse to talk to her at work, even followed her home once to see where she lived – a two-bedroom apartment near the westside bridge. She lived on the second floor of a two-story building, and sometimes at night he'd drive there, park, and watch her window, hoping to catch a glimpse of her. Sometimes he did. Most nights he didn't. Regardless, he'd always masturbate, once, sometimes twice if his dick was literally up for it. One night he'd fallen asleep in his car, and when he'd woken in the morning, he'd been terrified that she'd spot him. But he'd managed to get out of there before she exited her building. By the time he'd gotten back to his own apartment, showered, and dressed, he was forty minutes late for work. When he arrived, she'd asked him if he was okay, if something had happened to hold him up. He'd thought of how he'd jacked off while staring at the glowing square of her window, and said, *I held myself up, that's all.* His little joke amused him, and as it was – in a way – a subtle confession of what he'd done, it had excited him, too. He'd never asked Alexandra out, though. He'd wanted to, sure, *desperately*, but he'd never found the right time or the right words.

You sure you weren't just being a fucking coward, Jerky?

Jerome was horrified by Randall's words, and he looked at Alexandra to see how she'd react to them, but she continued typing on her computer, oblivious. Maybe she simply hadn't paid attention to Randall's words – she did have a tendency to hyper-focus on a task and tune out the rest of the world – or maybe Randall had prevented her from hearing his thought-voice. He *was* a ghost, after all. He could do what he wanted, right?

Answer my question, Randall said.

Jerome looked at Alexandra. He had been a coward, hadn't he? Not like Randall. Even as a high school student, Randall had known exactly what he wanted, and he'd gone for it, regardless of how society would view his actions or what they might cost him. That took serious balls. Jumbo-size.

Okay, next question, Jerky. What is it that you really want from this woman?

He continued gazing at Alexandra while she worked. What *did* he want from her? To fuck her? Maybe. He did find her attractive, but right this moment he felt no sexual pull toward her. Part of that was undoubtedly because he'd emptied his balls into all those dead women from the river, but he thought there was something more to it. He wanted her, God, so *much*, but he didn't want her in *that* way.

It wasn't about sex for me, and it's not for you, either. That's why we took a detour to the river. I wanted you to get all that sex stuff out of your system – literally! – so you could think more clearly at this moment. So I'll ask you one more time: what do you really want from her?

Jerome didn't have to think about his answer this time.

I want her life, he thought.

Good boy. Open The Book *and turn to the middle.*

Jerome did so, and this time he discovered that *The Book* had been hollowed out in the middle, and lying in a rectangular space was a boning knife. He gazed upon it for several moments, then touched the tip of a trembling index finger to the gleaming metal. It was cold, and something like a small electric shock jolted him. Surprised, he jerked his hand away and then looked at Randall.

Is this....

Yep. That's the same knife I used, Jerky. Not a copy. The real fucking thing. I considered using a butcher knife, but I wanted something that would give me both penetration and the ability to do detail work. Best decision I ever made. I sharpened it for you, too.

Jerome turned his gaze back to the knife. The way the light shimmered on the metal was the most beautiful thing he had ever seen.

Close it before she notices, Randall said.

Jerome closed *The Book* so abruptly that it made a loud *thump.* The sound broke Alexandra's concentration, and she looked up at him. *Of course, it* would *be a book that got her attention,* Jerome thought.

She smiled. "Hey, Jerome. Something I can do for you?"

Now there's a loaded question, Randall said.

Jerome ignored him, and since Alexandra didn't look at him, he assumed she couldn't see or hear him. Good. But before he could say anything, Alexandra noticed he held *The Book.*

"I see you're revisiting an old favorite," she said.

Her words caught him off guard. He'd had no idea she knew about *The Book.*

Of course she knows about it, Randall said. *Her goddamn cousin is in it, remember? She knows where it's shelved too, and its red cover is more than a little distinctive. How many times do you think she's noticed you go over there and drool over her cousin's photo when you should've been working?*

Christ, he'd been an idiot! He'd thought he'd been so careful, but from her desk Alexandra had a perfect view of the shelf where *The Book* was housed. Even if he'd kept his back to her while looking at it – which, now that he thought about it, he wasn't sure he'd always done – she still might've guessed which volume kept drawing him back to that particular location. *God, she must think I'm some kind of ghoul!*

Well, aren't you? Randall asked.

Jerome was still struggling to come up with words when a woman in her late thirties with three young children standing nearby at the checkout counter looked down at her phone and let out an ear-piercing scream. She dropped the books she was holding, snatched up the smallest child, and ran toward the exit. After a second's confusion, the other two children followed after her, crying, one of them calling out, "Mommy, Mommy, what's wrong, what's *wrong?*" Everyone looked at the woman and her kids, including Jerome and Alexandra. Everyone except Randall. He continued looking at Jerome.

Less than a year after her sister died in a car wreck, she married the sister's husband, and they started a family – this, after the husband had told the sister he 'wasn't ready for fatherhood' yet. The sister just sent the woman a video of her smashing her former husband's cock and balls with a hammer. The woman's rushing home to save her husband – spoiler alert: she's going to be too late. Then she will confront her sister, and this time she'll get to watch live as she bashes the kids' brains in. Homecoming – the fun doesn't end until you do!

Once the woman and her children had left the building, Alexandra said, "Lot of weird stuff going on this morning."

Jerome was glad to have a neutral subject to talk about.

"You noticed too, huh?"

She nodded. "People have been acting really strange ever since we opened. And social media has been blowing up with all kinds of bizarre stories! It's wild!"

Honey, you have no idea, Randall said.

Jerome wasn't sure what prompted him to ask Alexandra his next question. Maybe it was because it *was* such a weird morning. Reality itself was in flux, and anything seemed possible now, anything at all.

"Would you come with me for a few minutes? I have something I'd like to show you."

She gave him an appraising look and then slowly smiled. "All right."

She got up from her chair and came out from behind the reference desk. She walked up to him and stood closer than he expected, closer than she ever had before. When she spoke, he could feel her warm breath on his lips. "So…where are we going?" she asked.

Jerome didn't have a ready answer. He hadn't thought this far ahead.

The men's room, Randall said.

Jerome didn't give himself time to question this advice. Besides, Randall hadn't steered him wrong so far, had he?

"Come on," Jerome said softly, then he turned and started toward the restrooms, not looking back to see if Alexandra followed. He knew she would. He didn't check on Randall, either. He sensed his new mentor would hang back and let him handle this solo. His nerves jangled with anticipation, and a line of sweat broke out on his brow. He was doing it, actually *doing* it! He wasn't merely standing in the stacks, looking at photos in *The Book* and fantasizing about what it must be like to take another human being's life. He was about to find out, and he was so nervous he felt like he might piss himself.

The building was large enough to have several sets of restrooms – two sets for patrons, one for staff. Jerome led Alexandra to the closest pair, the one near the children's section, but when he reached the men's, he hesitated. What if someone was already in there taking a piss? Or worse, taking a shit? Then he thought, *Fuck it*, shoved the door open, and stepped inside. He put *The Book* down on the sink counter, then turned to see Alexandra enter, a decidedly naughty smile on her face. When the door swung shut, she turned around and locked it before facing him once more.

"It's about time," she said.

Jerome was at a loss. Had she been expecting – even *hoping* – that he would murder her? It didn't make sense.

"I don't understand."

She walked up to him and without preamble grabbed his crotch and gave it a hard twist. When he cried out in pain, she covered his mouth with hers and began exploring with her tongue. She took hold of his right hand and mashed it to one of her breasts. She let out a moan of pleasure, and Jerome felt the sound's vibration on his own tongue.

He was so surprised by Alexandra's sudden aggression that for a moment he did nothing as she released his genitals and began grinding her crotch against his. She wore a pair of thin black leggings, and when she brought his left hand down to knead her vagina through the cloth, he could feel how wet she was. Finally, he managed to get hold of himself and he took Alexandra by the shoulders and pushed her away from him, more roughly than he intended. She didn't seem alarmed by this. On the contrary, she became even more excited.

"You want to hit me, Jerome? Want to *bite* me? Do it! Just don't leave marks anywhere that shows."

"What's happening here?" he asked. All of his courage, determination, fire was gone now, wiped away by Alexandra's puzzling behavior.

She frowned. "What do you mean what's happening? *You* brought *me* here, remember? So let's get to it."

She stepped forward again and began unbuckling his belt. Without thinking, he slapped her hands away.

She grinned. "Do that to my tits," she said, her voice nearly a purr. "Slap them. *Hard*."

"I don't...I mean, I'm not sure...."

She scowled. "You want to do to me what Randall Beck did to my cousin, right? That's what I want too."

"You want me to...kill you?"

"Hell no! I want you to fuck me the way Randall fucked Tami *before* he killed her. I've fantasized about it ever since she died, but I've never been able to find a guy who really gets me, you know? Someone who understands the attraction of the dark and forbidden. So whip that cock out and let me have a look at it!"

This time when she started to undo his belt, he didn't stop her. What the hell was *wrong* with her? Randall hadn't had sex with any of the three girls he'd killed. There'd been no forensic evidence to suggest otherwise, and beside that, Randall himself had told him that he hadn't been interested in fucking the girls. Killing them, yes, cutting off their faces afterward, sure, but *fucking*? No way. It seemed to him that Alexandra had built her own fantasy around her cousin's murder without actually adhering to the facts. Some research librarian she was!

"Uh, Jerome, not that I'm judging or anything, but you kind of need an erection if you're going to do me, and right now, your dick is showing a decided lack of enthusiasm."

He looked down and saw that she'd undone his belt, unzipped his pants, and pulled down his underwear to reveal his very limp – not to mention extremely exhausted – penis. She could do whatever she wanted to the thing, but it wasn't going to respond. But even if this had been happening another time, he still might've not been able to get an erection. This was all wrong. Alexandra was supposed to be playing the part of a *victim*, not an *aggressor. He* was supposed to be dominating *her*, not the other way around. Rage blazed bright within him, and he turned around and snatched *The Book* off the counter. He opened it, took out the boning knife, and waved it in front of her face.

"I'm going to kill you," he said with as much menace as he could muster.

Alexandra's gaze fixed on the knife and her eyes widened. But then she laughed.

"No, you're not! If you don't have the stones to fuck me, you sure don't have what it takes to kill me."

She took off her sweatshirt and tossed it to the floor. Then she removed her black bra and discarded it as well. She tapped her fingers to a spot above her left breast.

"Put it right here, killer. Go ahead. I dare you."

He couldn't believe this was happening. Did she have some kind of death wish? Had she been fantasizing about Tami's murder for so long that she'd convinced herself that she wanted to die the same way too? Well...so what if she had? He wanted to kill her, didn't he, and here she was, practically throwing herself onto the knife. All he had to do was take her up on her offer. He clenched his teeth, tightened his grip on the knife, took in a couple rapid deep breaths to psych himself up. Then he sighed and relaxed. He couldn't do it. Maybe it was because she was still being the dominant one, and it turned him off. Or maybe – and this was much worse – he didn't have it in him to kill someone.

She sneered at him.

"You're pathetic, you know that?"

She bent down, grabbed her sweatshirt, and put it back on. Then she picked up her bra, wadded it up, and stuffed it down the front of her leggings. This made the bottom edge of her sweatshirt bulge, but it wasn't too noticeable.

"Don't talk to me anymore unless it's work-related, okay? And I don't know why you cut up the insides of that book, but you're going to buy a new copy to replace it. If you don't, I'll report you. Am I clear?"

Jerome heard Randall's voice then. *The Book.*

He caught movement out of the corner of his eye, and he turned to look at the mirror. Randall wasn't in the restroom, but his reflection was there in the glass, and he was holding up a copy of *The Book*, although the real thing still rested on the counter. The mirror book was open to the middle, specifically to a picture of the spot on the bank of the river where Tami's body had washed ashore.

Show her this.

Jerome placed the boning knife on the counter, picked up *The Book*, then turned to face Alexandra once more.

"Have you looked at the pictures inside?" he asked. "They're quite interesting. Especially this one."

He opened *The Book* to the middle. No longer was it hollow inside. It had been restored to its previous condition, except now the photograph of the river was in color instead of black and white, and the water was blood red.

"Why don't you take a closer look?" he said.

He held the book out toward her and a torrent of blood shot forth to strike her chest. The blast knocked her into the restroom door so hard that the lock broke, the door swung open, and her body – which was now quite broken – fell to the floor outside. Blood continued pouring out of the book, faster now, all of it moving away from Jerome as if drawn by powerful tidal forces. He looked back to the mirror, saw Randall there. He no longer held his version of the book.

The specter grinned. *Why don't you take a stroll, show everyone else what Alexandra saw?*

"That's an excellent idea."

Jerome walked out of the men's room, holding *The Book* out before him, blood shooting from it as if it were a fire hose, splashing onto the floor. Soon parts of bodies began to flow out as well, and they were quickly followed by entire corpses, although how these fit through the small rectangle of the river's photo, he had no idea. But that was a minor detail. Trivial. Unimportant. What *was* important was that he was having fun.

He began walking through the library, blasting anyone unlucky enough to get in his way. People screamed and ran, and those who didn't get caught in the blood blast slipped in the crimson stuff and fell to the floor, and then Jerome *did* get them, inundating them with crimson until they could no longer breathe. He was enjoying himself thoroughly when he felt *The Book* jerk and shudder in his grasp.

He heard Randall's thought-voice. *This is the big one – hang on!*

Jerome did so.

A gigantic wave of red rolled forth from *The Book*, the force of its passage staggering Jerome. He nearly lost hold of *The Book*, but he kept his grip on the tome, and he watched as the wave – which rose all the way to the ceiling – raced toward the library's main entrance, sweeping up patrons along with the dead bodies of naked women that the wave had brought with it. Jerome assumed Alexandra's body was in the mix somewhere, but if so, he didn't see her. The wave smashed into the entrance's glass doors, shattered them, and flowed out into the parking lot, losing none of its momentum in the process. The blood streaming from *The Book* began to lessen after that. It quickly became a trickle and then stopped altogether, save for a few last drips.

Jerome closed *The Book* and looked around. The library was in shambles. Shelves had been knocked down, books had been washed away, and those that hadn't were now soaked crimson. Furniture had been overturned or broken, and blood covered every surface.

While the wave itself hadn't touched him, he'd gotten quite a bit of blood on his clothes, hands, and face from the splash back, but he didn't care. He rather liked the feel of it, actually, and it seemed a fitting uniform for the new world that was in the process of being born. He didn't see Randall, but that was okay. He knew he was there. They were a team now – partners – and partners stuck together, no matter what.

He tucked *The Book* under his arm and began whistling merrily as he walked toward the shattered entrance, excited to see what waited for him out there.

CHAPTER THIRTEEN

Julie sat next to Emily Patton, monitoring her vitals, as Nick drove. The siren's wail was loud, but in its own way comforting. It was business as usual – it was *normal* – and right now Julie could use all the normal she could get.

The ride had been mostly smooth so far, although they'd run into a bumpy patch of road several minutes ago. Slick, too. The medic had skidded a bit, but Nick had quickly gotten the vehicle back under control, and everything had been fine since. Blood had soaked through the bandages wrapped over Emily's eye sockets, but not so much that the packing underneath needed to be changed. Best to leave it alone until they reached the hospital. Julie realized then that they'd forgotten to collect Emily's eyes, but considering they'd had to deal with a group of vengeful ghosts, they'd been lucky to get on the road at all. Plus, she'd seen the condition of those eyes, and she highly doubted that even the most skilled surgeon in the world would be able to do anything with them.

She'd given Emily a shot of morphine as soon as they pulled away from her house, but the woman still moaned in pain and struggled against the straps holding her to the stretcher. She spoke, so quietly that Julie almost couldn't make out the words over the siren.

"Demons…demons…."

Julie didn't know what the hell they'd encountered at Emily's house, but demons seemed as good a name as any. And as disturbing as it had been to see the apparitions of patients she hadn't been able to save – and make no mistake, it had been *highly* disturbing – seeing her dead brother had been far worse. The scene continued playing out in her mind on a repeating loop: the ghosts blocking the way to the medic, advancing toward them, obviously intending harm; Brian running up and shooting streams of bee stingers from his body – and how fucked up was *that*? – to repel the attack; the ghosts vanishing and Brian jogging off with a smile and a wave, his work complete. And then, as if a final grace note, the hand coming out of Oliver's laptop to stroke his face. If Nick and Oliver hadn't been there to witness the whole thing, she would've thought she'd gone insane. She still wasn't discounting that possibility.

She wondered if they'd made a mistake leaving Oliver behind to wait for his father. He'd undoubtedly been traumatized by seeing his mother gouge out her eyes, and then he'd witnessed the ghosts of the dead patients manifest, along with Julie's brother.... The boy had to be pretty fucked up right now, and she and Nick had just driven away and left him alone. Julie knew that none of them had been thinking straight at the time, but that was a poor excuse. She hoped Oliver's father would get home soon, and with any luck, both of them would arrive at the hospital not long after she and Nick got Emily there.

As nightmarish as the ghost attack had been, Julie thought it almost made sense that Brian had arrived to save the day. Her big brother had always put other people's wellbeing before his own, and that went double for her. He'd been there her entire life, defending her when she needed it, encouraging her when she doubted herself, soothing her when she was hurt, holding her when she was sad. He was her best friend, her champion, and her cheerleader all in one, and she'd chosen a career in the medical field in order to follow in his footsteps. His death – so stupid and senseless – had hit her hard. He'd had so much to give the world, and for all of that to be taken away by a single fucking bee sting seemed like a cruel joke. After he died, she'd fallen into a depression, began drinking too much and started contemplating ending her own life. She could never hope to live up to Brian's example, could only ever be a poor imitation, so what was the point of trying? But she'd known Brian wouldn't want her to kill herself, would've done everything in his power to help her overcome her depression. So she entered into therapy, started taking antidepressants, and slowly but surely, she'd gotten better. She still had her down days, of course, like anyone else, but they were fewer now and took less effort to get through. She'd finally gotten to the point where, while still grieving her brother's loss, she was able to focus more on all the good he'd done in his too-short life, and that gave her comfort.

And now he'd returned as a ghost that could shoot bee stingers out of his goddamn hands. She shook her head at the ridiculousness of it all. Brian had been a comic book geek growing up, and he'd no doubt love the idea that he was spending his afterlife as a sort of ghostly superhero: The Undead Stinger. Despite herself, she laughed, and if her voice held an edge of hysteria, it was only to be expected given the circumstances.

What in the ever-loving fuck had happened at the Pattons' house? She didn't believe in life after death, Heaven and Hell, gods and demons. And yet the supernatural seemed the only possible explanation for what had occurred. She wished she were riding up front with Nick so she could talk to him about this shit. Nick was Jewish, and while he wasn't fanatical about it, he attended synagogue regularly and considered himself a religious man. She wondered what his perspective on all this was. Then again, he was probably like her, still struggling to accept that he hadn't lost his goddamn mind.

Emily stopped moaning then and turned her head toward Julie. Although the woman no longer had eyes, Julie couldn't escape the feeling that she was looking directly at her.

"It's the End Times. They're not what I expected, of course, but you know what they say. God works in mysterious—"

The sound of crashing metal and shattering glass, a violent jolt, and the medic began to spin. Emily was safe enough – the woman's stretcher had been secured using the wheel locks once it had been brought aboard – and Julie made a desperate grab for the stretcher's metal railing in hope of steadying herself. She missed, though, and fell out of her seat. She hit the floor, struck the wall dividing the front of the medic from the back, then slid backward as the vehicle continued spinning. She pinballed around like this for several seconds before the medic finally struck something and came to a sudden stop.

She lay still for a second as she did a mental inventory of her condition. Her left hip hurt like hell, as did her right shoulder, and she must've hit the back of her head pretty hard because it throbbed like a motherfucker.

Could she have a concussion? Maybe. But nothing seemed to be broken, and she thought she could move without injuring herself any further. She rose to her feet, bracing herself with one hand on a wall. She hurt all over, but she ignored the pain as she turned to examine her patient. As she did, she saw that the medic's rear doors had come open during the crash, revealing a sidewalk, a public waste basket, a small tree – an elm, she thought, but she wasn't sure – and a bakery called Icing on the Cake. She recognized the place. She bought German chocolate cupcakes here once a month as a special treat. She turned her attention to Emily. The woman seemed okay – as okay as anyone could be after ripping their own eyes out of their head, anyway – and she murmured the words, "I told you, I told you, I told you, I told you," over and over, as if it were some kind of chant.

"You're going to be okay," Julie told Emily, then she moved forward to check on Nick. The wall that separated the front and back of the medic had a plastic window that could be slid open so that the person in the back could communicate with the driver. She slid the window open and said, "Nick? You doing all right, buddy?"

He didn't respond right away, and when she leaned forward to look through the open window, she saw why.

The medic's windshield had been completely shattered. A motorcycle was lodged partway into the driver's compartment, and its front tire was jammed against Nick's throat. His head was canted at a sickening angle, and blood trailed from his nostrils and mouth.

"Shit, shit, shit!"

She reached through the window and placed two fingers against the side of Nick's neck. His eyes were wide and unblinking, though, and she knew he was dead before his lack of a pulse confirmed it. When she pulled her hand back, it was shaking. How the hell had this happened? Did the motorcycle's rider jump a ramp or something, launch the bike into the air, and then…what? Nick accidently drove the medic into the bike's path as it was airborne? It didn't make sense.

She turned back to Emily and froze. Standing next to her was a man drenched in blood from head to toe. He was wearing coveralls that might have once been white, but they were so thoroughly sodden with gore that it was impossible to know for sure. He looked at Julie for several seconds before leaning over Emily. He pinched her nostrils shut, and when she opened her mouth to breathe, a torrent of blood gushed forth from his own mouth. Emily began choking, her body spasming beneath the stretcher's straps. Julie rushed toward her, intending to help, but the blood-soaked man – who continued to vomit blood into Emily's mouth – gestured with his free hand and Julie was thrown back against the wall. She tried to move forward again, but her body refused to obey her. All she could do was watch as Emily's exertions lessened, her coughing grew weaker, and finally she fell still.

The blood-covered man let go of her nose and straightened. He regarded Emily for a moment with an expression that was strangely loving. Was he her husband? If so, when had he died? The man gestured and the straps binding Emily to the stretcher unbuckled and fell to the sides. The woman remained still for a moment, but then she sat up stiffly. The blood-covered man held out a hand, she took it, and he helped her off the stretcher. She went into his arms, and they hugged each other tightly. When Emily pulled away, her front was slick with blood, too.

Good luck, she said without opening her mouth. Then she and the man clasped hands and together slowly faded away to nothing.

Julie stared at the empty space where the two had stood, heart pounding, her injured head feeling like it might explode any second. She decided she might just have to reconsider her atheism.

Once Emily and the blood-covered man were gone, Julie could move again, and she climbed down from the back of the medic. She immediately saw what had stopped the vehicle's spin: the rear quarter panel of the medic had slammed into a Pontiac parked in front of the bakery. She checked to see if anyone was inside the Pontiac, but luckily it was empty. Limping slightly because of her sore hip, she walked around to the front of the medic and tried to figure out what the hell had happened to cause the wreck. She saw the other end of the motorcycle jutting from the vehicle's broken window, and she thought, *At least you went fast, Nick.* She still didn't know how the bike had ended up colliding with the medic, but the rest seemed clear enough. When the motorcycle killed Nick, the medic had spun out of control and finally stopped when it struck the Pontiac. A thought nagged at the back of her mind then, but she couldn't get hold of it. Something about Nick and a motorcycle.... She wasn't thinking straight, and she assumed her head injury was to blame. Whatever it was, it would come to her eventually. She turned to the street, looking to see if she could spot the driver of the motorcycle, but she saw no one. Maybe the biker had been thrown clear during the crash, but if so, she didn't see any sign of him or her. She then checked if any other vehicles had been involved in the accident, but it appeared none had been. Traffic was flowing normally, although there were fewer cars than she would've expected for this time of day, and they were moving faster than the posted speed limit – some *much* faster. The sidewalks were empty, too. It was close to lunchtime, and there were a lot of funky little restaurants and coffee shops in this part of town, and there was usually a good-sized crowd here. Those few people who drove by barely glanced at Julie or the wrecked vehicles, seemingly too preoccupied with their own concerns. Some drivers cried with great racking sobs, while others laughed maniacally, eyes wide and terrified. Still others stared straight ahead, steering wheels held in white-knuckled grips, features slack, gazes haunted. She realized then that whatever was happening in Echo Springs, it wasn't just happening to her – it was happening to everyone.

Her thoughts – which up to this point had been hazy and unfocused – sharpened, and she was hit by the full emotional impact of what had happened. Nick, her friend and partner, was dead. God, what was she going to say to his husband? *I'm sorry to tell you this, Ray, but Nick caught a motorcycle in the face during a run today. Sucks, but that's how it goes sometimes.* Tears of her own came then, and with them a fresh explosion of head pain. Maybe she'd been injured more seriously than she'd thought. She decided to see if the medic's radio was still functional – or for that matter, if she could even get to it. If so, she'd call a medic for herself. She thought Nick would've appreciated the irony. She wiped away tears with the heels of her hands and then started limping toward the medic's passenger-side door.

Her mind cleared a bit more, and the thought she'd been grasping for earlier came to the forefront of her consciousness. She remembered something Nick had told her after their first month of working together. When he'd been seventeen, he'd driven alone to West Virginia to visit his grandmother. It had been night, raining fairly hard, and he'd been driving through the hills, up and down, curving this way and that. He'd made this trip with his folks dozens of times, but this was his first time driving it solo, and he feared he'd written a check that his ass couldn't cash. As he came around a bend, his headlights illuminated a pair of objects lying in the road in front of him. He slammed on the brakes, and his Chevy Silverado fishtailed to a stop. He sat there for a moment, breathing heavily, before activating the car's hazard lights and getting out. Rain pelted him, but he barely felt it. A man lay on the road, less than ten feet from an overturned motorcycle. He was slender, his features concealed by a black helmet, and he wore a black leather jacket, jeans, and brown boots. The jeans were torn and bloodied, and a splintered fragment of bone jutted from his left leg. Nick was scared shitless, but he ran to the man's side and knelt down. The man lay on his back, and even over the sound of rain hitting the asphalt around them, Nick could hear the man moaning.

Nick had no idea what do. He'd never received any sort of first aid training, and what little he did know about helping sick and injured people he'd picked up from movies and TV shows. He figured most of that shit was probably useless. He knew that you weren't supposed to move someone who was injured, because if you did, you might make their injuries worse. But he couldn't just leave the guy lying in the middle of the road like this, could he? What if another vehicle came around the curve too fast to stop in time? While he was trying to decide what to do, the man's body stiffened, he let out a strangled cry, and then fell still.

I didn't know how to revive him, Nick had said, *or if it was even possible to revive him. I called 911 on my cell, and eventually a state trooper arrived, followed by a medic. Turned out the biker was in his sixties and had a history of heart trouble. He'd had a heart attack right in front of me, and there was nothing I could do to stop it. That's when I decided to become an EMT. I never wanted to feel that helpless again.*

A cold chill shivered through Julie. She had no idea what kind of motorcycle the man had been driving that rainy night in West Virginia, but she felt certain it was the same make and model as the one that had just taken Nick's life.

Same make and model? Hell, it's the exact same goddamn bike!

The voice reverberated in Julie's already pounding head, and she winced in pain. She sensed the origin of the voice was behind her, and she turned around to see a man in a black helmet and leather jacket. He was dripping wet, as if he'd been caught in a rainstorm, and his jacket and jeans were scuffed and torn. There was a blood on his pants, and a jagged length of bone protruded from below his left knee. That leg was bent at an odd angle, and while it shouldn't have been able to support his weight, somehow it did.

That queer could'a saved my life, but he didn't do shit! Just knelt there like a fuckin' numbnut while my heart seized up in my chest like a worn-out carburetor. Man, I've been waiting a long time for payback! You surprised I was able to throw my bike like that? Don't let these skinny arms fool you, bitch. I'm a hell of a lot stronger these days. We all are.

As if his last three words were a summons, a number of figures began to materialize behind him. As their forms came into sharper focus, Julie recognized them. The suicide, Ed Clayton. Bonnie Reese, the girl with the broken neck. Geraldine Rowe, who, like the biker, had died of a heart attack. Bill Dawson, who bled to death after a chainsaw accident. And worst of all, little Jasmine Hunt, naked, her mutilated genitals dripping with blood. These were some of the dead patients who'd confronted her back at the Pattons' house, ones she hadn't been able to save. All of the people she'd lost as an EMT haunted her, but none more so than these five, and now they'd returned to take another shot at her, their skin swollen and discolored from the stingers Brian had shot into them.

Brought some friends with me, the biker said. *I settled my old score. Time for them to settle theirs. And don't think your fuckin' brother is gonna come runnin' to your rescue again. We're blockin' his ass this time.*

With that, the biker faded and was gone.

Nothing stood between Julie and the five ghosts now, and each of them grinned in dark anticipation. She wasn't sure if she could run given her injured hip, not to mention the goddamn bass drum pound-pound-

pounding in her head, but she sure as hell intended to give it a try. She took a step, the ghosts lunged at her, and in that moment, she knew they were too fast for her to escape. Within seconds they would be on her and tearing her apart, and there wasn't a goddamn thing she could do about it.

She heard an engine roar, caught a flash of movement in her peripheral vision, and turned just in time to watch a blue van slam into the ghosts. Instead of being knocked forward by the impact, the five spirits silently burst apart like human-shaped soap bubbles and were gone. The driver of the van braked then, skidding to a stop less than two feet from the medic.

The driver's-side window rolled down to reveal a Black woman behind the wheel.

"Are you okay?" she said.

Julie gave her a weary smile. "I've had better days. Thanks for the assist."

"You're welcome. I couldn't let them take you."

A lot of people would have, Julie thought.

A wave of dizziness hit her then, and she swayed on her feet, staggered, almost went down. Her rescuer got out of her van, hurried to her, and put an arm around her waist to steady her. Grateful, Julie put a hand on the woman's shoulder. Without asking, the woman began helping Julie around the front of her van toward the passenger side, and Julie let her. Together, they managed to get Julie into the vehicle and buckled into the passenger seat. The woman closed the door, the sound setting off a fresh burst of pain in Julie's head, then hurried back to the driver's-side. She climbed in, closed the door behind her —causing Julie even more pain – then put on her seatbelt. She'd left the van running when she'd gotten out to help Julie, and now she put it in reverse. She backed away from the medic, put the van in drive, and started driving.

"You want to go to the hospital?" the woman asked. "You look pretty banged up."

Julie thought of what it must be like at the hospital right now. How many patients had died there over the years? How many would return seeking, as the biker had called it, payback? Hundreds, at least. The place would be a madhouse. *No,* she thought. *A slaughterhouse.*

"Thanks, but I'll be all right."

The woman gave her a skeptical glance, but said, "Suit yourself," and kept driving.

Julie had been too focused on managing her head pain to notice before now, but she saw the woman had blood on her clothes, face, and the backs of her hands.

"Are *you* okay?" she asked.

The woman kept her gaze fixed on the street as she answered in a toneless voice. "I watched my husband get torn apart by my dead baby girl," she said.

"My partner was just killed by the ghost of a man he wasn't able to save. Guy threw a fucking motorcycle through our windshield."

They were silent for several moments after that. Eventually, the driver said, "I'm Mari."

"Julie."

They continued down the street.

CHAPTER FOURTEEN

Faizan stared at the rusty tools on the stainless-steel tray, paralyzed with indecision.

Just pick one, his father said. *It's not like you're going to be performing brain surgery, you know.*

Pliers, hammer, chisels, knives.... None of them were appropriate for what he needed to do. Then again, he didn't think the tool had been created for the task that lay before him. He turned back to the creature reclining in the dental chair, his nose wrinkling at the thing's stench. He wished he had a barrel full of mouthwash to douse the creature with. He doubted it would remove the stink entirely, but it might make the smell somewhat bearable. In the harsh glare of the dental light, the thing looked even more nightmarish than it had before – a conglomerate monster formed from hundreds of dirty and diseased teeth. Inside its mouth miniature living people protruded from its jaws, one of them his mother. She kept waving her hands as if to get his attention, her mouth moving as if she were speaking, but she was so small he couldn't make out her words. He knew what she was saying, though. She wanted him to leave this place before something bad happened to him. Maybe she feared the tooth monster would claim him the same way it had done to Smiles, Inc.'s staff and patients, shrink him down and add him to the collection in its mouth. But as frightened as Faizan was right now, he couldn't abandon his mother, nor could he leave the other people without trying to do something to help them.

A noble sentiment, his father said. *Foolish, but noble.*

"Be quiet," Faizan murmured. "I'm trying to think."

The people were embedded in the creature's jaws up to their waists. But the question was, how *strongly* were they embedded? Real teeth were firmly seated in the gums and attached by roots. But this creature appeared to be made only from teeth. It had no fleshy parts that Faizan could see. Were the people simply wedged into spaces between its teeth? If so, they had to be in there pretty tight, otherwise those hanging from the upper jaw would fall out.

Do you remember when you started to lose your first baby tooth? Asad asked. *When it became loose, I told you to wiggle it to loosen it further, but you were afraid and refused to do it. Eventually, I was forced to hold you on my lap, grip your tooth with my fingers, and wiggle and twist and pull until it finally came free. How you squealed in pain! It was so satisfying that afterward I began pulling your teeth before they became loose. I had to work much harder, and you screamed like you were dying. Those are some of my favorite memories of you.*

Faizan remembered those tooth-pulling sessions. How could he forget them? The pain, the blood, the feelings of helplessness as his father – so much bigger and stronger than Faizan was – did whatever he wanted to his son's body. But he didn't have time for these thoughts now.

"I believe I told you to be quiet."

None of the tools that had been presented to him seemed sufficient to free the people without harming them in the process. Could he use his fingers to take hold of them and pull them out? Unlikely. No matter how hard he tried to be gentle, he was so much larger than they were that he was bound to injure them, maybe even crush them, if he tried to remove them that way. But what if he put one of his fingers *close* to them? Their arms were free. If they could get a grip on his finger, use it as leverage, maybe they could pull themselves free. If necessary, he could withdraw his finger slowly to create more force, and if it became too much, the person could let go before they were hurt. The more he thought about it, the more it seemed like a plan worth trying.

Get on with it, please, Asad said. *This is becoming tiresome.*

Faizan ignored him. He decided to go for it. But who should he start with? He wanted to help his mother first, of course, but what if his plan didn't work? Worse, what if despite his best efforts, the person he tried to extract ended up getting hurt? He didn't want to harm anyone, but he didn't think he could live with himself if he hurt his mother. He needed to start with someone else, but who? He recognized a few of the people his mom worked with, but he didn't know any of them well, could barely remember their names. How could he choose from among them? But then he realized he didn't have to.

Faizan looked into the tooth creature's mouth, and when he spoke, he kept his voice soft so the volume wouldn't hurt the small people's ears.

"I'm going to try to get you out," he said, and he explained what he had in mind. "I have no idea if this will work, and even if we do get you out, I don't know if you'll return to your normal size or if you'll stay small. And I have to be honest – I've ever done anything like this before, and there's a chance you might get hurt. So I'm asking someone to volunteer. Anyone want to give it a try?"

He didn't know if anyone would agree to go first, but he was surprised to see that almost everyone raised their hands. He supposed if he was stuck in the jaw of a tooth monster, he'd be eager to take any chance at freedom too. His mother waved her arms frantically, trying to get his attention. She obviously wanted to be the guinea pig for his experiment, but he knew she wasn't volunteering for selfish reasons. She wanted to spare someone else from taking the risk.

She always did love playing the martyr, Asad said.

Faizan admired his mother's courage, but there was no way he was going to choose her. He picked a man embedded in the lower jaw, one wearing a white coat. Faizan assumed he was one of the dentists, although he couldn't remember his name. He was an older man with a full head of white hair and the whitest teeth Faizan had ever seen in his life. White coat, white hair, white teeth – Faizan decided to think of him as Dr. White.

How creative, Asad said.

Faizan felt good about Dr. White going first. After all, assuming the man *was* a dentist, who better to supervise an extraction? Faizan pointed to the man. "Okay, you and me. Let's give this a try."

He extended his right index finger toward Dr. White. He tried to remain calm, but his hand trembled nevertheless. He gripped his right wrist with his left hand to steady it, and that helped, but it didn't entirely eliminate the shaking. Moving as slowly as he could, Faizan edged the tip of his index finger closer to Dr. White. Closer…closer…. When he'd gone far enough, Dr. White raised a hand for him to stop, and Faizan did. The man reached out and wrapped his arms around Faizan's finger – his hands felt like an insect's touch – and he tapped the skin twice, a signal for Faizan to slowly begin withdrawing. Nervous sweat ran from Faizan's armpits and trickled down his sides. His mouth was dry as dust, and he could hear his heartbeat in his ears, pounding fast like the rat-a-tat-tat of a snare drum. Dr. White didn't cry out, and his grip didn't slacken, and Faizan began to think that this might just work after all.

Then something bumped his right elbow, causing his hand to lurch forward. Horrified, he turned to see Asad standing next to him.

Did I do that? How clumsy of me.

Faizan yanked his hand back and brought his index finger close to his face. He went cold when he saw a smear of blood on the tip. He didn't want to look at Dr. White, didn't want to see what had happened to the man, but he forced himself to turn and examine the tooth creature's mouth. The lower half of Dr. White's body remained stuck in the creature's jaw, but the top half of him was bent backward at a ninety-degree angle. His head was torn halfway off, and blood flowed from the neck wound. The other people trapped in the tooth creature's mouth were understandably upset. Some cried, some wailed in despair, some shouted at Faizan, blaming him for what happened, and some looked defeated, as if they now believed there was no chance they could be freed. Faizan's mother remained silent and still, gazing at him with deep sorrow.

Faizan was gripped by sudden fury over what his father had made him do. He turned to the dental cart where the tools lay, grabbed the hammer, and turned toward Asad. He raised the hammer above his head and took a step forward.

Asad's delighted laugh echoed in Faizan's mind.

That's the way to show some backbone, boy! Go ahead, hit me. You've wanted to for a long time. Come on! I deserve it! For everything I did to you, to your brother and sister – and especially for all the things I did to your mother….

Asad grinned as he thought these words, and his eyes glittered like ice.

Faizan knew why his father was taunting him. He was attempting to awaken his son's darker impulses, to make him give in to his anger, submit to the temptation to commit violence, satisfy his need to visit upon his father the same cruelty he'd shown to his family. Asad wanted to *conquer* him, break him down and remake him in his own image – and Faizan would be damned if he'd let him. Besides, he had a new idea how he might free the people trapped by the tooth creature.

He turned back to the dental table, snatched up a chisel with his free hand, then turned toward the thing sitting in the chair. He placed the chisel on the center of its chest, where the heart would be in a human being, then he raised the hammer and brought it down hard on the chisel's handle. Rusty metal struck rusty metal, and the impact drove the cutting edge of the chisel into the creature's chest. Shards of enamel shot through the air as a number of teeth broke off and slid onto the floor, striking the tile with soft clacks. Faizan smiled grimly. He'd been right. Nothing solid held the tooth creature together, just some kind of invisible force. And if he could disrupt that power with enough force of his own, the thing's entire structure might collapse like a house of cards, freeing the people trapped in its mouth. He raised the hammer for another strike, but the creature – which up to then had remained statue-still – shot out a hand and wrapped its fingers around Faizan's throat. Like the rest of its body, the creature's hand was formed from teeth, and some of the sharper edges pointed outward. The creature squeezed its hand, and those edges pressed painfully into Faizan's neck. He felt his skin break, felt blood well from a dozen small wounds. He tried to draw in a breath, found he couldn't, tried to pull away from the creature, but its grip was too strong.

You broke one of his teeth, Asad said. *It's only fair you replace it.*

Faizan's entire body began to tingle fiercely, as if an electric current ran through his system. Whatever power the tooth creature had used to shrink the staff of Smiles, Inc., it was using that same power on Faizan now. He would be shrunken down to tooth-size, the creature would pluck the dead Dr. White from his socket, and insert him. He knew he had only seconds to act, assuming it wasn't already too late. He yanked the chisel out of the creature's chest and brought it up to the thing's arm. He jammed the cutting edge into the inside of its elbow, brought the hammer up, and struck. The chisel bit into the elbow joint, and Faizan could feel the blow's impact judder down the arm and into the creature's hand. He hit the chisel a second time, then a third, and the teeth holding the arm together began to fall apart and rain to the floor. Everything from the elbow to the hand lost structural integrity and collapsed, and suddenly Faizan could breathe once more. He drew in a desperately needed gulp of air. His throat felt as if it was on fire, but he'd never known a sweeter breath in his life.

Not bad, Asad said grudgingly. *But I bet you didn't expect* this.

The tooth creature still had one intact arm remaining, and now it curled its fingers into a fist and jammed the hand into its mouth. There was a sharp sound of enamel scraping enamel, accompanied by a wet *smush* that made Faizan's stomach do a flip. Blood splashed from the sides of the creature's mouth, and then it began to grind its fist back and forth, reducing the tiny bits of bone and flesh inside it to red paste. Faizan stared, horrified, then he let out a cry of anguish and began hacking away at the creature with the chisel. He struck like a man possessed, each blow shearing away another group of teeth, and by the time he'd cut away a third of the creature's body, its form lost all cohesion and fell apart. More teeth fell to the floor to join those already there, but the teeth that had comprised the main part of its body lay in a pile on the chair.

Faizan took a step back, lungs heaving, body covered with sweat. The people were gone. His *mother* was gone. He hadn't been able to save them, not a single one. He turned to his father, intending to ask him if he was satisfied now—

—but Asad was gone.

Faizan let the hammer and chisel drop from his hands and onto the floor. Then moving slowly, head hung low, he shuffled out of the examining room.

★　　★　　★

As Karen walked out of Time for Tots, she was surprised to find herself having mixed feelings about her sister's death. As for all the others who had died at the school – in *spectacularly* gory fashion, no less – she had no feelings whatsoever. Kathleen had been responsible for those deaths, and they had nothing to do with her. Once Erika was dead, Kathleen vanished, her work evidently complete, leaving behind one hell of a mess for some poor sonofabitch to clean up. Karen should've been happy that Erika was gone, and she *was*. Mostly. But she also felt empty somehow.

Bennie walked at her side, and he spoke to her in his thought-voice.

You've hated your sister all your life. That hatred was a large part of your identity. Erika was your bête noire, *your black beast. The white whale to your Ahab. In a very real way, she gave your life purpose. Now that she's gone, it's only natural that you feel at loose ends. You'll adjust. It'll just take some time. You have so much more hate to give the world, Karen. You just need to find an outlet for it.*

His words made her feel a little better.

"Thanks, Bennie."

A thought struck her then.

"Bennie? Now that Erika is dead, does that mean she can come back like you? Like Kathleen?"

Bennie grinned. *I was wondering how long it would take you to think of that. You know how much I enjoy torturing you, right?*

She nodded.

So what makes you think I'd ever answer that question?

He began laughing then, cold and cruel, just like she remembered. Then he faded away, leaving behind the sound of his laughter, and several seconds later, it was gone too.

"Bastard," Karen muttered, but she wasn't really angry at him. She'd have done the same thing if she'd been him. She wasn't the sort of person to worry overmuch about the future anyway. She preferred to focus on the here and now. So until Erika returned to exact her revenge – if she ever did – Karen wasn't going to give her dead twin another thought. Besides, if Erika killed her, then she'd be a ghost too, which meant she'd be able to torment her sister for eternity. Cheered by this thought, she headed for her Explorer. She had no clue where she would go next, but the Homecoming, as Bennie had called it, was happening all over town. Maybe she'd drive around and enjoy the mayhem, stop and watch if she came across something good. Maybe even participate if she found something *really* good.

She had her hand on her car door, was about to open it and climb in, when she saw the boy come out of the dentist's office. He had brown skin, but he didn't strike her as a spic. An A-rab, more likely. He walked slowly, listlessly, his head down. Karen was, in her small way, a predator, and like any predator, she could smell pain and weakness a mile off, and this kid reeked of both.

She smiled. This was going to be fun.

She ran her hands through her hair to muss it, put on a suitably distressed expression, and began shouting.

★   ★   ★

"Help me! Please, help me!"

Faizan turned toward the sound of the woman's voice. She was his mother's age, maybe older, and was running across the parking lot toward him. She had blood on her clothes, face, hands, and hair, and at first he thought she was another ghost come to attack him. But then he realized that he'd actually *heard* her voice. She'd spoken aloud, something neither his father nor the tooth creature – which Asad claimed had once been a human woman – had done. Of course, encountering two ghosts didn't exactly make him an expert on their species. For all he knew, they came in different varieties, like ice cream. Still, the woman *seemed* real enough, and after failing to save his mother and the rest of the people in Smiles, Inc., the opportunity to help someone, and perhaps by doing so redeem himself, was irresistible.

He started jogging toward the woman, and he met her halfway between the preschool and Smiles, Inc. She practically collapsed in his arms, and her solidity reassured him that she was, in fact, alive.

"It was horrible!" she said. "She appeared out of thin air.... A teacher who'd died a while back. Kathleen's her name. She was so *angry*! She started going around the school and...and...." The woman drew in a hitching breath, then closed her eyes and paused for a moment, as if she was trying to compose herself. She opened her eyes and continued, her voice steadier now. "People began *exploding*! Like water balloons filled with blood. Teachers, staff, and the...the children." Her voice cracked, and whatever control she'd managed to assert over her emotions collapsed. She buried her head against Faizan's chest and let out a sob.

Tentatively, he reached up and patted her back. He felt ridiculous trying to comfort her like this after what she had experienced. He tried to imagine what it would be like to see someone literally explode – especially a *child* – and he was glad he couldn't. He understood why she had blood all over her, though. He didn't know if she worked at Time for Tots or if she had a grandchild who attended classes there and she'd merely been visiting. If the latter, she'd sure picked a hell of a day to drop in.

A thought occurred to him then.

"How did you get away?" he asked.

She kept her face against his chest as she answered.

"I...I don't know really. I started running when I saw what Kathleen was doing, and I guess I managed to get outside before she caught up to me."

Faizan looked at Time for Tots's entrance, half expecting to see an angry ghost come rushing out, point a finger at them, and reduce them to two red stains on the asphalt. But no one appeared, and he was relieved. He'd had more than enough of ghosts for one day.

He took hold of the woman's shoulders and gently pushed her away from him.

"Are you okay? Are you hurt?" he asked.

"I don't think so." She looked down at her shirt, examined the backs of her hands. "This isn't my blood. It's.... It's...."

He feared she was going to break down again, so he quickly changed the subject.

"Can I take you someplace? Your home? Or maybe a relative or friend's house?"

The woman wiped at her eyes, but Faizan didn't see any tears. Then again, her face was spattered with blood, so maybe he'd simply missed them.

"I don't have anywhere to go," the woman said. "Do you?"

The question brought Faizan up short. He hadn't considered what he was going to do once he'd rescued his mom, and he *certainly* hadn't thought about what his next move might be after he'd failed to save her. What could they do? If the reports were true, if this really was happening all over the world, then nowhere was safe. He supposed they could try to go to a holy place. The mosque he and his family attended was in Oakmont, but that was about a thirty-minute drive, and that was under good conditions. Somehow, he didn't think traffic would be cooperative today. There were plenty of Christian churches in town, as well as a synagogue. Any port in a storm, right?

"Yeah, I think I might."

CHAPTER FIFTEEN

Mari had continued driving aimlessly after escaping Noelle, partly because she feared her daughter's spirit would attack again if she stopped, but also because she wasn't ready to deal with Lewis's death. Driving gave her body something to do, which in turn kept her from thinking too much. If she could, she'd travel aimlessly through the streets of Echo Springs like this for the rest of her life, going nowhere, thinking and feeling nothing.

She'd witnessed a number of disturbing incidents since fleeing her home, the dead preying on the living in ways both shocking and unbelievable, but each time she'd driven on by, without even considering stopping to help. But when she saw the woman – Julie – about to be attacked by a group of ghosts, she'd been compelled to intervene. She wasn't sure why. Maybe it was because Julie was an EMT, someone who helped others and now needed help herself. Or maybe the emotional numbness that had clouded her mind since she'd watched Lewis be torn apart by his unborn baby was beginning to fade. Either way, she'd driven her van into the group of spirits attacking Julie and repelled them. Afterward, she'd continued on without a specific destination in mind, only now she had company.

"Do you need to return to your fire station or the hospital or something?" Mari asked. "Wherever you need to go, I can take you there."

Julie thought for a moment.

"There *is* one place I'd like to go. I left somebody there and I'd like to check to make sure he's okay."

That sounded to Mari like as good a destination as any.

"Tell me the address," she said.

★   ★   ★

As they approached the house, Mari saw a white pickup parked in the driveway with the words *Precision Paint* on the side.

"The truck wasn't there before," Julie said.

"It probably belongs to the boy's father," Mari said. "You said Oliver had called him before you and your partner arrived."

"And I saw the father's ghost in the back of the medic. At least, I think it was the father. If so, that means he died after coming home. The front door's still open, too."

Mari hadn't noticed this detail, but now that Julie had pointed it out, she saw the front door to the house *was* wide open. In February.

"The father would've rushed inside to get Oliver and take him to the hospital," Julie said. "He planned on leaving immediately, so he wouldn't bother closing the door, especially as frantic as he must've been."

"But they didn't leave," Mari said. "His truck is still here."

"Which means he was probably killed inside."

Which means Oliver might have been killed here too, Mari thought. She didn't want to say this aloud, but she was certain Julie was thinking the same thing.

She pulled into the driveway behind the pickup, killed the engine, and she and Julie got out. The cold air made her shiver, but Julie didn't seem to notice the temperature. She ran to the door without waiting for Mari and went inside. Mari hurried after her, and once she was inside, she closed the door to keep the cold out.

"Oliver!" Julie called. "Are you here? Are you okay?"

When she didn't receive a response, she began searching the house, moving quickly from room to room, still calling Oliver's name. She limped a bit, but not as badly as when Mari had first found her, and Mari was glad the woman was starting to feel better. She decided to help Julie search for the boy, and she headed for the kitchen. Nothing there, so she moved on to the dining room. Once in the doorway, she froze and stared at the blood on the floor. There was so damn *much* of it, and seeing it reminded her of how blood had fountained from Lewis's mutilated body as he died. Then she thought of what Oliver's mother had done to herself here. On the way over, Julie had told her about the call she and her partner had received and what they'd found when they got here. How could a person *do* that to themselves? And once they started the job, how could they withstand the pain enough to finish it?

She turned away from the dining room, rushed back into the kitchen, ran to the sink, and threw up the remains of her breakfast. When she was done, she ran the tap to wash the vomit down the drain. She heard Julie calling Oliver's name deeper within the house and knew she was likely checking bedrooms and bathrooms. Mari was beginning to think they'd find Oliver dead, if they found him at all, and although she'd never met the boy, she felt sad for him. To die so young....

He's still alive. But if you and your friend don't get your asses in gear, he won't be for much longer.

The voice startled Mari, and she turned to see a petite woman with curly black hair standing in front of the refrigerator, door open, a small plastic storage bag in her hand. The front of her clothes was soaked with blood – there was a lot of that going around today, Mari thought – and bloodstained bandages were wrapped around her eyes. Mari knew at once that she was looking at the ghost of Oliver's mother. Her gaze focused on the plastic bag, and she saw it was filled with ice and bits of bloody flesh that were...were....

The ghost removed the bandages from her head and dropped them to the floor, revealing empty red hollows where her eyes had been. She opened the bag and the eyes within jumped out of it as if possessed of a life of their own. They flew up to the woman's head, optic nerves slithering into her skull, and then the eyes sealed themselves in place. She blinked several times, rolled her eyes around to test them, and then smiled.

Much better. Now go save my son. He's in the basement.

The woman then disappeared. The bag of ice hung in the air for a moment longer before falling to the floor to join the bloody bandages.

Mari, gaze fixed on the bag, drew in a deep breath and shouted Julie's name.

★ ★ ★

Oliver sat at the river's edge, Delia next to him, her arms wrapped around him so tight he could barely breathe. They were both still naked, and their special place – which Oliver now understood wasn't exactly real – had changed. The river was no longer filled with blood and bodies, but it hadn't resumed its previous state, either. The water, now greenish-black, had stopped flowing and become still and stagnant, stinking of rotting meat and decaying plant matter. Things swam beneath the surface, large sinuous forms that didn't reveal themselves but left ripples to mark their passage. The grass they sat on was dry and lifeless, the ground beneath hard and uncomfortable. The sky was the purple of a fresh bruise, and the air was as still as the water, stuffy, heavy, and stale, like the air you'd find in a small windowless room that had been kept closed for too long. The trees were gnarled, twisted, leafless, and instead of bark, they were covered with what looked like crusty red scabs. No longer did a bright summer sun hang in the sky. In its place was an obsidian circle surrounded by a slowly swirling ring of multicolored light. The blackness within that circle was deeper and darker than anything Oliver had ever imagined. Looking at it filled him with a sense of absolute despair, and so he kept his gaze averted.

Delia sighed in contentment. "Isn't it beautiful?" she said.

Oliver didn't reply.

"Tell me you love it," she said.

Oliver still said nothing.

"Tell me you love *me*," she said, her tone vaguely threatening.

"I love you" Oliver said. "But you're not the same Delia I remember. What happened?"

Her arms tightened around him further, cutting his air off entirely. She held him that way for several moments – long enough to make him think she was going to kill him – before finally releasing him. She stood, put her hands on her hips, and scowled at him. Oliver got to his feet and took a couple steps away from her, wanting to put some distance between them. When Delia saw this her scowl deepened.

"What happened? I fucking *died*! You think I look like *this* now?" She gestured to her body. "I recreated this for *you*, and believe me, it's not easy to maintain. It takes *effort*. Maybe you'd like to get a look at the real me these days."

As Oliver watched, Delia's body rippled, distorted, blurred, and when it came into focus again, she no longer looked like the beautiful young woman Oliver had spent so much wonderful time with by the river. Her father had killed her with a fireplace poker, and her flesh was covered with contusions, cuts, and puncture wounds. He'd attacked her breasts and vagina – the parts he'd viewed as sexual – with special fury, savaging them to the point where they were nothing but ragged, bloody tatters. He'd also attempted to obliterate her face, as if he'd wanted to erase Delia's identity entirely. The left side of her head was caved in, as was everything from her forehead down to her mouth. Her lips had been torn to shreds, most of her teeth had been knocked out, and her tongue had been slashed to ribbons.

Delia could no longer physically speak, and once more Oliver heard her words in his mind.

Hot, right? Wanna fuck some more? Wanna eat this out?

Delia placed her hands on the sides of her ruined crotch and stretched the remains of her vagina wide. A thick dark clot of blood fell out and hit the ground with a sickening *splat*.

Oliver experienced a wave of deep revulsion, and all he wanted to do was look away from the horrible sight of his dead girlfriend taunting him with her mutilated genitals. But whatever transformation she'd undergone in the afterlife, this was still Delia, and he did still love her. He stepped forward, raised a hand, touched his fingers gently to her cold cheek, and looked into the holes where her eyes had once been. Was that why she'd forced his mother to gouge out her eyes, because she had none of her own?

"I'm so sorry this happened to you, Delia. You didn't deserve this, no one does."

You're damn right I didn't deserve it! And it never would've happened if I hadn't met you! Would you like to know what it feels like? Would you like to know what it's like to be me?

Pain beyond anything Oliver had ever imagined gripped his body and he crumpled to the ground. He could no longer see, could barely breathe through the ruin his mouth had become. His chest and genitals felt as if they were aflame, and his thoughts were muddy and slow.

Hard to think when half of your skull's been crushed, Delia said.

Oliver moaned in agony as he writhed on the ground. The pain was so all-encompassing that even if his brain hadn't been damaged, he still wouldn't have been able to think clearly. Even so, a spark of awareness remained in his mind, tossed about like a moat of dust in a windstorm. And in this tiny portion of his self that remained Oliver, he didn't blame Delia for what she was doing to him; he understood that being imprisoned in a boundless universe of suffering like this would drive anyone insane.

He gasped out four words.

"I...still...love you."

And then just as swiftly as the pain had hit him, it was gone. He could think and see again, but he was so weak that all he could do for the moment was roll over onto his back and wait for his strength to return.

Delia, once more looking as she had in life, knelt by his side, took one of his hands, and placed it between her breasts.

Over her heart, Oliver thought.

Now that she'd returned to the guise she'd been wearing in their special place, she could speak aloud once more. Or at least she *seemed* to do so.

"If you love me – *really* love me – then you'll want to be with me. I can visit the world of the living, but I can't stay. If you want us to be together, you have to come with me to *my* world. And there's only one way you can do that, Oliver. You have to die. Are you willing to do that for me? For our love?"

Oliver looked into Delia's eyes. He saw love there, yes, but he saw something else as well, an inhuman hunger that frightened him to the core of his being. Delia was in there too, he believed that now, but she wasn't the *only* thing there. He knew it didn't matter what answer he gave her, though. Either way she was going to kill him, and given the power she possessed, he couldn't stop her from taking his life. She'd caused his mother to mutilate herself and she'd killed his father, all because she thought they might stand between the two of them. And if Delia thought Oliver himself stood in the way of getting what she wanted, she wouldn't hesitate to kill him as well. Whatever he chose, the end result would be the same: he was going to die.

"Get the fuck away from him!"

Both Oliver and Delia turned toward the voice and saw two women standing at the top of the basement stairs. Oliver recognized one as the female EMT who had come to help his mom. The other was a Black woman Oliver didn't know. The EMT had been the one who yelled, and she glared challengingly at Delia. The other woman was taking in the details of the dark world Delia had created within the basement, and from the expression on the woman's face, she was having difficulty processing what she saw.

The EMT came rushing down the stairs, taking them two and three at a time until she reached the bottom. She then came charging toward Delia, and if the strange surroundings bothered her at all, she didn't show it. Delia watched her come, anger clouding her face. Oliver struggled to stand, but he was still weak and only managed to get up on one knee.

"Get out of here!" he shouted. "She's too dangerous!"

Without bothering to look at him, Delia swept her right arm backward and struck him on the jaw. The blow knocked him off balance, and he fell to the ground. His jaw hurt, but the pain was nothing compared to what he'd experienced several moments ago, and he barely noticed it.

"He's mine," Delia said. "You can't have him."

Delia gestured and the scab-covered trees bent over – their crusty growths breaking open and oozing clear fluid – and their branches burst into motion. Wooden limbs whipped toward the EMT like thrashing tentacles, and she had to throw herself to the ground to avoid their grasp. Delia had created this place, and that meant she controlled every aspect of it. There was no way the EMT could keep from being captured for long, and once Delia had hold of the woman, she was as good as dead. Unless Oliver found a way to distract Delia.

Oliver forced himself to his feet. Fighting dizziness, he stepped forward, bent down, grabbed hold of Delia's bare ankles, and yanked her legs backward. She fell forward and her chin slammed hard against the ground. Oliver didn't stop there. Before she could recover, he jumped onto her back, straddled her, grabbed her head with both hands, and began repeatedly smashing her face into the ground. The animated tree branches went wild, flailing and thrashing, reflecting their mistress's pain and confusion. The EMT stayed down to avoid being struck by one of the wooden tendrils and crawled toward Oliver and Delia.

Oliver didn't let up. He continued bashing Delia's head against the ground, encouraged to see blood on the dead dry grass where her head hit. He didn't know if it was possible to kill whatever it was that she had become, but he was damn sure going to try. He still loved her, but he couldn't allow her to harm anyone else, and if that meant she had to lose her life for a second time, then so be it. Delia, however, did not intend to go down easily.

She heaved herself to her feet, and the sudden motion dislodged Oliver. He flew off of her and landed hard on his back, the impact driving the air from his lungs. He fought for breath as he struggled to rise, and he saw Delia coming toward him, features twisted into a mask of pure hatred. He glanced toward the EMT, saw one of the tree tendrils had wrapped around her right leg and had pulled her to the ground. Other tendrils rushed toward her, and Oliver knew the woman would be dead within the next few seconds. She'd returned to help him, and now her kindness was going to be rewarded with an agonizing death. He wished the woman had forgotten about him and stayed away, had gone on to help others who had a chance of being saved, but it was too late now.

When Delia reached him, she grabbed hold of his left wrist, spun him around once, twice, and then hurled him into the air. His arms and legs thrashed wildly, as if desperately searching for something, anything to grab onto to stop his flight. The world became a jumble of images – the riverbank, the great black hole in the sky, the animated trees, the EMT, the woman at the top of the stairs, Delia watching him tumble, and the motionless stagnant water below. And then Oliver plunged beneath the surface of the river, the water cold, thick and foul. As he sank, he took a reflexive breath and water rushed down his throat, some going into his lungs, some into his stomach. He coughed, inhaled, drew in more water, sank further. As he descended, he thought it was a shame that he'd never learned to swim.

CHAPTER SIXTEEN

Julie was fighting to free herself from the tree limb that had wrapped around her ankle when she saw the naked girl throw Oliver into the air. She watched as he fell into the river – and what the hell was a goddamn *river* doing in the kid's basement? – with a loud splash and disappeared beneath the surface. She hoped he could swim, but even if he was an excellent swimmer, hitting the water that hard would've stunned him. He might be unconscious, and if so, he would drown. She needed to get to him, but in order to do that she first had to get loose from this fucking tree.

The wooden tendril had pulled her off her feet when it grabbed hold of her, and she'd moved into a sitting position so she could get her hands on it and pry it off her leg. The damn thing was wrapped around her ankle tight as an iron band, though, and she couldn't budge it. It didn't help that her head still pounded like a sonofabitch, and her hip felt like it was on fire. It was an effort to concentrate past the pain, but she had to, for Oliver's sake. She clawed at the tendril around her ankle more frantically, knowing that every second that passed increased the chances of Oliver dying. She ignored the fact that she was in some kind of nightmarish world located within the Pattons' house, a world where trees came to life and grabbed hold of you like octopus tentacles, where a horrible black thing hung in the sky in place of a sun. Whether this place was real, an illusion, or some combination of the two didn't matter. All that mattered was getting free so she could go to Oliver's aid. She thought of the ghosts that had confronted her, the angry spirits of those patients she'd been unable to save. She was determined not to add him to their number today.

She continued tearing at the tendril around her ankle, wishing she had a knife, or better yet, a chainsaw, when a second tendril wrapped itself around her right wrist. It was followed by a third, which caught hold of her left ankle, and a fourth, which encircled her left wrist. Then working in concert, the tendrils lifted her into the air several feet. She thrashed, trying to shake herself free, but it was no use. She was held fast and helpless.

The girl came walking toward her now, blood flowing from a wound on her forehead. Oliver had done that when he'd bashed her head into the ground, and Julie was glad he'd at least gotten a few licks in. There was nothing about the girl's physical appearance to indicate she was a ghost, but Julie had seen enough spirits today to know that unless they had any obvious injuries, they often looked like ordinary humans. But she'd seen how the trees had come to life at the girl's command and how easily she had hurled Oliver out over the river, and she had no doubt this girl wasn't alive. She remembered the last sight she'd had of Oliver as Nick drove the medic away from his house: him standing outside, holding a laptop, a hand emerging from the screen to stroke his cheek. She felt it was a good bet she was looking at the owner of that hand now.

"Oliver's mother told us he was down here," Julie said. "She didn't say he had company, though."

The girl stopped a foot away from Julie and regarded her, waves of hatred rolling off of her like heat blasting from a raging bonfire. Julie understood then that this girl was the demon that Emily Patton had been raving about when she and Nick had gotten her ready for transport. She'd been the one who'd compelled Emily to tear out her own eyes.

"That bitch came back?" the girl said, sounding surprised. But then she shrugged. "It's not important. She's obviously too chickenshit to come down here and face me herself, so she sent you and your friend to deal with me." She smiled. "Lucky you."

The girl's mention of Mari made Julie wonder how her new companion was doing. She glanced toward the stairs and saw that Mari had descended them and was slowly making her way to the river, keeping her eye on the girl as she went. She was going to try to help Oliver, but in order for her to succeed, Julie needed to keep the girl distracted.

"So who are you?" she asked. "Oliver's crazy ex-girlfriend?"

"My name is Delia, and I'm not his ex. We're still together. He just doesn't know it yet. But when he's dead he'll understand." She paused "You all will."

Julie looked over Delia's shoulder and saw that Mari had reached the river's edge. She kicked off her shoes, glanced over to make sure Delia was still occupied, then began to quietly make her way into the water. Her features pinched in disgust as the liquid touched her skin, and her nose wrinkled at the noxious smell. Julie wasn't sure which of them – her or Mari – had it worse right now. She decided it was probably a toss up.

Mari was up to her waist in water now. She took a deep breath and dove under, barely making a ripple as she did so. Julie focused her full attention on Delia.

"What will we understand?" Julie asked. "Enlighten me."

Delia cocked her head to the side as she considered Julie's words. Finally, she said, "I don't think so. It would spoil the surprise, and what would be the fun in that? You know, when I was little, I never pulled the wings off an insect. I always thought it sounded like a terribly cruel thing to do. But in the back of my mind, I always wondered what it would be like to have ultimate power over something so small and helpless. It's the end of the world. If you can't indulge your curiosity then, when can you? I think I'll start with your left arm."

Delia gestured and the branch wrapped around Julie's left wrist began to retract. Sharp pain lanced up Julie's arm, and she let out an agonized cry as she felt her shoulder pop out of place. She wondered if, once her arm was torn off, she'd bleed out before Delia could tear off the rest of her limbs. She hoped so. That would spare her some pain at least.

The air behind Delia shimmered and Brian – still dressed in his running clothes – appeared. His shirt was torn, his face bruised, one eye swollen shut, his lower lip split and bleeding. She remembered what the ghost biker – one of the patients she hadn't been able to save – had said to her just before Mari had come to her aid. *And don't think your fuckin' brother is gonna come runnin' to your rescue again. We're blockin' his ass this time.* From the looks of it, Brian had fought his way past those ghosts to get to her. Without speaking a word, her brother grabbed Delia's shoulder, spun her around, and punched her in the jaw. The blow staggered the girl, and she took several lurching steps to her right. Her concentration faltered and the tree branch stopped pulling Julie's arm. It slackened, as did the other three branches, and while their coils did not release her entirely, they did loosen considerably. She literally had wiggle room now, and she began thrashing her body, working to free herself. Her dislocated shoulder screamed at her to stop, but she gritted her teeth against the pain and continued trying to get loose.

Brian didn't give Delia a chance to recover. He moved toward her, struck her face with a hard right cross and followed it up with a powerful left to her stomach. It was so strange for Julie to see her brother fighting like this. He'd dedicated himself to helping others, not hurting them. But she was grateful for his newfound toughness. She, Oliver, and Mari needed it right now.

The punch to the stomach caused Delia to hunch over, and while she was reeling from the blow, Brian held his palms out toward her. As he did, the flesh peeled back to create a pair of orifices, he tensed his arms, and twin streams of stingers blasted forth to rake Delia's body. This assault broke the last of her concentration, and the tree tendrils let go of Julie, and she fell to the ground. She didn't have far to go, and she managed to land on her feet, although her right ankle gave a sharp twinge as she hit. She hoped she hadn't twisted it. Her dislocated shoulder hurt like a bitch, and that arm hung limp at her side. She wasn't overly worried about the injury, though. Dislocated shoulders were easy enough to fix.

The front of Delia's naked body was covered with stingers from head to toe. They were embedded deep in her flesh, and lines of blood ran from the puncture points. The flesh around them was already beginning to blacken and swell, and a couple of the thorns had struck her left eye, which was reacting similarly. Julie was glad. Served her right after what she'd done to Oliver's mother. Too bad she still had one undamaged eye left.

In life, Brian had always been calm, even in the most stressful of situations. Julie used to call him the Eye of the Storm, and although she was teasing him when she said this, she'd meant it too. It was a perfect description of him, and that emotional equilibrium had served him well throughout his life and especially in med school. He was far from calm now, though. His eyes blazed with fury, and his hands curled into white-knuckled fists.

You can't have her, Delia. She's mine!

These words disturbed Julie. She'd never heard Brian refer to her like this before, as if she was his personal property. When he'd first manifested and had driven off the dead patients who wanted revenge on her and Nick, she'd thought her big brother the protector had come to her rescue one more time. Now she wondered if she'd misjudged his motive for aiding her.

She looked toward the river and saw a very wet Mari helping an equally wet Oliver out of the water. Oliver was walking, a little shaky-legged but functional, and Mari had an arm around his waist to steady him. Mari looked to Julie, then jerked her head toward the stairs. Julie nodded.

Delia glared at Brian with her one good eye, hate coming off of her as hot as a blast furnace. She drew in a deep breath and then flexed like she was a body builder. The stingers popped out of her flesh and streaked toward Brian too fast for him to evade. He was able to raise his arms in time to shield his face, however. The stingers struck him as they had Delia, but other than bleeding, his flesh showed no reaction to them. It appeared death was an excellent cure for allergies.

This is MY world! Delia said, reverting to her thought-voice. *I created it, and that makes me god here!*

She began growing then, her size increasing rapidly. Eight feet. Ten. Twelve. Twenty. Twenty-five…. Brian held out his palms, intending to send another barrage of stingers hurtling toward her. But before he could release them, Delia – now close to thirty feet tall – covered the distance between them in a single step and then kicked him in the chest with her massive foot. There was a horrible crunching sound as Brian's ribcage and spine shattered, and the impact sent him flying out over the river. As he arced down toward the water, a huge dark shape leaped up toward him. The thing resembled a cross between a fish and lizard, with a bit of crustacean thrown in for good measure. It opened a tooth-ringed lamprey-like mouth, caught hold of Brian, and fell backward into the water with a monstrous splash.

For the second time in her life, Julie mourned the loss of her brother, but she was also glad Mari and Oliver had managed to avoid being devoured by the leviathan. Christ, what a way to go! And speaking of going....

Mari and Oliver had reached the top of the basement stairs, and Mari ushered the boy into the house without a backward glance. Julie decided it would be a good idea to join them. She tried running, but between the pounding in her head and the searing agony in her shoulder, the best she could manage was a half-jog, half-walk. Behind her, Delia continued growing, and she raised her fists to the dark sky, threw back her head, and shook her private little universe with a scream of rage and frustration so loud, it was like someone jammed white-hot needles into Julie's ears. She hoped her goddamn eardrums wouldn't burst. She'd sustained more than enough injuries for one day.

With every step she took, she expected Delia to kick her, step on her, smash her with a fist, or swat her like an insect, but the gigantic girl didn't seem to care about her anymore. She began grabbing hold of the gnarled, leafless trees, ripping them out of the barren soil, and throwing them into the river. The trees were still animated, and their limbs flailed as Delia uprooted them, and Julie thought she could hear their cries of pain. Delia was throwing an absolutely epic tantrum, and Julie was grateful she was distracted. She increased her pace, though, regardless of how much it hurt to do so. If Delia were to throw one of those trees in the direction of the stairs, she could destroy Julie's only way out.

Julie made it to the stairs and steadied herself with her good hand on the railing as she ascended. Her twisted ankle complained, but it was nothing compared to the pain in her shoulder and head, and she barely registered it. Her vision went hazy, and for a moment she thought she might pass out, but when it cleared she found herself at the top of the stairs, standing in front of the open doorway.

Hey! I didn't tell you you could leave!

Julie sensed movement behind her, and she threw herself through the open doorway. Air gusted from the basement, as if displaced by an extremely large object – say, the gigantic hand of a titanic teenage girl ghost. This was followed instantly by the sound of splintering wood, and

Julie knew Delia had destroyed the stairs. She'd angled to her right as she'd jumped through the doorway and hit the sunroom floor on her good shoulder. The impact still jostled her injured shoulder, and the pain was so bad she screamed. Suddenly Mari and Oliver were there. The boy was still naked, but he seemed to have recovered from his near drowning experience. Together, the two helped Julie to her feet – after she warned them to be careful of her dislocated shoulder – and they helped her toward the dining room. They went as fast as they could, through the dining room, where Emily's blood was still on the floor, the kitchen, the hall, and the vestibule. Cold February air hit them in their faces when they reached the open front door. The cool air felt good, and it helped center Julie, sharpened her focus.

"We need to get to the van before she—"

Behind them came a sound like a wrecking ball slamming into the side of a building.

"—comes after us," Julie finished.

The three of them hurried outside and rushed toward Mari's minivan. Oliver was shivering in the winter air, and when they reached the vehicle, Julie insisted he get in first. He wasn't happy about this, but he did as she said, and Julie climbed in after him. Between the dueling agonies in her head and shoulder, she came near to passing out again, but she managed to hold on to consciousness, if only just. She reached toward the passenger door with the hand of her good arm, grabbed the handle, and pulled it shut. Mari had hurried to the driver's-side door while they'd gotten in the van, and she was already behind the wheel and turning on the engine when Julie closed the passenger door. None of them even thought about putting on seatbelts. There wasn't time to do anything more than hold on and pray. Even Julie, who wasn't exactly the praying type, sent up a request for any benign powers that might be out there somewhere to give them a break.

Mari put the van in reverse and hit the gas.

The vehicle lurched backward just as Delia's hand – which was now twice the size of the van – came slamming down on the driveway. Concrete exploded into fragments, and the Precision Paint truck was crushed. *That could've been us,* Julie thought. *Still could be if we don't haul ass.*

Mari reversed out of the driveway, slammed on the brake, put the van into drive, and hit the gas once more. The vehicle shot forward, and Julie thought how it hadn't been all that long ago that she and Nick had raced away from this house, hoping to get Emily Patton to the hospital in time to save her life. Now both Nick and Emily were dead, and the rest of them were in imminent danger of being flattened by Oliver's angry dead girlfriend. *Life,* Julie thought, *sure is fucking weird sometimes.*

As the van roared down the street, Julie looked at the rearview mirror. She expected to see Delia's gigantic form lumbering after them, but there was no sign of the girl at any size. The Pattons' house looked like someone had dropped a bomb on it, though.

"Is she going to come after us?" Mari asked. She glanced at Oliver and turned the van's heater on full blast. He nodded gratefully.

"I don't know," he said. "I have no idea what she's capable of."

Julie thought of something Delia had said.

"Do you remember what Delia said before she attacked my brother?"

Oliver frowned. "That guy was your brother?"

"Yes. Delia told him that the basement was her world, that she made it, and in it, she was god. I don't claim to know what the hell's going on or how these ghosts or whatever they are work. But it seems as if Delia's power was limited to the basement, or close to it, anyway. I don't know if she'll still be able to come after us, but I don't think it'll be as the Fifty-Foot Teenager."

Julie shifted her weight and hissed as a fresh bolt of pain lanced through her shoulder.

"Mari, once we're sure Delia's not following us, would you mind pulling over so I can pop my shoulder back into place? After that, I can give Oliver my jacket so he doesn't have to keep running around naked."

Mari looked at Julie, then at Oliver.

"*He?* I don't...." She trailed off. "Oh. Yes. Of course. He." She smiled at Oliver, and he smiled back.

Oliver then turned to Julie.

"Thanks for coming back for me. Did you get my mom to the hospital? Is she okay?"

Julie didn't want to have this conversation right now, but she knew she had to. She took a deep breath and began.

"My partner and I were on our way to the hospital...."

CHAPTER SEVENTEEN

It was cold out, and Jerome wished he'd thought to grab his coat before leaving the library, but all in all, he was enjoying his stroll. He walked alone, and while he missed having Randall to talk to, Jerome figured he probably had important ghost stuff to do and would return when he could. The sun was just beginning to peek out from behind the clouds, and while it didn't do much to warm things up, it did make the day seem more pleasant, cheerful, carefree…. He supposed much of this feeling came from the satisfaction of finally having popped his cherry, murder-wise, with Alexandra. As he walked, he replayed her death in his mind: a torrent of blood shooting from *The Book*, slamming her into the restroom door so hard it tore from its hinges, the impact leaving her broken and lifeless. It wasn't as intimate a murder as the ones Randall had committed – a lot more hands-off than using a knife – but it had a theatrical flair that Jerome thought compensated for that lack. And there was plenty of time for him to hack someone to death with a blade if he really wanted to. He was just getting started, after all.

After walking out of the library, *The Book* tucked securely under one arm, Jerome had headed east down the sidewalk, leaving a trail of bloody footprints behind him on the cement. He had no specific destination in mind, was only following Randall's suggestion that he show people what Alexandra had seen right before her death. He thought of himself as a kind of missionary, out to spread the dark gospel of *The Book* to an undeserving world. He would continue walking until *The Book* told him when and where to stop. In the meantime, he intended to simply go with the flow. He thought of waves of blood gushing from the pages of *The Book*. *Go with the flow.* Very funny.

Next to the library was a small shopping center containing an RX Direct pharmacy, a photographer's called Lenscaps, a burger joint called

Brew and Chew, a used bookstore called Book Barn, a license bureau, and a pet store called Paws and Claws. *The Book* remained silent as he walked past, and he knew that none of them was the place he was looking for. As he traveled, he heard screams, saw clearly injured people running from buildings, witnessed ghostly manifestations of one kind or another pursuing them. The atmosphere was highly charged, and Jerome found it invigorating. Anything was possible on this day – the Homecoming, Randall had called it – and it was wonderful.

He continued walking several more blocks until a church came into view. Jerome wasn't a religious man – unless you counted his devotion to Randall and his victims – but he drove by this church every day on his way to work, and it was a familiar part of the landscape to him. It was an old-fashioned-looking church: white with a black roof, a steeple, stained-glass windows. A smaller, more modern-looking building sat next to it, this one made of salmon-colored brick with a flat roof. Jerome assumed this was a more recent addition, with a fellowship hall and classrooms for Sunday school. There was a digital message board placed on the front lawn. It displayed the church's service times – Sundays 9:00 a.m. to 10:00 a.m. and 11:00 a.m. to 12:00 p.m. – along with an inspirational message that changed every week. Today's said, *There's Power in the Blood.* And the name of the church? *New Life.*

Jerome felt *The Book* twitch beneath his arm and he smiled. This was the place.

The parking lot was jam packed, so much so that people had been forced to double park or pull onto New Life's lawn. More than a few vehicles showed signs of recent damage, and Jerome assumed their drivers had encountered trouble on their way here. On any other weekday afternoon, he would've been surprised by the number of people in attendance. He doubted the church drew this large a crowd even on Sundays. But today was the Homecoming, and where else would confused and frightened people gather? *It'll be like shooting fish in the proverbial barrel,* Jerome thought, and practically salivated at the notion.

He wended his way through the maze of vehicles as he crossed the parking lot. He listened for the sound of organ music, of hymns being sung, but he heard nothing. Were they all sitting quietly inside, terrified by what their world had become in the space of a few short hours? Were they talking amongst themselves, sharing stories of their encounters with the dead? Were they desperately praying for help from a god that might have inflicted this strange plague on them in the first place? He didn't know, but he couldn't wait to find out.

The front doors of the church were unlocked, and he entered. He had blood on his clothes, but he wasn't worried about this. He had a feeling much of today's congregation would have similar issues with their clothing, and that today's service would most definitely be come as you are. He knew this was a Christian church, but he wasn't clear on the denomination, and there was nothing about the interior that provided any indication. The narthex had a bulletin board on one wall that was covered with fliers printed on various colors of paper, providing details on different church programs and resources, and on another wall was a sign giving information about where various rooms were located. The church office was nearby, down a hallway to the left, and the nave – which modern churchgoers often referred to as the Sanctuary – was straight ahead. The narthex was empty, but the door to the nave, as well as the walls on either side of it, was made of clear glass, and Jerome could see that it was standing room only inside. Even the aisles between the pews were full, people sitting cross-legged on the wooden floor, some with children in their laps. At the front of the nave, on the raised platform called the chancel, a man with brown hair and a neatly trimmed goatee stood at a lectern. Behind him was a large minimalist painting of a cross, two big black strokes – one vertical, one horizontal – on a stark white background. The man wore a rumpled flannel shirt and jeans with a hole over one knee. Was he the church's pastor? Perhaps he hadn't had time to don a suit and tie before beginning what was surely an impromptu service. Then again, if the man's morning had been like everyone else's in Echo Springs, he'd been lucky to get out of his house alive, regardless of how he was dressed. The man was speaking, but Jerome couldn't hear what he was saying, so he opened the nave's door and entered. There was no space in any of the pews, and people stood along the walls. There was a small spot in front of the wall on the nave's right, and he walked over to it, squeezed in, and listened.

"—can't tell you with any certainty why this is happening or even *what's* happening." The pastor paused, ran a trembling hand through his hair, scanned the faces of the crowd as if he hoped they might have some answers.

As the assemblage waited for the pastor to continue, a thought occurred to Jerome. What if some of the people here were ghosts? Randall had appeared to be a normal human with a physical body. If Jerome hadn't known Randall was dead, he wouldn't have been able to tell him apart from a living person. Any of the people in the church could be ghosts. Maybe most of them. Maybe *all* of them, including the pastor. Jerome could be the only one in New Life who was actually alive. The notion was exciting in a way, but it was also disturbing, unsettling, disquieting.

The pastor found his voice again and continued.

"Those of you who come here regularly know this is a modern church, not some holy-roller, fire-and-brimstone kind of place. I've always thought the *Book of Revelations* was either a *really* hard to understand metaphor or else the ravings of an unbalanced mind. But I have to tell you, after some of the shit I've seen today, I'm about ready to believe in the Beast, the mark, Armageddon, the whole nine fucking yards."

Jerome was a bit surprised by some of the man's language, but he certainly seemed to be speaking from the heart, which was what a good preacher was supposed to do, right? It seemed some people agreed with Jerome's assessment. They said, *Woo-hoo!* and, *You tell 'em, Steve!* and fist-pumped the air. Others, however, most definitely did not approve. They gave Pastor Steve dark looks and whispered to each other, clearly unhappy with the man's swearing. But the majority of those who'd gathered here today displayed no reaction. They sat quietly, faces blank, and Jerome wondered if they were even aware Steve was speaking. Most of the people in attendance had obviously had a rough time of it before making their way to New Life. Many were bloodied, wounds inexpertly bandaged, clothes torn and stained. They stared straight ahead, eyes barely blinking, still as mannequins. Jerome knew he was witnessing the effects of trauma, and found it very interesting. With any luck, he'd get a chance to witness more of it, up close and personal.

A stout balding man sitting in a pew near the front stood up. He wore the remains of a winter jacket that looked to have been shredded by the claws of some large beast. *Maybe it was,* Jerome thought. It was a brave new world they lived in, after all. Everyone focused their attention on the man, and they all watched as he began to speak, his voice eerily calm.

"Remember me, Steve? Dean Carlson. You counseled me after my wife and kids died in a car crash. Hit by a fucking drunk driver who walked away without a goddamn scratch. You told me that their deaths were part of God's plan, that they were in a better place, that they'd be waiting for me when I died, that until then it was important that I went on with my life. Well, my family visited me this morning, and I barely recognized them. They'd...*merged* with the car they died in. It was horrible. They were furious with me for not dying with them in the wreck and they tried to kill me. I escaped, barely, but I know they're still out there somewhere, waiting to get another chance at me. All the stuff you preachers say about heaven and how God's watching over us, loving us and protecting us? It's all bullshit! If there is a God and he's watching right now, I guaran-damn-tee you that he's laughing his ass off over this sick joke he's played on us. I'd rather put *my* faith in a god you can trust."

The man reached into a coat pocket, withdrew a pistol, and aimed it at Pastor Steve.

"My wife and daughters say hi."

The man squeezed the pistol's trigger. The gun bucked in his hand as he fired, the sound of the shot echoing in the nave like thunder. A crimson flower bloomed in the middle of Pastor Steve's forehead, and his brains sprayed out the back in a V-shape to splatter the black-and-white painting of the cross. Jerome thought the mix of gray and red was an improvement on the painting's color scheme. Steve jerked backward then fell to the floor of the chancel. A number of people in the crowd screamed while others began yelling. Many jumped up from their seats and started heading toward the back, jamming the aisle and stepping on people who'd been sitting there. An Asian woman sitting against the wall in the rear of the nave rose to her feet and tried to fight her way through the fleeing crowd to reach the aisle. She wore a long-sleeved white shirt, blue slacks, and black shoes. There was an insignia on the left side of the shirt. Jerome stood too far away from the woman to make out the insignia clearly, but it looked like some sort of official city logo. She was likely a paramedic, he decided, and she wanted to check on Pastor Steve's condition. Not that there was any real need. There wasn't a surgeon on the planet that could put the red-and-gray slurry that used to be his brains back into his skull. Professional training died hard though, he supposed.

"Julie, don't!"

A young man wearing a dark blue jacket and apparently no pants jumped up. He'd been sitting next to the paramedic, and now he started after her. An older Black woman who'd been seated on the other side of the paramedic got up, grabbed hold of the boy's arm, and held him back. He tried to pull away, but the older woman draped an arm around his shoulder and held him in place. They watched with worried expressions as Julie fought her way into the aisle and slowly began pushing against the tide of terrified people trying to get the hell away from Mr. My-Gun-Is-God as fast as they could. Too many people were trying to fit through the doorway at once, and because of this no one was getting through. People shoved and hit and clawed at each other, their fear reducing them to little more than animals. Some gave up on going through the door and were pounding their fists against the glass walls between the nave and the narthex, hoping to break the glass and create alternate exits for themselves.

Julie had managed to get farther up the aisle than Jerome expected, but she was fighting a losing battle. There were too many panicked people trying to flee, and soon the inevitable happened. She was knocked down, fell to one knee, and Jerome knew that within seconds she'd be driven all the way to the floor and trampled. But a young man who looked to be of Middle Eastern descent was sitting in the pew next to where Julie had gone down. He stood, reached for her, caught hold of her arm, and hauled her into the pew with him. She fell into his arms, exhausted, and gave him a grateful smile. An older woman stood next to the young man, and she was looking back and forth, taking in all the chaos, eyes glittering and mouth stretched into a cruel, satisfied smile. She noticed Jerome looking at her, and they locked gazes, each taking the measure of the other. In that moment, Jerome realized he was looking at someone like him, a woman for whom today wasn't a nightmare made real but rather a day of liberation, a day that her true self could be born.

Takes one to know one, he thought.

He nodded to her, and after a second's hesitation, she nodded back.

Notice anything special about the EMT?

Jerome looked to his left and saw Randall standing there. His personal deity had returned.

Jerome looked at Julie, trying to understand what Randall was talking about. Then he saw it. Julie resembled one of Randall's teenage victims – Linh Choi. They were both Asian, but it was more than that. They exuded a similar strength and confidence, although Julie's was much more mature. Looking at her was like seeing what Linh might be like if she had lived to grow into full adulthood. Jerome had always found Linh to be the most attractive of the three victims, and Julie was equally as pretty. More so, because of her age. Her beauty had a chance to ripen where Linh's hadn't. Jerome felt his cock begin to stiffen. His dick still ached after fucking all those bodies by the blood river, but the pain felt good now, almost a turn-on in itself

Nice, huh? Randall said.

"Yes. Very."

Then the sound of two more gunshots cut through the pandemonium, and everyone fell silent and froze.

Mr. My-Gun-Is-God had stepped up onto the chancel and taken Steve's place at the lectern. He held his weapon pointed toward the ceiling, and Jerome realized these shots had been meant solely to get everyone's attention. It was a waste of ammunition as far as Jerome was concerned, but it was the man's show, and he could do as he pleased.

It won't be his show for much longer, Randall said.

"Listen to me, everybody! We have to band together and fight back against the ghosts. It's the only way we'll have a chance to survive."

"How are we supposed to fight them?" a woman in the congregation shouted. "They're already fucking *dead*!"

This elicited murmurs of agreement from others in the crowd.

"If they're real, then they can be fought," Mr. My-Gun-Is-God said. But he sounded unsure, as if he didn't fully believe his own words.

A man toward the back of the nave – one of the people who'd been trying to break the glass walls – called out, "You're just a pussy who's afraid of his own wife and kids!"

Mr. My-Gun-Is-God lowered his pistol and aimed it at the man who'd spoken. He didn't fire, though.

"Damn right I am! If you'd seen the thing they'd become, you'd be afraid too!"

That's your cue, Randall said. *Let* The Book *be your guide.*

Jerome smiled. It was time to share the new gospel with the good people of Echo Springs.

He started toward the chancel.

CHAPTER EIGHTEEN

Mari watched in disbelief as Dean Carlson gunned down Pastor Steve. It seemed unreal, not least because it was so ordinary compared to what she'd experienced with Noelle and in Oliver's basement. No ghosts, no nightmarish distortion of reality, just one man, one gun, and one bullet.

They'd stopped halfway between Oliver's house and New Life so Julie could get out, brace herself against the van, and pop her shoulder back into place. Mari knew the woman was far from one hundred percent, but you couldn't tell it by the way she jumped up now, clearly intending to go to Steve's aid. But even without any medical training, Mari knew the poor man was dead. Oliver tried to stop Julie, but the Sanctuary had exploded into chaos, and Mari didn't want the boy to be caught in the stampede of frightened people trying to escape. She stood, grabbed hold of him, and held him back. Together they watched as Julie tried to fight her way to Steve, but eventually she was knocked down. Mari feared she would be trampled, but a young man a few years older than Oliver helped Julie into his pew, getting her out of danger – at least for the moment. Mari wasn't sure any of them would ever truly be out of danger again.

After Julie had told Oliver what happened to his mother, the poor boy had broken down sobbing. Mari almost told him about seeing his mother's ghost in their kitchen and how she had urged Mari to save her son, thinking the knowledge might give the boy some comfort. But she decided to save that for later. Oliver had enough to deal with as it was.

The three of them had no idea where to go after that, and it was Mari who suggested the New Life church. It was where she and Lewis attended services, and she thought if there was ever a time she could use some spiritual guidance, it was now. When Mari suggested this, Julie seemed less than enthused about the idea, but Oliver responded more positively. Mari had seen the painting of Jesus in the Pattons' vestibule, and she'd figured it was a good indication that Oliver's family was religious. She assumed Oliver's parents were progressive Christians given that they had a trans son, and New Life was a progressive church, so the boy should feel right at home.

When they reached New Life, she'd been surprised at first to see how crowded the parking lot was, but of course she wasn't the only one who'd felt the need to seek out the comfort of church today. And more than that, the spiritual manifestations the three of them had experienced so far – with the possible exception of Julie's brother – had turned out to be malevolent. Why would it be any different for everyone else in town? So if evil powers were trying to torment and kill you, where else would you go but a place that was dedicated to all that was holy, a place where you might be safe? But Dean had just reminded them all of a primal truth about the universe: safety was an illusion.

Mari didn't know Dean well, but she'd been friends with his wife. She'd served with Adrienne on the summer picnic committee, and she'd been devastated when the woman and her two daughters had been killed. She and Lewis had attended their combined funeral, and they'd given Dean their condolences, though she knew it would do nothing to blunt the force of the man's grief. That had been less than a year ago. Obviously, Dean was still struggling with sorrow, and the day's events had metastasized his pain, turning it into madness. Everyone, herself included, was probably crazy now, at least a little.

She was startled when Dean stepped up to the lectern and fired two shots into the ceiling, abruptly ending the chaos. Everyone stopped moving, fell silent, and turned to listen to what the man had to say. He told them they needed to work together to fight the ghosts, but people in the audience challenged his words. Dean ended up aiming his pistol at one of these challengers, and Mari feared Dean was going to take a shot at the man. But then another man started walking toward the front of the Sanctuary. He was middle-aged, had curly rust-red hair, wore a dark-blue turtleneck, slacks the same color, and black shoes. He carried a book with a blood-red cover in his right hand, and he made his way through the crowd with a sense of purpose, as if he was a man on a mission. People looked at him as he passed but no one did anything to stop him. Maybe they figured if he wanted to get killed it was his own business. But there was something about him that said he was just as dangerous as Dean, maybe more so, and people remained very still as he went by, like prey animals hoping to avoid attracting a predator's attention.

When Dean saw the red-headed man approaching, he swung his gun toward him.

"I don't know who you are, but you need to stay the fuck back, buddy," Dean said.

The red-headed man smiled. "My name is Jerome Gallagher. I used to be a librarian, but now…well, I guess you could call me a prophet."

Jerome continued walking toward Dean, seemingly unconcerned that a man who'd just committed murder in front of the entire congregation had a gun trained on him.

Dean scowled, angered by Jerome's words and the implicit challenge his approach constituted. But Mari thought he looked afraid too, and that worried her. Fearful people and guns were a dangerous combination.

"I'm warning you one last time," Dean said. "Back off or I'm going to put a bullet in you too."

"Guns will be powerless in the new world," Jerome said. He stopped at the edge of the chancel, opened the red book, and held it out before him as if it were a talisman, pages facing Dean.

Red water – no, *blood* – gushed forth from the book in an arcing stream. It splashed onto the chancel next to Dean, splattered his pants legs as it formed a puddle. Jerome snapped the book shut, cutting off the blood stream. Dean stared at the crimson puddle, as if trying to make sense out of what he was seeing. Then three forms rose forth from the blood, the puddle shrinking as they ascended, as if they were being formed from it. When the process was finished, the puddle was gone, and three young women stood next to Dean. They were naked, covered with blood, hair wet and matted with it. The skin of their faces had been removed with surgical precision, leaving lidless eyes and lipless teeth surrounded by raw red muscle. They had one more thing in common: each held a knife in her hands.

"Behold the Sisters of the Blade," Jerome said.

Blood ran from the top of the painting behind the lectern, completely obliterating the image of the cross. The blood reconfigured itself on the canvas, and when it was finished a crimson dagger had replaced the cross.

A number of people gasped in horror, and several pointed at the painting. Dean lowered his weapon and turned to see what they were looking at. When he saw the altered painting, he stared at it. Mari could only see the back of Dean's head, but she could imagine the expression of fear on the man's face. Dean then turned abruptly to the faceless girls and raised his gun.

"Fuck you, ghost bitches!" he shouted and began firing.

Even upset as he was, his aim was good, and the rounds struck the faceless women in their chests and abdomens. Their bodies jerked with the bullets' impact, but they did not cry out in pain, and no blood ran from their new wounds. Dean continued firing until his gun ran out of ammunition, and he squeezed the trigger several more times before realizing what had happened.

"Where's your god now?" Jerome asked.

The Sisters of the Blade raised their knives and Dean paled. He ejected the cartridge from his gun and jammed his hand into his pants pocket. He pulled out a fresh cartridge, but before he could put it in, the Sisters rushed forward. They fell upon him like ravenous animals, forced him to the floor of the chancel, and plunged their knives into him over and over. He screamed, high and loud, but not for long. After he'd fallen silent, the Sisters continued their grisly work, their enthusiasm unabated. No one in the Sanctuary spoke, no one seemed to even breathe. The only sounds were the *chok-chok-chok* of steel repeatedly violating flesh.

Jerome stepped up onto the chancel, and as he took Dean's place behind the lectern, the Sisters of the Blade finally stopped savaging Dean's corpse. They stood and lined up behind Jerome, knives held at their sides, blood dripping from the blades. Jerome then put his red book on the lectern and opened it.

"Today, my friends, is the Homecoming." He beamed at the congregation as if he was spreading the good news. "This is the day that our dead have returned to free us from our petty, selfish lives. They've come to share with us the greatest gift of all – the gift of death. Life is an aberration, a mutation, a *mistake*. The dead have come to rescue us, and the only way they can do that is by destroying us. They love us, they miss us, they want us to join them, and the only way they can do that is to kill us."

Jerome gazed upon the faces of the assembled once more, as if he were a teacher waiting to see if anyone had any questions or comments. Mari looked at Oliver, saw the boy was staring at Jerome with wide-eyed horror. Julie looked back at them, and Mari met her gaze. An unspoken exchange passed between them: How much worse was this day going to get?

Unfortunately, they were about to find out.

"Some of you might recognize the Sisters of the Blade," Jerome said. "Even without their lovely faces. They're three of the most famous citizens Echo Springs has ever known, all victims of *the* most famous – Randall Beck, a.k.a. the Skintaker."

Jerome gestured toward a blond-haired teenage boy standing against one of the Sanctuary's walls. He wore a Sonic Youth T-shirt, old jeans, and even older sneakers. Mari hadn't grown up in Echo Springs. She and Lewis had moved to town after she'd landed her teaching job. She wasn't as familiar with the story of Randall Beck as lifelong residents were, so she didn't experience the same shock of recognition that many of those in the Sanctuary did. But she heard their gasps, saw the expressions of disbelief on their faces, and she knew this boy was – no pun intended – a dead ringer for the infamous killer. She had no problem believing the boy truly was Beck, though. After the things she'd seen this day, she could believe any damn thing.

Randall smiled and gave everyone a small wave of greeting. His eyes remained flat and emotionless, and Mari saw little humanity in them.

"Randall and people like him – Bundy, Dahmer, Gacy, Gein, Ramirez, Chikatilo, and so many more – were harbingers of the new age that we are now on the cusp of," Jerome said. "They paved the way for the Homecoming with offerings of blood and flesh. Randall has come among you today to bring you the great gift of Oblivion. And I, as his prophet, have the honor of presenting this gift to you."

Jerome tilted his head back to look at the ceiling and raised his hands palms up, as if appealing to the heavens. The book on the lectern began to shake, and then a geyser of blood shot upward from its pages to strike the church's ceiling. The blood spread across the surface of the ceiling without a single drop falling, and as the book sent more blood gushing toward the ceiling, the layer grew thicker, and still none of it dripped on the people below. The sight was almost hypnotic, and everyone stared at the ceiling, entranced, Mari included.

It's almost beautiful in a way, she thought, and she wondered if maybe Jerome was right, that the dead *had* come to free them from the burden of living. The thought had its appeal…after all, isn't that what the words *rest in peace* meant? An end to suffering, worry, fear, regret, all the things that the world's religions promised humanity would be free of in the next world. For her and the rest of those gathered in the Sanctuary, it could start here and now. She heard the faint, distant sound of a baby crying and a tear ran down her cheek. She could be with Lewis and Noelle. For the first time they could be a family, and they could remain one for all time.

Like the others, Oliver included, she gazed in wide-eyed awe at the expanding blood lake on the ceiling. Because she was in the back, she didn't have to look straight up to watch the ceiling, and Julie remained in her field of vision. She saw the air next to Julie blur, and suddenly her brother, Brian, was standing next to her. He was worse for wear after having been snapped up by the huge creature from Delia's dark river. His left arm was partly detached and now dangled uselessly at his side. Half of his head was gone, torn away by the monster's teeth, revealing brain and bone, and his T-shirt and shorts were ripped, the flesh beneath shredded and bloody. Twice before Julie's dead sibling had appeared to save her, and now here he was for a third time, having somehow escaped the belly of a massive nightmarish beast to come to his sister's aid. Julie drew back in horror upon seeing her brother's condition, but Brian seemed unaffected by her reaction. He grabbed her hand and pulled her out of the pew. Julie in turn caught the hand of the young man who'd saved her from being trampled and pulled him along after her. In turn, he took the hand of the older woman who'd been standing next to him, and she followed the other three. The Sanctuary was no less crowded than before, but everyone was immobile, frozen wherever they sat or stood – everyone except those in contact with Brian, that is – staring up at the blood gathering upon the ceiling. Because of this, Brian was able to lead Julie and the others toward the back of the nave swiftly and without difficulty. Mari was as entranced as everyone else in the Sanctuary and she couldn't move, could barely think of anything except the beautiful crimson lake above. But part of her mind recognized that if Brian had returned to aid Julie, something seriously bad was about to happen. If she'd been in full possession of her body, she would've turned and hauled ass out of there, taking Oliver with her, but all she could do was watch as Brian, Julie, the boy, and the older woman approached. For an instant it appeared that they were going to exit the Sanctuary and leave Mari and Oliver behind. But Julie reached out with her free hand as she passed and snagged Mari's. Her touch instantly broke the spell Mari had been under, and she was able to grab Oliver's hand. Oliver returned to his senses just as she had, and now Brian led the entire group toward the door.

People were no longer fighting to get out, were instead looking at the blood gathering on the ceiling, expressions of worshipful awe on their faces. They still blocked the exit, though, and as the group drew near, an unseen force took hold of them and hurled them out of the way. They flew a dozen feet, some hitting the floor with the sound of snapping bones, others colliding with people standing close by, again with the sound of breaking bones, only twice as loud. They all went down, leaving Brian and his charges a clear path to the door and the narthex beyond. Mari assumed that Brian had used some kind of ghostly power to smooth their way, and while she wasn't happy that those poor people got hurt, she was also terrified for her life, so she wasn't too broken up about it.

Brian was the first to pass through the Sanctuary door, and while Mari knew she shouldn't look back, like Lot's wife, she was unable to stop herself.

Three shapes extruded from the ceiling, crimson cylindrical things that stretched downward toward the mass of people below. They took on more definition as they grew, becoming slender, feminine arms several times the size of human limbs. Hands emerged, fingers sprouting outward, and the arms bent in the middle as elbows formed. And then, as a final touch, slender objects extended for each of the hands, thin and sharp.

"Dean had it wrong," Jerome said. "God isn't a gun. God is a *knife*."

Behind Jerome, the Sisters of the Blade began slicing their knives through the air, and the giant arms mimicked their movements, large red blades swinging in swift, vicious arcs. The blood-blades bit into flesh, and the paralysis that had gripped the congregants broke and the screaming began.

Brian passed through the doorway and into the narthex, pulling Julie and the rest after him. Mari saw one of the blood-blades come sweeping toward the older woman, who was wearing a black microfleece jacket. The giant knife was on course to stab her in the back, and Mari didn't have time to call out a warning. But at the last instant, the arm stopped its swing, paused as if reconsidering its target, then turned and with a single swipe cut a very pregnant mother down the middle, from crown to crotch. Mari turned away as the two halves of her body fell to the floor, and she tried not to think of what had happened to the baby she'd been carrying, tried not to think about her own Noelle.

The ravaged corpse that was Brian continued dragging them forward until they reached the church's front entrance, passed through the doors, and into the chilly air. When the last of them was outside, he released Julie's hand, turned to look at her with his single remaining eye, and then faded away. The screaming inside the Sanctuary was loud enough to hear out here, but it quickly began to diminish in volume, and Mari knew only a few people remained alive inside, but they wouldn't stay that way for long.

"We've got to get out of here," Julie said, "before that maniac with the red book decides to come after us!" Before Mari or Oliver could respond, Julie turned to her two new friends. "We've got a van. We'll all fit inside."

The young man seemed hesitant at first, but then he gave a single quick nod. The older woman – who seemed unaffected by the slaughter they'd barely escaped – said, "Sounds good."

Julie turned to Mari and smiled grimly.

"Lead the way," Julie said.

Mari started running toward the parking lot, and the others followed. As she ran, she started to ask God to protect them, but she stopped before the thought was fully formed. After what she'd witnessed in the church, she didn't know if she'd ever be able to pray again.

★   ★   ★

Jerome gazed upon the remains of New Life's congregation, feeling quite pleased with himself. He'd done good work here today. Randall – who, of course, had been untouched by the giant blade-wielding hands – began slowly clapping.

Bravo.

Jerome grinned and executed a bow.

When he straightened, the arms flowed back up into the main mass of blood on the ceiling, and when that was accomplished, the blood ran back down into *The Book* in a reverse geyser. When it was finished, *The Book* slammed shut. The ceiling was clean, but the same could not be said for the rest of the nave. The floor, walls, and pews were covered with blood, and mutilated bodies lay everywhere. Jerome picked up *The Book* and tucked it under his arm.

"Our new lord thanks you for your sacrifice," he said.

He turned to acknowledge the Sisters of the Blade. They bowed their heads to him in unison and then disappeared.

Jerome stepped off the narthex and walked over to Randall, doing his best to keep from stepping in the worst of the mess spread across the floor. The air stank of blood, piss, and shit – the scent of a new world, and he inhaled its perfume deeply.

When he reached Randall he said, "Five of them got away." Including the EMT who'd reminded him of Linh.

Yes, Randall said.

When he didn't elaborate further, Jerome said, "One of them – the older woman – was almost struck by one of the blades, but she was spared at the last moment."

Yes, Randall said again.

"Why were they allowed to leave?"

The EMT is reserved for you, Jerky. She is to be your first true kill. As for the others...."

The air nearby rippled and four figures appeared: an older man wearing an airline pilot's uniform, a Middle Eastern man in a three-piece suit, and a naked black-haired teenager holding a baby, a swollen length of umbilical cord protruding from the infant's belly.

They are already spoken for, Randall said.

CHAPTER NINETEEN

Mari's van had six seats. Julie drove, Mari sat in the passenger seat, Oliver was behind Julie, Faizan behind Mari, and Karen sat all the way in the back. In order to fit everyone, they'd had to unfold the two rear seats, and as they'd done so, they quickly exchanged names. Now they were on the road, heading away from New Life.

Talk about an ironic name, Faizan thought.

No one spoke as they drove, and Faizan figured they were all doing the same thing he was – trying without success to shut out the images of people being slaughtered in the Sanctuary. He wondered if similar scenes were happening in places of worship across the world, if all the people who had gathered for comfort and support in this time of great crisis were being cruelly cut down by whatever force was behind the ghostly attack on the planet. He thought of the mosque he and his mother attended, of his friends who went there, and he prayed he was wrong about people in other churches being killed, but he feared he wasn't.

He was sad about leaving the Rolling Banana behind, but he was glad to be around more people than just Karen. At first she'd seemed genuinely traumatized by what she'd experienced at Time for Tots, but once they'd gotten on the road and started heading for New Life, her demeanor had become distant, almost cold, and a couple times he heard her chuckle softly upon witnessing atrocities taking place in the neighborhoods they passed through. He told her what had happened inside Smiles, Inc., of the Tooth Fairy and how his mother had died. Karen had taken the information in and said only, "That sucks, Fay-jen." He hadn't bothered to correct her pronunciation of his name. He'd tried to tell himself that he shouldn't judge anyone by their behavior, not right now, when so much insanity was happening all around them. You couldn't expect anyone, not even yourself, to act normally during such a time. Still, he couldn't escape the feeling that there was something wrong about Karen, maybe even dangerous.

He'd only just met the others, but Julie, Mari, and Oliver seemed nice enough. They certainly projected a more positive energy than Karen. But if he couldn't judge her in the current circumstances, how could he judge them? Perhaps Karen would turn out to be an angel and they devils. There was no way to know, so he had no choice but to go on faith, even if the world had become a place where faith seemed to hold no meaning. Still, the three of them seemed just as shaken by the horrors they'd witnessed inside New Life as Faizan was, but they each had a sadness about them too. *They've lost people today,* Faizan realized. Just as he had. He didn't get the same sense of loss from Karen. Maybe she'd been lucky, and she hadn't lost anyone yet. Or maybe she had and just didn't care.

Oliver had puzzled him at first, but then he'd realized Oliver was trans, and that was cool. Faizan's father hadn't been tolerant of different sexualities and gender identities – he hadn't been tolerant of anything, really – but his mother had been, and Faizan had a number of gay and trans friends growing up, as well as in college.

"I just realized something," Karen said.

Her voice startled everyone out of their thoughts, and they gave her their attention.

"I'm the only regular person here," she said. "You know – *normal.*"

"I don't think *normal* means much anymore," Julie said.

Karen scowled at that, but she didn't respond.

So Karen wasn't just emotionally off, Faizan thought. She was racist and transphobic too. *Fantastic.* Even if he'd known this, he wouldn't have left her in that parking lot to fend for herself. But she wasn't the sort of person he'd choose to experience the end of the world with, either.

He leaned forward in his seat so he could see Julie's face.

"Would you mind turning on the radio?" he asked. "I'm getting all kinds of national and international news on my phone, but not much local stuff. I figure the more we know about what's happening in Echo Springs specifically—"

"The better we'll be able to make some kind of plan," Julie finished. "Sounds good."

"I'll do it," Mari said. She turned on the radio and began searching through the channels. There was a great deal of static, which Faizan assumed meant a lot of stations were off the air. Maybe all of them. But Mari eventually found a signal, and when she had it tuned in well enough, she turned up the volume. The speaker was male, but Faizan didn't recognize his voice.

"—really knows what the hell's happening, but people are callin' it Judgment Day, and given the things I've seen since I woke up this morning, it's hard to argue with them."

"It's the Homecoming," Oliver said. He looked at the others. "At least, that's what the guy in the church called it."

Faizan found the term more than a little ominous. *Homecoming* implied a return to a place you belonged, and unless it was going to be followed by a *Leavetaking*, the world would soon belong entirely to the dead, if it didn't already. But maybe there was some cause for hope yet. From what he'd gathered, the weird ripped-up ghost that had gotten them out of New Life safely was Julie's brother. So maybe some of the ghosts were good. Or maybe they weren't good *or* evil, but something else altogether.

"I don't know if you've been checkin' the news on the Internet and social media, but it seems that every city, town, and village on Earth is under attack by these things. It's bad here in Ash Creek. Okay, that's a gross understatement. It's a fuckin' nightmare! I've seen a few reports that it's better out in the country. Safer. Almost like the dead things don't want to leave the cities. I don't know if this is true, though. Could be total bullshit. But I tell you what, when I'm done here – which is gonna be sooner rather than later – I'm gonna haul ass out of town and take my chances in the woods!"

Ash Creek was located forty-five minutes from Echo Springs. It had a couple radio stations – one classic rock, one country – and Faizan figured they were listening to one of those. A DJ or station manager had gotten on the air and was doing a local version of the Emergency Broadcast System.

"Do you think that's true?" Oliver asked. "That it's safe in the country?"

Karen responded. "He said *safer*, dear. Not *safe*. He also said it might be bullshit."

Faizan didn't like the inflection Karen had given the word *dear*. Maybe he was reading too much into it, but it seemed as if she'd used it in the way one woman sometimes referred to another, as if she was purposely misgendering Oliver. Oliver must've suspected the same thing because he'd frowned when Karen had called him *dear*, but he didn't make an issue of it. Faizan figured that somewhere along the line, Oliver had learned the same lesson his mother had once taught him: you have to pick your battles.

The sorrow over the loss of his mother welled up in Faizan once more, and he began crying. He looked at the window so the others wouldn't see. Not that he was ashamed of crying, but they had their own grief to deal with. They didn't need to be consoling him right now.

The man on the radio continued his rant.

"What's gonna happen to the spirits of those poor people who died so far in today's attack? There have been no reports of them returnin'. And as for the ghosts who have returned, it seems only those who have current connections to the living – like one of your relatives or your third-grade teacher – come back. It's not like George Washington and Shakespeare are runnin' around killin' people. And how come only human spirits return? Why don't we have animal ghosts? Or dinosaur ghosts? There should be a hell of a lot of those suckers stompin' around and munchin' on folks, right? Insects, plants, even goddamn germs and viruses.... None of them have come back. Why? And why did my wife and I wake up with our dead three-year-old in our bed this mornin', and why did she decide to tear out her mommy's throat with her fuckin' teeth? Why? Why-why-why-why-WHY?"

The man broke down sobbing then, and Mari quickly switched the radio off.

"Sweet Jesus," Mari whispered.

"Fucking brutal," Karen said, and Faizan thought she sounded almost gleeful.

They continued driving in silence for several moments after that. Julie was the first to speak again.

"I think we should do what the man said – get out of town. Maybe it's safer there, maybe it isn't, but I don't see how it could be much worse. What do you guys think?"

No one answered right away, but then Oliver said, "I would *love* to get the fuck out of this town."

"Same," Faizan said.

"We have to do something," Mari said, which, while maybe not definite, seemed to indicate agreement.

The last one to chime in was Karen. When she spoke, everyone turned to look at her, except Julie, who watched her reflection in the rearview mirror.

"Why not?" Karen said. "If nothing else, it should be interesting."

She sat back in her seat then, a small smile on her lips. Faizan didn't like that smile.

Not one bit.

★　　★　　★

Now this is traveling in style, Jerome thought.

He sat behind the wheel of a brand-new Mercedes Benz, which was a hell of a step up from the Honda Civic he usually drove. He never could've afforded a car like this on a librarian's salary. One more perk of being a prophet in this new world.

He drove down North Avenue at a leisurely forty miles per hour, only five miles above the posted speed limit. He could've gone as fast as he liked since the Echo Springs police – those who still survived, that is – had more important things to do right now than pull over speeders. But there was no need to hurry, so why not enjoy the ride? It wasn't as if anyone would ever make a car like this again after today, or any cars, for that matter. Best to appreciate it while he could.

After the church service was over, Randall directed Jerome to take the car keys from the pocket of a man whose head, right shoulder and arm had been sheared off by one of the Sisters' blood-blades. Randall then led him into the parking lot and to the Mercedes.

This is your new ride, Jerky, Randall had said.

I love the color, Jerome had said. *What is it? Burgundy?*

Randall had shrugged. *It looks like the color of deoxygenated blood to me.*

After Jerome had gotten into the car, turned on its engine, and revved it a few times to luxuriate in the feel of its power, Randall spoke to him through the open driver's door.

They're heading down North Avenue right now. They're going to try to get out of town, and it's your job to stop them. You can have Julie, but the rest you are to leave untouched. Do you understand?

Jerome didn't, not completely, but he nodded. He realized something then.

I don't have a knife. I left the one you gave me in the library restroom.

There are knives everywhere, Randall said. *You just have to know where to look.*

The ghost leaned forward and touched an index finger to Jerome's forehead. Electricity sparked somewhere deep in his brain, and his body spasmed briefly.

You'll be able to track them now. All you need to do is concentrate. Randall grinned. *Happy hunting.*

And then he was gone.

Jerome turned on the radio. He couldn't find any tunes, but he came across a station where a man was talking about how his daughter had ripped out his wife's throat with her teeth. That was almost as good as music. He continued driving, the man's wails of sorrow and despair filling him with dark joy.

★　　★　　★

Julie wasn't sure there was any place in the world that qualified as *safe* anymore, but at least they had a plan. They would take North Avenue to Orchard Street, and from there they'd get on Route 2, which would lead them out of Echo Springs. This had been Faizan's suggestion. It was the route he took to get to college every day, and not only was it the most direct way out of town, it was the closest to their current location. Where they'd go once they escaped Echo Springs, Julie had no idea, but they could worry about that later – assuming any of them actually made it out of town alive.

She felt guilty for not being out there on the streets, driving around in the medic, attempting to help whomever she could. The bizarre nature of it aside, what was happening right now was a disaster – she supposed it qualified as an *un*natural disaster – and as an EMT, she should be out in the thick of it, same as if a series of tornadoes or an earthquake had struck the town. But she couldn't save everybody. That was a truth any first responder had to learn and accept early on in their career if they didn't want to go crazy, and it was even more true this day. She was here, now, driving Mari's van, and trying to help Mari, Oliver, Faizan, and Karen survive. That would have to be enough.

The traffic was much lighter than it had been when they'd driven to New Life, and Julie feared this was because so many more people in Echo Springs had died since then. How much longer would it be before the roads were entirely empty? A couple hours? Less? Most of the vehicles they saw were headed in the same direction they were. She figured their drivers had heard the same radio broadcast they had and were leaving Echo Springs as fast as they could. Cars, vans, and pickups passed them, some traveling at reckless, even dangerous speeds.

At one point, a red Porsche zipped by them, the driver doing close to sixty, Julie guessed.

"Why aren't we hauling ass like that guy?" Karen asked.

Before Julie could answer, the Porsche entered an intersection just ahead of them, only for a city bus – old, rusted, body dented, windows cracked – to suddenly materialize and slam into its side. The Porsche crumpled like paper, spun across the road, and crashed into a light pole on the opposite corner. The collision had no appreciable impact on the bus, didn't even slow it, and the driver was able to make a sharp left turn onto North Avenue and come barreling toward the van. A turn like that should've been impossible given the bus's size and speed, Julie thought, but then, this wasn't an ordinary bus, was it? As it bore down upon them, Julie swung the van's steering wheel to the right, causing the passenger-side wheels to jump the curb and go onto the sidewalk. The bus roared by them, missing the van by less than a foot, and they got a good look at the driver and passengers as the vehicle flashed by. Their bodies were broken and bloody, as if they'd been through a crash of their own, and every one of them was laughing.

After they were safely past the bus, Julie looked at Karen's reflection in the rearview.

"And that's why we're not going any faster," she said.

Karen pursed her lips in what looked like irritation, but she didn't reply.

Julie knew it wasn't fair to make any kind of judgment about Karen. They'd only just met the woman and Faizan, and knew almost nothing about them. So far, she liked Faizan, but Karen? Not so much. Maybe Julie would like the woman more once she got to know her, but right now she doubted it. Still, she'd helped plenty of assholes during her time as an EMT. She didn't have to like someone to believe their life had value.

"I hate to do this," Mari said, "but I really need to use a restroom."

"Me too," Oliver said.

"There's a Qwik-Mart that I stop at sometimes on my way home from classes," Faizan said. "It's on our route. We could get some supplies there too — water and something to eat."

"We could gas up the van too," Mari said.

Julie wasn't sure stopping anywhere was a good idea. But she hadn't peed since before she and Nick had been dispatched to the Pattons' house, and she hadn't had anything to eat since breakfast. Not that she had much of an appetite. Still, they had to keep their strength up, and she doubted any of the others had eaten since this morning either. She knew which Qwik-Mart Faizan was talking about. She stopped there herself on occasion, and Faizan was right — it *was* on the way out of town. It would be a risk, but if they could keep their stop short....

"All right," she said. "A fast restroom and supply run — emphasis on *fast*."

She couldn't escape the feeling that this was likely to be a mistake. She just hoped it wouldn't prove to be a fatal one.

CHAPTER TWENTY

Karen was starting to get bored.

The day had started off great. First she'd watched as the Sleepy Lizard burned down, killing everyone inside. Then she'd throttled her bitch of a sister while everyone else in Time for Tots was reduced to bloody mist. And after meeting Faizan, she'd enjoyed listening to him talk about how his mother had died, crunched inside the mouth of a monster made of teeth. How fucked up was *that*? And it wasn't just that the woman had died but that Faizan had *failed* to save her. His grief and guilt had been a delicious combination. The bloodbath in the church had been a hell of a thing to witness, even if she *had* almost gotten sliced and diced with the rest of the congregation. And now here she was, riding in a minivan, on her way out of town with a bunch of losers. Where was the excitement in that? Where was the *fun*? She wished Bennie was here. He'd liven things up. Then again, he'd been the one to suggest she talk to Faizan in the first place. Maybe he'd planned all along for her to end up here, riding with a bunch of goody-goods, bored out of her fucking mind. It was just the sort of devious torture the fucker would come up with for her.

And if they succeeded in getting out of Echo Springs, what then? Were they going to start living in the woods – in fucking *February*? No way was she doing that. She'd never been an outdoors kind of gal, and she wasn't about to start now. She wished she'd stayed behind at New Life to talk to that Jerome guy. Now *there* was someone who'd be a ton of fun to hang out with – assuming you could keep the fucker from killing you.

She decided she'd remain with these four for a little while longer, but if things didn't pick up soon, she'd ditch them and look for someone else to hang with. Someone with more pizzazz, with a little pep in their step.

Karen didn't patronize convenience stores as a rule, not even to buy cigarettes. The stuff they sold was way overpriced, and the people who worked there were often foreigners – most likely illegals – who'd come to this country to steal American jobs. It was a goddamn shame. But she'd driven past Qwik-Marts many times over the years, and the one Faizan directed them to looked like all the others…with one with very notable exception. The parking lot was littered with spherical objects. At first she couldn't figure out what the damn things were, but as Julie pulled the Odyssey into the lot, she got a closer look. The larger spheres were made of bent metal, cracked plastic, and torn black rubber. *Those are cars,* she realized. The fucking things looked like they'd been through some kind of junkyard compactor that, instead of crushing cars into cubes, turned them into spheres. The smaller objects were also sphere-shaped but formed from less sturdy material – cloth, flesh, and bone.

"Those are made of people," Oliver said.

The 'boy' sounded decidedly queasy, and Karen wondered if he was going to throw up. Not that she gave a shit if he did. It wasn't her van.

"What in the world could *do* something like that?" Mari asked.

"Nothing from this world," Faizan said.

As bizarre as the spheres were, one of the stranger things that struck Karen was that no liquid had leaked from either the cars or the people during their transformation. No blood, no gas, coolant, transmission fluid, or brake fluid…. It was like instead of being crushed into spheres by some powerful force, they'd been changed *into* that shape. Gross, but definitely interesting. Karen wondered if the reshaping had hurt, and if so, what sort of sounds the people had made while it was happening. Screams? Whimpers? Thick, wet gurgles? Too bad they hadn't gotten here earlier. Maybe they could've watched it happen.

Julie pulled the van up to the front of the store and parked. She didn't turn off the engine right away, though. Instead, she turned halfway in her seat so she could look at everyone.

"It's not too late to change our minds and leave," she said. "We have no way of knowing if whatever did…*that* is still close by. We could be in a lot of danger."

"At this point, we're going to be in danger wherever we go," Mari said. "But I'm going to wet this seat if I don't get to a restroom fast."

Without waiting for anyone to reply, she removed her seatbelt, opened the door, and got out.

"I guess that settles that," Julie said, and turned off the van. After that the rest of them got out. Karen didn't mind being last, and in this case, she preferred it. If there was anything nasty waiting for them outside, she'd rather it attacked the others first. Not only would that give her a greater chance for survival, she'd get to watch the others die. So being last could be both educational *and* fun. She hoped Mari or Julie would fall prey to whatever power had made the spheres, but nothing happened to them as they headed for the store entrance. *Too bad,* she thought, and then quickly consoled herself. *Maybe on the way out.*

Karen exited the van through the side door, closed it after her, and followed the others into the store. She wasn't too worried about being gripped by a supernatural force and mushed into a flesh ball. Only the good died young, after all, so the odds were definitely in her favor.

★　★　★

Even though it had been Faizan's suggestion to come to Qwik-Mart, now that they were here, he was reluctant to enter – and not just because there might be a sphere-making monster inside.

The last time he'd been here, he'd encountered the spirit of his father, and after what had happened in Smiles, Inc., he didn't want to see Asad Barakat ever again. Once more, he heard the awful crunching sound as the Tooth Fairy rammed its hand into its mouth, and he had to close his eyes and concentrate hard for a couple seconds before the sound receded into the background of his mind. It didn't go away entirely. He didn't think it ever would. He also didn't want to enter because he was afraid of finding Roy's body inside. It wasn't as if he was best buddies with the store clerk, but he did know him, at least a little, and he didn't want to discover the man had suffered an agonizing death. He expected to hear the thought-voice of his father taunting him for being afraid, but if Asad was here, he said nothing – which was fine with Faizan.

Aside from a parking lot full of the spherical remains of people and cars, there were a couple other ominous signs. Qwik-Mart's front window had been broken, and its door hung half off the hinges. These details weren't enough to stop Mari from entering, and Julie and Oliver from following. Faizan went in after them, hoping they weren't all walking to their deaths.

Inside, it looked like hurricane-force winds had blown through the store, knocking over shelves and scattering items everywhere. The glass of the cooler doors was broken, just like the front window, and bottles and cans had fallen out and lay strewn about the floor. The small hallway that led to the restrooms was located near the coolers, and Mari made a beeline for it. Julie went with her, and Oliver headed for the men's room. Faizan had to pee as well, but he didn't follow Oliver – not because he had any aversion to being in a restroom at the same time as a trans boy, but because he'd noticed something out of the corner of his eye: a pair of shoes sticking out from beneath one of the overturned shelves. Shoes with feet in them.

"Looks like he's having a bad day."

Startled, Faizan turned to see Karen grinning at him. His attention had been so focused on those feet that he'd momentarily forgotten about her. He wanted to tell her that this wasn't something to joke about, but he held his tongue. People dealt with difficult events in all sorts of ways, and black humor was one of them. Faizan glanced toward the front register. The TV behind the counter was still on, although now the screen displayed a PLEASE STAND BY message instead of news. There was no sign of Roy, Master of the Universe. Unless, of course, that was him beneath the shelf.

Faizan made his way through the debris over to the body. Maybe the person was alive and needed help. He had no medical training, but he didn't want to wait for Julie to come out of the restroom. He knelt and reached out for one of the feet. He hesitated a second – he'd never touched a dead person before – and then wrapped his hand around the ankle. He had no idea if you could take a pulse this way, but since the feet were the only body parts sticking out, he didn't have a lot of choice. Whoever it was wasn't wearing socks and the flesh felt warm. That didn't necessarily mean anything, though. It had only been a couple hours since Faizan had been here, not enough time for a body to grow cold. He didn't feel a pulse, so whoever it was might be dead. That, or Faizan simply couldn't detect the pulse because he didn't know what he was doing. If this person *was* dead, at least he or she had experienced a more normal demise than being compacted into a sphere. Faizan figured that was something, at least.

Karen had followed him to the overturned shelf, and now she gave it a hard kick.

"Hey!" she shouted. "You alive under there?" She kicked the shelf twice more for good measure.

No response.

Faizan stood and turned to Karen, angry at her for treating a dead person with such disrespect. But before he could say anything to her, she bent down, picked up a snack-sized package of sour cream potato chips, straightened, tore the package open, pulled out a chip, tossed it into her mouth, and chewed noisily. "Looks like it's our lucky day," she said, spraying pieces of chip. "It's an end-of-the-world sale, and everything must go." She snorted, amused at her own joke, and started walking, head down, examining the items strewn about the floor, munching chips as she went.

"I don't think too many people would consider this day to be lucky," he said.

Karen ignored him and continued searching for goodies.

He knew it was an uncharitable thought, but he was beginning to regret taking Karen with him when he'd left Smiles, Inc. He wanted to go to the restroom and leave her to scavenge alone, and he almost did. But he decided it wasn't safe for any of them to be by themselves right now, so he stayed until the others came back from the restroom. He showed Julie the body, and she checked for a pulse the same way he did, and she came to the same conclusion: the person was dead. Faizan almost suggested they remove the shelf from the body so they could see if it was Roy, but he decided there was no point to it. They'd seen enough horrors for one day.

He told the others about the 'no one goes anywhere alone' policy, and they agreed it was a good idea. Everyone but Karen, that was. She was too busy gathering packs of cigarettes from behind the counter and stuffing them into plastic shopping bags. Oliver accompanied him to the restroom, and when they returned, the others had gathered armloads of supplies. Julie had bottled water and healthy snacks like trail mix, and Mari had the same, although she also had several packages of honey roasted peanuts. Karen had her cigarettes, along with sugary sodas and snack cakes. Faizan and Oliver hurriedly grabbed some stuff as well – their armloads a mix of healthy and unhealthy food – and they started toward the door. Faizan was more than ready to get out of here and back on the road. But when they stepped outside, they stopped. A young boy, five years old at the most, stood in the parking lot looking at Mari's van. He had black hair and wore a *Star Wars* T-shirt and jeans. Despite the temperature, he had no coat and his feet were bare.

"Are you all right, sweetie?" Mari said. "Do you need help?"

The boy didn't look at them. He lifted his hands and began moving them as if he was making a snowball. The van began to shake and then, with a sound of crumpling metal, it curled inward to form a sphere. When he was finished, the boy smiled then turned to look at them.

Your turn, he said.

*   *   *

Jerome reached Qwik-Mart in time to see the child – who he assumed was a ghost – crush a minivan with his telekinetic powers.

That's Sammy Butler.

Randall had reappeared and now sat in the Mercedes's passenger seat.

He drowned in his family's swimming pool while his mother and father – who were both drunk as hell – were fucking in the downstairs bathroom. He was a very artistic child, and one of the things he liked best was to play with modeling clay. The first thing he did when he returned this morning was combine his parents into a single sphere. He's been amusing himself like this ever since.

At first Jerome feared that the EMT – Julie – had been inside the van when Sammy crushed it. But then he saw her standing outside Qwik-Mart with her companions, all of them holding armloads of products taken from the convenience store, and he was relieved. Julie had been promised to *him*, and that little bastard Sammy couldn't have her.

Jerome whipped the Mercedes into Qwik-Mart's parking lot and brought the vehicle to a screeching halt less than five yards from Sammy. Randall handed Jerome *The Book*, and he got out of the car and started toward the ghost child. Sammy looked at Jerome as if he wasn't quite sure what to make of him. He was human, but he traveled with a ghost. Good. The little fucker's confusion would work to his benefit.

Jerome stopped, opened *The Book*, and held it out before him, its pages facing Sammy.

"Say goodbye, kid."

The Sisters of the Blade emerged from *The Book*, swimming on a stream of blood suspended in midair. They reached Sammy, grabbed him, and before the boy could react, the stream reversed course, pulling the Sisters and their young captive back into *The Book*. When the four were gone, Jerome slammed *The Book* shut and tucked it beneath his arm.

Jerome glanced at the spherical remains of the minivan.

"I'd say I was sorry I didn't get here before he ruined your ride, but since you're all going to be dead in the next few minutes, it doesn't really matter."

Randall materialized at his side. He grinned as he regarded the humans standing in front of Qwik-Mart, but he said nothing.

Julie and the others looked scared, but they held their ground. Jerome respected that.

"What the hell do you want with us?" she demanded.

The young Middle-Eastern-looking man said, "And how did you even find us?"

"I had a little help, assistance, support." Jerome nodded to Randall. "And it's not just what *I* want. It's what *they* want too."

He gestured to his left and four figures coalesced from nothingness. Thanks to Randall, Jerome knew all their names: Bennie, Asad, Delia, and

Noelle. As before, the naked teenager held the baby, but now the infant's umbilical cord swished back and forth, like the tail of an angry cat.

Jerome was pleased to see expressions of horror on the humans' faces – all except for Bennie's wife. She didn't look afraid in the slightest. If anything, she appeared to be excited as if she couldn't wait to see what happened next.

Better get a move on, Randall said. *The Homecoming isn't going to last forever. If you don't kill her now, you won't get another chance.*

"Kill who?" the Black woman said.

Noelle's umbilical cord shot toward the woman, lengthening as it went. The woman made a choking sound as the cord whipped around her throat. She dropped her drinks and food packages and reached up to try to loosen the cord. But before she could, both she and the baby vanished.

Asad became a blur and raced toward his son. When he reached him, he grabbed his shoulders, and the two of them disappeared as well. The boy's packages remained hovering in the air for a second before falling to the ground.

Delia ran to her ex-lover, threw her arms around him, kissed him, and then they were gone too, his food and drink remaining behind just as the others' had.

That left only Bennie's wife. Instead of waiting for her husband to go to her, she discarded her shopping bags and went to him.

"Let's get it over with," she said. She took his hand and they faded from view.

Only Julie remained.

"What happened?" Julie asked. "Where did they go?"

"Honestly? I have no idea," Jerome said. "But wherever they went, I'm sure it's not going to be much fun." He smiled. "Certainly not as much fun as *I'm* going to have."

He started toward her.

CHAPTER TWENTY-ONE

"Higher, Mommy! Higher!"

Mari pushed Noelle on the swing, and the girl giggled and kicked her feet as she soared upward. Her daughter's joy was contagious, and Mari couldn't help but laugh herself.

"Not too high now," Lewis said, sounding a bit nervous.

"I'm a superhero, Daddy!" Noelle said. "Nothing can hurt me!"

Mari gave her another shove, and the girl squealed with delight as she went up again.

The three of them had stopped at a small playground after church. They still wore their nice clothes – suit and tie for Lewis, dresses for Mari and Noelle. Normally Mari would've insisted on Noelle going home and changing into everyday clothes before taking her out to play, but when they'd driven past the playground, Noelle had begged to stop, and Mari had thought, *What the hell? You're only young once.* Plus, it was an absolutely *gorgeous* day: temperature in the low seventies, gentle breeze blowing, white cotton-candy clouds drifting in a robin's-egg-blue sky. It was the sort of day that made a person glad to be alive.

The playground was a small one, nestled between an apartment complex and a suburban cul-de-sac, with swings, monkey bars, slide, merry-go-round, and jungle gym. Cedar chips were spread all around the equipment, and a modest grove of trees formed a lovely green backdrop. The area was so small, it was barely visible from the road, and Mari was surprised Noelle had spotted it. Mari had driven past this area many times over the years without noticing the playground. *Young eyes are the strongest,* as her grandmother used to say. They had the playground all to themselves. There were no other kids or parents in sight, and aside from the sighing of the wind, there was no sound. No traffic passed by on the road, no one rode bikes or bounced basketballs in the cul-de-sac, no one went in or out of the houses and apartments on either side of the playground. No birdsong, no movements of small animals in the trees. It was as if they were the only three beings in the entire world, and Mari thought, *This must be what heaven is like.*

She loved being a mother, loved everything about it, even the hard parts. It could be physically and emotionally demanding, and she second-guessed herself much of the time. She experienced doubts and recriminations, compared herself to her own mother and constantly came up short in her own estimation. But when she saw Noelle like this – so full of light and life, a miniature sun in girl form – it was all worth it.

She gave Noelle a big push, and at the apex of her flight, Noelle let go of the swing's chains and launched into the air, laughing. Mari's heart seized in her chest, and she started forward, hoping to somehow catch Noelle or at least break her fall, knowing she wouldn't be able to reach her daughter in time. For an instant, Noelle seemed to hang motionless in the air, and then she plummeted downward. She landed solidly on her feet, and Mari feared momentum would cause her to pitch forward onto her face, but it didn't. She stood there, clapped several times as if applauding her own dismount, then ran toward the jungle gym.

Mari let out a relieved breath then walked over to Lewis, shaking her head.

"I swear, that child will be the death of me yet," she said.

Lewis looked at Noelle climbing on the jungle gym, a nervous expression on his face. He kept his gaze fixed on their daughter as he spoke.

"I don't have much time," he said. "The moment she realizes what I'm doing, she'll exert control over me, and I'll be her puppet again, doing and saying what she wants me to."

Mari didn't know what Lewis was talking about, but his words made her uncomfortable.

"Hush now," she said. "Don't spoil the day." A thought occurred to her. They usually stopped at Bob Evans after church, and Lewis could get a bit cranky when he hadn't eaten for a while. "Are you getting hungry? Let's give Noelle five more minutes to play, and then we can—"

Lewis took hold of her arm, his grip firmer than she was used to, almost painful.

"Listen to me!" he said, keeping his voice low. "All of this – the playground equipment, the park, the trees, even the sky – none of it is real. It's all make-believe. Pretend."

"I don't want to hear this." She jerked free from Lewis's hand, turned, and started walking toward the jungle gym. All she wanted to do was watch her daughter play, just for a few more minutes. Was that too much to ask?

He hurried to catch up with her and walked at her side.

"Noelle isn't a little girl of four, no matter what it looks like," he said. "She was never *born*. Don't you remember?"

She stopped, spun toward him, and slapped him hard across the face.

"Don't you say that to me. Don't you *ever* say that!"

"What's wrong, Mommy?"

Mari looked down and saw Noelle standing there, looking worried.

"Everything's okay, baby." She turned to Lewis, a warning in her eyes. "Isn't that right, hon?"

Lewis opened his mouth to speak, but nothing came out. He tried again, brow furrowed and body shaking, as if the attempt took intense effort. Finally, his body relaxed and he let out a long, frustrated sigh. Then he smiled brightly, and said, "Everything's fine. Better than fine – it's *wonderful*."

He swept Noelle up in his arms, swung her around, and she giggled happily.

Despite herself, Mari thought of what Lewis had said.

The moment she realizes what I'm doing, she'll exert control over me, and I'll be her puppet again, doing and saying what she wants me to.

Lewis stopped swinging Noelle and held her in his arms. He turned toward Mari so both father and daughter could face her. Noelle scowled and spoke in a stern voice.

"You shouldn't think about such things, Mommy. They're bad things, and if you think about them, that makes *you* bad too."

A shadow fell over the playground. Mari looked up and saw a dark cloud now blotted out the sun. Where had it come from? There hadn't been even a hint of storm clouds in the sky only a few moments ago. The air grew cooler and the wind picked up strength. Gooseflesh rose on her arms, and she crossed them over her chest and shivered. She realized a remarkable thing then. She was afraid of her daughter.

"I'm sorry," Lewis said. "There's nothing I can do. The Monad won't let me."

"Damn right it won't," Noelle said, her voice sounding far more adult than it should.

She began to change then. Her dress aged, its colors fading, the cloth becoming threadbare and fibrous. Gaps appeared in the fabric as the dress disintegrated, and within moments it fell to dust that was carried away by the increasingly angry wind. Noelle was naked now, and she began to shrink in upon herself, limbs growing shorter, torso compacting, hair retracting into the skull, teeth receding into gums. An umbilical cord burst from her navel with a spurt of blood and flopped down between her legs like a hideous parody of a limp penis, swollen and sore, pus dripping from its end. The cord lay there for a moment, as if asleep, and then it rose into the air and began to sway like a hungry serpent.

Did you like being part of a family? Noelle asked, no longer speaking with her mouth. *That's what you could've had in real life if you hadn't cast me out!*

Memories come back to Mari then, scattered and hazy, difficult to make sense of, but enough to let her know that this creature that claimed to be her daughter was far more powerful – and more deadly – than she looked.

"I didn't expel you on purpose," Mari said. She spoke loudly to be heard over the sound of wind and rustling trees. "Something was physically wrong with one of us, maybe *both* of us. Whatever the reason, I couldn't keep carrying you. I wanted to, *god* how I wanted to! But it wasn't meant to be."

MEANT TO BE?

Noelle's thought-voice slammed into her brain like a sledgehammer. She staggered back, felt hot blood gush from her nostrils and run from her ears. Her vision went gray for a moment, and she thought she might pass out, but then it cleared and she realized she was still standing.

You were meant to be my mother, and I was meant to be your child. That's what was supposed to happen, but it didn't! And it's all your fault. You can't blame me — I was the size of a plum!

The umbilical cord shot toward Mari, but she dodged to the side, leaving the swollen spiral tubing to lash at empty air. But she wasn't out of danger. She was too weak from Noelle's psychic blast, and if her daughter managed to wrap the cord around her neck, she wouldn't be able to escape this time. She wasn't sure where this place was — or if it was a real place at all. Most likely it was a realistic illusion, like the river in Oliver's basement, only this one had been created by Noelle. Mari didn't know if it was possible to hide from a spirit in a place like this, but she saw no other option. So she ran, her steps halting, stumbling, feet threating to slip out from beneath her with each movement. She headed for the woods behind the playground, not knowing how deep they went, but hoping she'd find some sort of cover within.

Her vision blurred in and out of focus as she ran, and she knew she shouldn't look back over her shoulder, knew she didn't need to in order to know that Noelle was coming after her, but she couldn't stop herself. Lewis acted as Noelle's steed, holding her in his arms as he ran after Mari. Noelle's umbilical cord whipped the air like the tentacle of some furious sea creature, one determined to ensure that its prey did not escape. Hatred poured off Noelle in waves of almost physical force, and for an instant, Mari considered stopping where she was and letting the girl have her. What was the point in going on? The entire world was under attack by creatures like Noelle, and there was no way to stop them. Based on the way things had been going in Echo Springs so far, Mari doubted there'd be anyone left on Earth by tomorrow's sunrise. Anyone living, that was. And while her rational self knew that what she'd told Noelle about the miscarriage not being anyone's fault was true, secretly she'd always feared that she'd done something to cause it to happen. She hadn't eaten enough of the right foods, hadn't taken the right supplements, hadn't seen her OB/GYN often enough, had stood too close to other teachers who were outside taking a smoke break…. She could've done — or failed to do — a million different things, and any one of them, or perhaps some combination, had resulted in her having a miscarriage. This guilt, admittedly irrational, gnawed at her day in and day out. If she let Noelle kill her, at least the guilt would be gone, and if the child thought she'd gotten justice, maybe she'd go back to wherever it was that ghosts came from without hurting anyone else.

She almost did it. What stopped her was the thought of Lewis watching her die. She was certain he was real and not part of Noelle's illusion. She'd watched him die only a few short hours ago, and she did not want to put him through that – especially when he would be unable to so much as lift a finger to help her. Noelle would most likely catch her anyway, but at least Lewis wouldn't have to watch Mari make it easy for their daughter.

When she reached the woods, she leaned against the trunk of an oak tree for a second to catch her breath, and to give her vision a chance to clear. When the world came back into focus, she saw that there were no more trees beyond the few dozen that formed the playground's backdrop. In fact, there was nothing at all, just endless white, an entire empty universe. Why did the woods just stop like this? Because Noelle didn't need any more trees to complete her playground illusion? Or was she running low on power and attempting to conserve her strength? Or was it something more basic than either of those things? Despite the way that Noelle expressed herself as if she was older, she was still just an infant – even younger, since Mari's pregnancy had ended in the first trimester. Noelle's spirit had learned to navigate the physical world to a degree, but there was still much she didn't understand. To Noelle's simple mind, there was nothing behind the trees because she couldn't conceive of things she couldn't see. To her, the woods were like a picture in a book, flat, two-dimensional. And what was behind a picture? *Beyond* was a completely alien concept to Noelle. Because of this, Mari had nowhere – literally – to run.

She looked back over her shoulder one more time. Noelle and Lewis had almost caught up to her now, were only a few feet away. Another couple seconds and Mari would be within reach of the umbilical cord, and once it streaked forward and caught hold of her, that would be the end. So she did the only thing she could do. She moved away from the tree she'd been leaning on, took three steps forward, reached the edge of Noelle's illusion, and jumped into Nothing.

★   ★   ★

"Now remember, Asad. Don't throw the ball – you *roll* it!"

Faizan watched as his son, a skinny ten-year-old who lacked even the most rudimentary physical coordination, ran up to the foul line, skidded to a halt, heaved the bowling ball into the air, and observed it come crashing down onto the lane. It bounced several times before veering sharply to the left and rolling into the gutter. Faizan stood in front of the scoring pad, and he sighed as he entered another zero for Asad. The boy hadn't gotten the spare. What a surprise.

The boy watched his ball roll all the way to the end of the gutter, then disappear. He remained standing there, waiting, and when the pinsetter machine swept away his pins, he clapped his hands and grinned, as excited as if he'd knocked them down himself.

Asad wore a dark blue polo shirt, khaki shorts, and rented bowling shoes. Faizan wore a red polo shirt and navy-blue slacks, but he owned his own shoes. There was no way he would put on filthy rental shoes that a hundred other people before him had worn. The very thought was disgusting. But Asad didn't deserve his own pair of shoes, not with bowling like *that*. If the boy got foot fungus, it only served him right.

Asad stopped when he reached the ball return. He loved to watch his bowling ball – one of the smaller, lighter ones available here – come rolling out of the return's aperture. It seemed to mesmerize him, almost as if he thought it a magic trick of some kind.

Faizan walked to the opposite side of the ball return and looked at his son.

"You were born and raised in this country, Asad. You should understand plain, simple English, but obviously you do not, else you would've done as I told you and *rolled the damn ball!*"

Faizan shouted these last four words, and Asad flinched as if he'd been struck. Inwardly, Faizan smiled at the boy's reaction, but outwardly, he kept his demeanor stern.

Asad glanced around, as if to see if anyone was watching his humiliation. But all the others lanes were empty. Today, Faizan and Asad had the place all to themselves.

"I'm sorry, Father. I will do better next time."

"You'd better. Now go to the seating area."

Asad did as he was told. *At least he can manage that much,* Faizan thought sourly. He went to the ball return, used the hand dryer, then picked up *his* ball – of course he'd brought his own – stepped forward, and rolled a strike. This was the seventh frame, and so far he'd gotten a strike every time. It was so easy, like he didn't even have to try. He thought he could approach the lane with his eyes closed, drop the ball, and it would still end up knocking down all the pins.

What can I say? he thought. *When you're good, you're good.*

A small niggling voice in the back of his mind said, *No one's that good.*

He chose to ignore it.

He expected to hear Asad enthusiastically clapping for him, perhaps cheering as well. But the boy was silent, his head bowed. Seeing his son like this filled Faizan with rage. How could he have ever sired something as weak as that pathetic creature? If the boy *was* his. Who's to say his slut of a wife hadn't gotten pregnant by some other man? It would explain a great deal. He walked up to Asad, stopped, regarded the boy for several moments. Asad did not raise his head.

"Look at me," Faizan said, voice tight with anger and disgust.

Asad continued looking at the floor.

"I said *look at me!*"

Asad flinched again, but he still refused to obey.

Faizan could not tolerate such blatant disrespect. The boy needed to learn that when he was told to do something, he did it, immediately and with no questions asked.

Faizan's lips drew back from his teeth in a sneer as he raised his right hand, ready to strike his son. He pictured hitting the boy on the side of the head so hard that he was knocked to the floor, imagined him lying there, crying, hand pressed to his face where he'd been hit, the skin red, swollen, and painful. That would be a most gratifying sight indeed.

But he did not bring his hand down.

He stood there, hand raised and trembling, looking at the spineless coward that called itself his son. But the longer he gazed upon the boy, the more his rage evaporated, replaced by deep sympathy. Faizan knew what it was like to feel small, scared, worthless, and unloved. He knew what it was like to be this boy. He continued to keep his hand raised, though.

Come on.... You know you want to.

He heard the voice in his mind, a sly, sinister purr.

Asad lifted his head to meet Faizan's gaze. His eyes shone with dark delight, and his mouth stretched into a mocking smile.

I'm small and weak. You're big and strong. You can do anything you want to me, anything at all, and there's nothing I can do to stop you. How long have you waited for a chance like this, Faizan? A chance to finally strike back at me, to repay me for every harsh word and cruel remark, every smack, slap, pinch, kick, and punch. To show me what it was really like for you growing up. Teach me a lesson that I'll never forget. I deserve anything you can do to me and so much more. Hurt me, Faizan. I guarantee you'll feel a hell of a lot better afterward. His smile widened. *I always did.*

Faizan wanted to, but he was beginning to remember who he was, and more importantly, who *Asad* was. Yes, Faizan knew what it was like to be preyed upon by someone bigger and stronger, someone who should've loved and protected him, the man who the world called *father* but who'd never truly been one. He allowed his arm to drop to his side and hang there.

"I know what you're doing," Faizan said. "You're trying to make me cold, selfish, and hateful, just like you. But I'm nothing like you, and I never will be."

The child version of Asad looked at him for a long moment, before finally speaking.

There are only two types of people in this world, Faizan. Those who hit and those who get hit. I gave you a chance to become the former, but you've chosen to live as the latter. So be it.

Asad stood, and as he did his form shifted, grew, and he became his adult self once more. He walked past Faizan to the ball return, used the hand dryer, then picked up his bowling ball. But instead of stepping up to the lane and rolling the ball, Asad gripped it one-handed, drew his arm back, then hurled the ball with great force straight toward Faizan's head.

CHAPTER TWENTY-TWO

Oliver was fairly confident that he still existed – *I think, therefore I am* – but he couldn't feel his body. Couldn't see it, either. For that matter, he wasn't sure if he was 'seeing' with his eyes or with some other sense that he didn't have a name for. He was surrounded by a slowly swirling gray mist threaded with softly pulsing veins of blue light, but he wasn't afraid. Disoriented, yes, but not scared. This place – if it could be called that – was suffused with a calming, peaceful energy that he found both relaxing and comforting. He thought he could stay here for a while, for the rest of his life and beyond, and be quite content.

I was hoping you'd react this way.

The thought-voice was Delia's, but Oliver didn't see her in the mist. He could sense her presence now, but he couldn't pinpoint her precise location. It was like she was simultaneously everywhere and nowhere.

Where are we? Oliver asked. The last thing he remembered was standing outside Qwik-Mart with Julie, Faizan, Mari, and Karen, all of them looking at that crazy guy from the church. What was his name again? Oliver thought the man had said it at one point....

Jerome, Delia supplied. *But he's not important right now. All that matters is you and me. As for where we are, I thought I'd try something different this time. I already created a version of our special place, and while it was nice for a time –* very nice *– it didn't last. How could it? It wasn't real. But this place is as real as it gets. This is where we go when we die, love. This is the Monad.*

Oliver recognized the word, but it took him a moment to remember its definition.

Doesn't that mean 'unit' or 'one', something like that?

Yes, Delia said. *The Monad is one. The Monad is all.*

You're starting to sound like Jerome, Oliver said.

He sensed more than heard Delia laugh. *I suppose I am. When humans obtained sentience, we became permanent. Our consciousness imprints itself upon the energy of the universe, and since energy can neither be created or destroyed, it has to go somewhere. Our energy coalesced – like calling to like – and from this the Monad was formed. It's the closest thing to God there is.*

Oliver struggled to wrap his mind around the concept. He didn't doubt Delia's words. Here, in this place, in this state of being, deception – of others, of the self – was impossible.

So the afterlife is that we get to merge into a giant fog bank? Oliver asked.

Delia laughed again. *Essentially. We become the Monad and the Monad is us. But I didn't bring you here only to tell you these things. I wanted you to see what it was like inside the Monad. Notice anything special about it?*

Oliver pondered Delia's question. The answer had to be something beyond the obvious, else there would be no point in asking it. This appeared to be a realm of pure thought, a place made entirely of mental energy. It was like being inside a gigantic brain, the glowing lines of energy the equivalent of neurons communicating with one another. Neither he nor Delia had physical form here. They were spirits, unencumbered by flesh, free from the constraints of material existence. Which meant....

That's right, Delia said. *Without bodies, we have no physical gender. All that matters is who we are as individuals, not what we have between our legs. And without bodies, the joining of souls is far deeper and more intense. Let me show you.*

Delia's presence grew closer, brushed up against Oliver, pressed into him, as if she were giving him the psychic equivalent of a bear hug. He felt pressure build, and for the first time since finding himself within the Monad, he was afraid.

Don't resist, Delia said. *There is no danger. Only love.*

Oliver sensed the truth of Delia's words, and he relaxed and gave himself over to her. He felt a soundless *pop*, as if a barrier had given way, and then Delia's spirit flooded into him. What he experienced next was beyond anything he ever could've imagined, beyond all language, thought, and sensation. He was a universe unto himself, as was Delia, and now their two realities merged into one, and Oliver understood then that every way humans had found to be close – the entwining of bodies, the sharing of thoughts and experiences, the joining of lives – were merely feeble attempts to reach the state he and Delia were now in. This feeling of completion, of *oneness*, was what people longed for and sought from the instant of their birth to the moment of their death. They sought it in love, religion, work, family, service to others, devotion to country or ideology, but no matter where they searched or for how long, there was only one place they could find it – within the Monad.

Delia withdrew from Oliver then, and he fought desperately to prevent her from leaving. But he couldn't hold on to her, and she pulled away, leaving him feeling more alone than he would've thought possible. Despair took hold of him, and his essence reached for her, but she held him at bay.

That was amazing, right? she said. *And that was just the two of us. Now imagine merging with every human who has ever lived throughout all of history – billions upon billions of separate minds and hearts coming together as one. That's the Monad, that's heaven. That's what I'm offering you, Oliver. All you have to do is accept, and you'll be one with us – for all time.*

Oliver wanted that, wanted it more than he'd ever wanted anything in his life. He sensed that it wouldn't take much, all he'd have to do was say yes, and it would be done. But he said nothing.

Is something wrong? Delia asked.

If the Monad is so wonderful, why is the Homecoming happening? Why all the killing and suffering?

Delia didn't respond.

Why are you making this offer to me now? Why not just wait until I die naturally? What's the Monad's hurry?

Again, Delia said nothing.

Deception might not be possible here, Oliver realized, but that didn't mean all truths were immediately revealed. There was more going on here than what Delia had told him. A lot more.

Take me back, Oliver said. *Back to the real world.*

I don't think so. It might take a century or two, but you'll come around eventually. See you then, love.

Delia's presence withdrew, and Oliver was alone.

He'd been alone before during the course of his young life. Alone in his crib at night when his parents were asleep. Alone in his room, playing with toys, reading, or lying on his bed, staring up at the ceiling, thinking. He'd been alone when feeling that the him inside didn't match the him outside. And he'd been alone after Delia's father had beaten her to death for the sin of loving him. But if you combined all the loneliness he'd felt during those times, it wouldn't come near to what he experienced now. Because even though he'd *felt* alone then, he hadn't truly been alone. There were others close by that he could turn to if he wished. And if he didn't wish, just the fact of their presence, of their *existence*, was some comfort. But now he was absolutely, utterly alone, an entire universe unto himself, with no one else, and he'd never experienced anything more awful.

Delia! Come back! Please....

If she heard his mental plea, she didn't respond, and although he had no physical eyes with which to cry, he wept.

★   ★   ★

Julie didn't know what was happening, but at this point, she was starting to get used to that.

A second ago, Mari, Oliver, Faizan, and Karen had been standing next to her, and now they were gone, vanished into thin fucking air. For a horrible instant, she wondered if her companions had been ghosts all along, if maybe *everyone* in the world was a ghost and she was the only living person left. Her and Jerome, that is. That bastard hadn't gone anywhere, and now he was coming toward her, a hungry gleam in his eyes. He didn't scare her, though. She'd experienced too much weird shit over the last few hours to get worked up over being approached by a human male, no matter how strange he was. Then again, he had that magic book of his, and that thing *did* scare her.

She thought she could handle herself against Jerome, probably even kick his ass. But she wasn't exactly in tip-top condition right now. Her head still throbbed like a sonofabitch – she was confident she had a concussion, maybe a serious one – her hip still ached, and her shoulder, while back in place, still hurt. She might not be a complete mess, but she was damn close to it. Jerome wasn't a physically imposing man, but he appeared uninjured, and that gave him a decided advantage over her. In different circumstances, she would've remained out in the open where she could better maneuver to fight and, if necessary, escape. But she needed to find a way to level the playing field, so she turned and went back inside Qwik-Mart.

She didn't know if the ghost boy who'd molded those people and cars outside into spheres was also responsible for the destruction inside the store. Maybe some other unearthly force had passed through before or after the boy. She'd likely never know what caused the wreckage, and its origin didn't matter. What mattered was that Jerome would have as difficult a time getting around inside the store as she would and that, if she was lucky, she'd find something she could use as a weapon among the debris.

She picked her way through the store, placing her feet carefully, head down, scanning the scattered items for anything she could use to defend herself. She heard Jerome enter, immediately slip on something and curse. He didn't go down, though.

"You're making this harder than it needs to be, Julie," he said. "And quite frankly, this isn't where I pictured my first time taking place. Not to put too fine a point on it, but it's a fucking *mess* in here."

First time? What did he mean by that? Was he planning to rape her? The idea seemed almost ludicrous. Of all the horrible things that had occurred in Echo Springs this day, rape seemed so...ordinary. Although she doubted she'd feel that way when it was happening.

Whatever had knocked down the shelves had tossed around the items in the store, and there was now no rhyme or reason to where they were located. Cereal lay next to pain medicine, peanuts next to sunscreen, work gloves next to bread.... Then an object caught her attention, one half-buried beneath a bag of spicy corn chips: a metal object attached to a black piece of cardboard with the word *Corkscrew* printed at the top.

Yes!

She bent over to retrieve the corkscrew, ignoring the pain in her head and hip, but as she reached for it, she heard debris rustle. She reflexively looked in Jerome's direction and saw his foot coming at her. Before she could react, his foot slammed into her belly, driving the air out of her lungs. He kicked her hard, and the impact knocked her onto her side – the same one where her injured hip was located. Something cracked when she hit, and the pain became blazing hellfire. She would've screamed if she'd been able to draw breath.

Pain-tears blurred her vision, but she could still see well enough. Jerome knelt, laid the red-covered book down next to him, and picked up the corkscrew. He held it up to his face to examine, smiling.

"Randall told me many things could be used as a knife. Let's see if he was right."

Jerome pulled the corkscrew free of the packaging and tossed the cardboard aside. This corkscrew was of the twist variety, with a black plastic handle from which extended a spiral length of metal with a sharp point on the end. Julie had intended to use it as a weapon herself, but now it looked like it was going to be wielded against her. She tried to sit up, but her hip shrieked in protest. It did the same when she tried to scoot away. If she had a few minutes to lie here and rest, she was confident she could get back on her feet, but she knew Jerome wasn't going to give her the time she needed. With nothing else left to her, she began grabbing objects at random and throwing them at Jerome. She knew she wouldn't hurt him this way, would only slow him down a little and annoy him, but she refused to simply lie there and let him do what he wanted to do to her without putting up some kind of fight.

She hurled a candy bar, a package of gum, a large bag of pretzels, all of them striking Jerome on the face and chest.

"Fuck! Stop it!"

He turned away and raised a hand to shield his face. Julie kept the pressure up. Crackers, donuts, light bulbs....

Her hand closed on a metal canister.

She raised it to her face, saw that it was painted black, with a black plastic cap, and it had an image of a cartoon bug lying on the ground, X's where its eyes should be, hands folded over its chest, a lily clutched in them. Above the bug's head were the letters *B-GONE* and below them, in smaller letters, *World's Number One Pest Killer!* Jerome certainly counted as a pest – the biggest goddamn one that she'd ever had to deal with.

She pulled off the cap, tossed it aside, and held out the canister. "Jerome!" she shouted.

As she hoped, the idiot lowered his hand and turned to look at her. She pressed her index finger down on the nozzle and gave him a full-face blast of B-GONE. He screamed, recoiled, dropped the corkscrew, and started slapping at his face in a frantic – and mostly ineffective – attempt to clean off the pesticide. He was still facing her, though, so she gave him another shot. His eyes were squeezed shut, but this time his mouth was open, and not only did he get a good taste of the B-GONE, he inhaled a quantity of it and started coughing, deep racking spasms, as if he was trying to vomit forth a lung.

He groped blindly for his book, and while Julie didn't want to go near the goddamn thing, let alone touch it, there was no way she was going to let him get his hands on it again. With an effort, she sat up. Her head and hip seemed to hurt less now, but she knew this was the result of adrenaline. She needed to make the most of the effect before it wore off. She snatched up the book with one hand, grabbed the corkscrew with the other, and pushed herself up onto her feet. Her first impulse was to head for the parking lot, but she knew that if Jerome managed to regain even partial vision, which she thought likely, she still couldn't outrun him in her condition.

She was able to breathe freely now, and she headed toward the back of the store, her head and hip only protesting mildly, her shoulder silent.

Jerome shrieked with pain and frustration, his cries punctuated with words like *bitch*, *cunt*, and *whore*. His rage frightened her more than even the book she clutched in her hand. She'd gone on numerous runs to homes where a woman had been physically assaulted by a man, and she knew the damage males were capable of inflicting when their perceived superiority was challenged or they were denied what they believed was rightfully theirs – which was usually a woman's blind obedience and unrestrained access to her body. She needed to put a barrier between herself and Jerome, and there was only one place in the store where she could do this: the restrooms.

Once she reached the small hallway where the restrooms were located, she automatically started toward the women's, but then she realized that was the first place he'd look for her. So she went into the men's. She'd had to go into men's rooms on calls before, so being inside one wasn't any novelty for her. She pushed the door shut behind her, locked it, and stood with her back against it, breathing heavily. The pain in her head and hip was coming back – despite what happened in movies and on TV, adrenaline never lasted long – and her legs started to shake. She slumped down to a sitting position, still holding on to both the corkscrew and the book, and she listened.

Jerome had been temporarily blinded by B-GONE, and he'd been yelling so loud, it was possible he didn't realize where she'd gone. If that was so, he'd most likely figure she'd left the store, and he'd go outside to try and find her. Although at this point, she thought he might be more eager to retrieve the book than to get his hands on her. The book, after all, seemed to be the source of whatever power he possessed. She heard him stumbling through the store, the sounds growing louder as he drew closer. This still didn't mean he knew where she was. He could be flailing about blindly, hoping to catch hold of her. But a few moments later, she heard him approach the restrooms, and whether he knew she'd come here or was simply being methodical in his search, the moment he discovered the men's room door was locked, he'd know where she was. He'd kick the door in then, and she'd have a fight on her hands. She rose unsteadily to her feet and stepped away from the door. She placed the book on the sink counter, gripped the corkscrew tight, and turned to face the door, ready for whatever happened next.

She heard him push open the door to the women's restroom and step inside.

"You in here, Julie?" he called. "Did you need to powder your nose?"

She heard him kick open the bathroom stalls, one by one. Then after a couple more moments, she heard him step back into the hallway. She held her breath and pictured herself ramming the corkscrew into his carotid artery as he came at her. She'd plunge the metal spiral deep, give it a twist, and then yank it out as hard as she could, altering the angle to cause maximum damage. If everything went right, the fucker would bleed out in seconds.

She waited....

And waited....

And then she heard Jerome's footsteps as he moved away from the restrooms. She listened a while longer, expecting him to realize his mistake and come running back, but he didn't.

She almost let out a laugh. Either the B-GONE had gotten to his brain and he wasn't thinking clearly, or he was stupidly sexist – but either way, it appeared it hadn't occurred to him that a woman would seek shelter in a men's room. She'd wait here for a while, give him a chance to get far away from her, then she'd leave and start looking for her friends, although she didn't have the first clue how she might find them.

It's not your friends you should be worried about.

She turned slowly and saw Randall standing by the sink, the three faceless Sisters of the Blade behind him.

CHAPTER TWENTY-THREE

"Would you like something to drink?"

Karen looked over at the flight attendant. The woman was Black, young, pretty, and thin, with short hair and conservatively applied makeup. She wore a blue uniform, the skirt rising just above her knees, and a light blue scarf tied around her neck. She stood behind a metal beverage cart, smiling at Karen as if they were best friends.

Karen sat between two other people – an Asian man in his twenties wearing a sweatshirt with some cartoon character on it that Karen didn't recognize, and a petite, middle-aged Indian woman wearing a sari. The Asian, who had the aisle seat, lay back, earbuds in, eyes closed. His seat tray was down and a plastic cup filled with soda sat on a square napkin. The Indian, who had the window seat, had a bottle of water on her tray.

"A cup of coffee," Karen said. "Black."

The flight attendant's eyes widened in surprise.

"Excuse me? Did I hear what I just *thought* I heard?"

Karen wasn't sure what she'd done to upset the woman. "I said I wanted black coffee."

The Asian man pulled out one earbud, opened his eyes, and turned to look at her. "That was pretty racist, dude."

"Yes," the Indian woman said. "Very much so."

Both of her seatmates were scowling at her, as if she'd said or done something reprehensible.

"I...I don't know what I did wrong."

The flight attendant leaned forward to put her face closer to Karen's. "I asked you if you wanted something to drink. You said, 'A cup of coffee. Black.'"

The woman was speaking loudly now, and people in the surrounding seats were starting to look in their direction to see what was happening. Karen noticed that none of them were white. Mexicans, Asians, Blacks, A-rabs.... Not a single regular person among them. She half stood and looked around the cabin. It was difficult to tell since she couldn't see everyone's faces, but she thought she might be one of the few white people on this flight. Maybe the only one.

She sat back down and looked at the flight attendant.

"I meant that I would like black *coffee*. No cream, no sugar. That's all. Why do you people always have to make everything about race?"

The Asian man rolled his eyes. "How come racists always say *you people*?"

There were murmurs of agreement from the passengers in the surrounding seats, and most of them were scowling at Karen now. She was starting to get angry.

"I don't want to hear any liberal bullshit about how minorities have been persecuted by white people throughout history. I just want a fucking cup of coffee!"

"It's not bullshit," the Indian woman said. Her voice was strained, as if she was working hard to control her temper.

Karen turned to the woman, intending to tell her to mind her own goddamn business, but when she saw the woman's face, the words died in her throat. The woman's black hair had turned white and become as dry and lifeless as old straw. Her eyes, now a cloudy white, had receded into their sockets, and her lips had pulled away from teeth grown yellow and jagged. Her skin had turned a sickly gray and drawn close to her skull, white bone showing through wide cracks in the flesh.

Karen turned away in disgust only to see the Asian boy and the flight attendant had undergone similar transformations – and not only them. All the people in nearby seats had become horrid gray things too.

The flight attendant leaned in closer to Karen, as did the Indian woman and the Asian boy.

"*You people* think you own the fucking world," the attendant said, voice dry as parchment.

"You take and take and take and take," the Indian woman said.

"You think it's your *due*," the Asian boy said. "That it's your *right*."

"You've taken too much for far too long," the Indian woman said.

"And now we're going to take some back." Thick drool ran from the flight attendant's mouth, as if she was suddenly ravenously hungry. She raised a gray-flesh hand, the nails long and sharp as talons, and reached for Karen. The Indian and Asian were slavering too, and they also reached for her with claw-like hands.

Fuck this, Karen thought.

She rose, grabbed the back of the Asian's head, and slammed his face into the seat in front of him. She pushed him back in his chair and shoved past him. She angled her shoulder toward the flight attendant and struck her in the chest. The woman reeled backward and Karen pushed her into the seat on the opposite side of the aisle. She sprawled across the lap of a Mexican man – who was also now a gray-skinned monster – and with the path clear, Karen reached the aisle and started making her way to the front of the plane. She didn't know what was happening and she didn't care. All she wanted was to get away from these greedy fucking monsters.

Gray-skins rose from their seats as she passed, hissing and swiping at her with their claws. Some of them managed to tag her, slice through her shirt and into the flesh beneath. The cuts burned like fire, but no one got a solid grip on her, and she was able to keep going. She looked back over her shoulder and saw a mass of the gray-skinned creatures coming down the aisle after her, the flight attendant in the lead.

"We're coming for *you people*," the woman said. "We're going to invade your neighborhoods, take everything you have, destroy your way of life, and there isn't a fucking thing you can do about it!"

The gray-skins roared in agreement with the flight attendant's words, and they surged forward, claws raking the air, eager to get the pound of flesh they thought Karen owed them. If there hadn't been so many of them and the aisle hadn't been so narrow, they would've caught her easily. As it was, she was barely managing to keep from being pulled down by the gray-skins in the seats she passed. She had no thought of escape – she was on a fucking plane in midflight, after all – but she hoped that if she could reach the restrooms at the front, she might be able to lock herself inside and find some temporary safety. It wasn't much of a plan, but it was all she had.

When she reached the restrooms, she tried both the men's and women's and found them each locked. She shook them anyway, earning her twin cries of "Occupied!" from whoever was inside. The horde of gray-skins was almost on her now, and she turned and ran toward the control cabin. The door was closed and locked, of course. The days of leaving control cabins open ended after 9/11. Bennie had used to complain about that. *Makes you feel cut off from the rest of the plane. It's like you're piloting a little tin box with only three guys in it.*

She pounded her fists on the door.

"Let me in!" she screamed. "For the love of Christ, let me in!"

She looked back over her shoulder again and saw the flight attendant and the slavering gray-skins advancing slowly toward her. She was trapped now, and they could take their time, draw this out, *enjoy* it. Where was she going to go?

The flight attendant gave her a hideous grin.

"We *love* the taste of white meat," she said, and the rest of the gray-skins laughed.

"I hope you fucking choke on it!" Karen said.

The gray-skins rushed toward her—

—and there was a soft *snik* as the control cabin door was unlocked. The door opened and she fell backward onto her ass. Hands gripped her beneath the arms and pulled her away from the doorway, then a man in a pilot's uniform stepped forward, shut the door once more, and locked it. When he turned to Karen, she thought she'd see another gray-faced monster, but it was her Bennie.

Get off your fat ass, sweetie, he said.

He didn't offer a hand to help her up – and she didn't expect him to – so she did it herself. She looked around and saw that the cabin was empty except for the two of them. Through the cabin windows she saw blue sky and white clouds, and despite the current situation, she couldn't help but think how beautiful the view was. Despite being a pilot's wife, she'd never flown on a flight when Bennie had been working, and even if she had, she didn't think he would've been permitted to bring her into the cabin while the plane was in the air. So this was what he'd seen the majority of the time when he'd been flying. She thought she could get used to a view like this.

Honestly, it gets pretty fucking boring after a while.

Karen could hear the jet's engines, feel the floor vibrate beneath her feet. What she didn't hear, though, was the sound of angry gray fists pounding on the outside of the cabin door.

"I'm surprised those damn things gave up so easy," she said.

Now that you're with me, they'll leave you alone.

She gave Bennie a suspicious look. "Did you do that? Were they some kind of illusion or something that you created to torment me?"

He smiled. *I invited them to come torment you, yes, but they aren't illusions. If they'd managed to catch you, they would've torn you limb from limb and feasted on you like you were a goddamn Thanksgiving turkey. Good thing you outran them, eh?*

"How come none of them were white?" she asked.

Nothing scares racists like the thought of Black, brown, and yellow people coming to destroy them.

"When did you get so woke?" she demanded.

Everybody's the same color in the grave.

"Profound," she said, though she found his words chilling. "So if you're talking to me and there's no one else in the cabin, who's flying this thing? Autopilot?"

No one's flying it, and the autopilot's disengaged.

She found these words far more disturbing than his remark about the grave.

"This is some kind of dream, right? The plane's not real."

It's real, all right. At least, as real as it needs to be. This is a recreation of the last plane I flew before I retired.

"You didn't retire. You had a heart attack on the crapper and died."

Bennie continued as if she hadn't spoken. *The passengers are the spirits of people who died during plane crashes. Now that their part in our little drama is finished, they've returned to their seats to await the climax.*

Karen didn't like where this seemed to be heading. "Cut the shit and get to the point, Bennie."

The Homecoming is almost complete, my dear. It's time for everyone to join the Monad. Including you.

She frowned. "What the fuck is a Monad?"

He ignored her question.

Right now we're cruising at an altitude of 35,000 feet above Ohio, on a direct course for Echo Springs. We'll be there in just a few minutes. That's where we're going to land.

"Are you nuts? Echo Springs doesn't have an airport. The nearest one's in Cincinnati!"

He grinned. *I know.*

★　　★　　★

Mari plummeted through white space. Wind whipped past her, so she knew there was air here, and there was light, otherwise she wouldn't have been able to see anything. Why a place that seemed to be the epitome of nothing should possess these two qualities – these two *somethings* – she didn't know. Ever since the moment she first heard Noelle crying this morning, logic had ceased to have any meaning. Or maybe the Homecoming, whatever it was exactly, had its own insane brand of logic. She decided it didn't really matter. She'd be dead soon and she'd never have to think about anything again. Unless, of course, she returned as a damn ghost to join all the others that were running amok across the planet. She vowed never to come back from whatever netherworld she ended up inhabiting. Let the other spirits cause their mayhem. She wanted no part of it. All she wanted was to rest, to finally be free of the sorrow and guilt that had eaten away at her heart since the miscarriage.

But there was one problem with that. While this nothingness clearly had an up and down – not to mention gravity – she couldn't see anything even close to resembling a bottom, just more whiteness. She supposed that if the bottom was white, it would blend in with everything else, making it difficult, if not impossible, to detect. But what if there *was* no bottom? What if she kept on falling forever? No, that couldn't happen. She'd die of thirst within a few days. Unless…. The rules were different here in this non-place. She still breathed, but maybe she no longer needed to eat and drink. And if that was the case, then she could keep falling forever, with nothing but her own thoughts – and regrets – for company.

It would be her own personal hell.

Something blurred past her face, moving so fast she couldn't tell what it was. It wrapped around her midsection, pulled tight, and her entire body jerked as her fall was slowed, then stopped. She dangled in space for several moments, slowly spinning right, left, and then she began rising. She turned her head, straining to see what had taken hold of her, and she was not surprised to see an incredibly long length of umbilical cord stretching upward, so far that she couldn't see where it ended. But she didn't need to see. She knew. It ended at her daughter's belly.

She wasn't certain if she could manage to maneuver herself into position to bite through the cord, as she'd done to escape Noelle back at the house. She wasn't a damn acrobat. And even if she could manage to get her teeth on the cord, she wasn't sure she wanted to sever it this time. *How's that for a little Freudian symbolism?* she thought. Since Noelle had manifested in her bedroom this morning, Mari had been running from the ghost of her unborn daughter, and what good had it done? There were some things in life – and she supposed in death – that you couldn't outrun, and those things needed to be faced, regardless of the consequences.

Eventually, Mari was able to see Lewis and Noelle standing on the edge of a blurry landscape that indicated the demarcation between Something and Nothing. The cord was shrinking or retracting or whatever the hell it did to grow smaller, and Lewis still held Noelle, both of them looking down at her and monitoring her ascent. She wasn't sure how Lewis was managing to stand there without her weight pulling him over the edge, but he was a ghost now, so the laws of physics were probably more like suggestions to him than hard and fast rules.

As Mari drew near the top, Lewis moved back to make room for her. The cord lifted her up and then, with unexpected gentleness, put her feet down on the grass-covered ground and released her. It slithered the rest of the way back to Noelle and disappeared into her navel with a wet *schlurp*.

Lewis gazed at her sadly, but Noelle's face was dark with anger.

You're a bad mommy! A very bad mommy!

"No, I'm not," Mari said. "I'm just a woman who had a miscarriage and wishes to god she hadn't. And you're not a bad girl. You're just a sad, angry spirit who never got the chance to be born into flesh."

Smiling, Mari walked over to Lewis and their daughter. She held out her arms and, after a moment's hesitation, Lewis handed Noelle to her.

No! Bad mommy! Bad, bad, bad!

Each *bad* was accompanied by a burst of psychic force that exploded in Mari's head like a miniature bomb, but she endured the pain. She drew Noelle to her chest and held her close.

"I love you, little one," Mari said. "I loved you when you were just a hope, and I loved you when you became a reality and started growing inside me. I loved you and grieved for you when you were gone, and despite what you did to your daddy and tried to do to me, I love you still." She bent her head down and kissed her daughter's forehead. She found the skin warm and velvet soft. Noelle looked like a normal newborn now, and she gazed up at her mother with wide, wondering eyes. Mari held out her pinky finger, and Noelle wrapped her own tiny fingers around it.

Mari smiled. "It's time for the three of us to be a family now." She held out her hand to Lewis. Smiling, he stepped forward and took it.

The trees and the playground beyond them slowly faded away, leaving the three of them surrounded by white nothingness. The ground – or whatever it was – felt solid enough beneath Mari's feet, so she wasn't worried that they'd fall, but she didn't know what they should do next.

We don't have to do anything, Lewis said. *The Monad is coming for us.*

She remembered Lewis using that word before, back on the playground when she hadn't realized Noelle had trapped them in an illusion.

"What *is* a Monad?" she asked.

But then it was there, surrounding them, filling them, and Mari understood.

Yes, she said in her new thought-voice. *I see.*

As Mari, Lewis, and Noelle began to merge with the Monad, Mari had only one regret – that she wasn't going to get a chance to say goodbye to her new friends. She wished there was something she could do to help them get to safety.

She became aware of other presences around her then. Other people.

You don't have to wish, one of them said.

And you don't have to do it alone, another said.

Mari saw them clearly now, all of them, and when she realized who they were, she laughed.

CHAPTER TWENTY-FOUR

Faizan had played dodgeball throughout his public school career. He'd read somewhere that a lot of school systems were phasing out the game because it institutionalized bullying, and because most of the kids, especially those who were eliminated early, really didn't get much exercise. Unfortunately, Echo Springs wasn't one of those school systems, and Faizan – with his skinny arms and legs – had been forced to suffer through barrages of large red rubber balls during many a gym class. He'd never been much good at hitting other kids with the ball, but he'd quickly become an expert at avoiding getting hit himself. This was partly due to the fact that he'd been born with good reflexes, but it was primarily due to his father paying Faizan's gym teachers to deliver weekly unofficial reports on his son's performance. If Asad learned anything in these reports that disappointed him – such as Faizan getting eliminated early in a game of dodgeball – he'd teach Faizan a lesson that night. A very painful and memorable one. So Faizan learned how to dodge extremely well, so well that he was often one of the last two kids standing during a game. He couldn't throw a ball fast enough to hit the other kid, so the games would end in a draw. Asad wasn't thrilled with that result, but it was good enough for Faizan to avoid getting a 'lesson' at home, and that was all he cared about.

So when the bowling ball his father had thrown came flying directly toward his face, Faizan didn't have to think about avoiding it. His body simply reacted, swiftly turning to the side, head leaned back, and the ball flew through empty space. It crashed into one of the seats behind Faizan, hitting so hard it tore the chair back completely off. The ball kept going until it struck the front of the snack counter, where it smashed into the wood siding with a loud *crack* and became stuck.

Faizan heard his father's shoes *thump-thump-thump*ing on the smooth wooden surface of the lane, and he turned in time to see Asad's open hand streak toward his face. Bright light flashed behind Faizan's eyes, and he staggered, almost falling to the floor. He had no idea how he managed to remain on his feet, but he did. The left side of his face was numb, but he knew from experience that the pain would hit him any second.

Asad hovered over him like a wrathful deity.

You are the most useless thing that God ever created! A maggot feasting on roadkill has more backbone than you! A dog licking its own balls in public has more dignity. A dung beetle rolling shit across the ground has more purpose! I wish I'd had the sense to pull my cock out of your mother and spurt you out onto the sheets so you would never have been born!

Asad grew taller with every word he shouted, until he loomed over his son like a giant. Then Faizan realized his father hadn't changed at all. Rather, Faizan had grown smaller. He was in a child's body, helpless before Asad's superior strength. Asad leaned down until his face was only inches from Faizan's, and he bared his teeth as he spoke, nearly snarling.

If I could prevent you from joining the Monad, I would. The same with your bitch of a mother. The two of you will be like pimples on our ass, painful and ugly, and of no value whatsoever. Just as you were in life.

Faizan looked into his father's eyes and remembered how the man had stood off to the side in the dentist's examining room as Faizan had struggled to save his mother. He remembered something Asad had said to him before the Tooth Fairy had crushed her in its mouth. *She always did love playing the martyr.*

Cold, steely anger took hold of him. He turned away from Asad and calmly walked toward a storage rack where a half-dozen balls that anyone could use were stored. With each step, he grew taller, and by the time he reached the rack, he had returned to his normal adult self. He selected a pair of balls, and inserted his fingers into their holes. He curled his fingers in order to grip the balls, then he lifted them from the rack and started to walk back toward his father. Asad watched him warily, as if unsure what he was doing.

Faizan stopped when he reached his father.

"Shut up, Dad," he said softly, then he brought the bowling balls up and swung them toward the sides of Asad's head with all his strength. When the balls struck, the man's head collapsed inward with a sickening wet hollow sound, like a watermelon might make if thrown off the roof of a building to splatter on the concrete below. Blood, brains, and fragments of bone decorated the air, and Faizan smiled as pieces of his father flew toward him.

Then his vision blurred and he could no longer feel the weight of the bowling balls on his hands. When the world came back into focus, he was once more standing outside Qwik-Mart, no bowling balls in sight, no blood or bits of brain on his face or clothes, and best of all, no Asad. He didn't know if he'd killed his father – could a ghost even die? – but he was relieved to be free of that bowling alley and, for the moment at least, Asad's presence. That was enough.

He looked around for Mari, Julie, Oliver, and Karen, but he didn't see them. Had they also been sucked into ghostly psychodramas like he had? If so, there was nothing he could do to help them. As he had, they would have to find their own way back.

He sat down on the walkway in front of the store, crossed his legs, leaned forward to put his elbows on his knees, and rested his head on his hands.

Come on, he thought. *If I can do it, so can you guys.*

*   *   *

Okay, so you're stuck inside the mind of some sort of…of…super ghost. Now what?

Oliver – alone and bodiless – floated within the gray mist that comprised the Monad's mind. The pulsating arcs of energy that continually passed through the mist, which he assumed were the thoughts of the Monad, were the only signs of life and movement around him. He wondered what had happened to his body. Had it been destroyed during his transition from the world of the living to this place? Was it stored somewhere, in some sort of pocket dimension, waiting for him to reclaim it? And if he couldn't retrieve it, or if it was gone for good, would he continue to drift within the Monad's mind until he finally broke down and gave Delia what she wanted? He remembered what she'd said before she'd left.

It might take a century or two, but you'll come around eventually.

The thought of being trapped here like this for centuries, or longer, was terrifying. How long would it take him to go mad? A year? Two? He had to find a way out of here and reclaim his body, not only for the sake of his own sanity, but because his new friends might need him. They'd all suffered losses this day. Well, maybe not Karen. She hadn't shared much about herself, and she hadn't seemed particularly upset about the Homecoming. Oliver had the suspicion that the woman was secretly enjoying the death and destruction, although he had no idea how anyone in their right mind could possibly feel that way. But Mari, Julie, and Faizan had told him of the friends and family they'd lost today, just as he'd shared the loss of his parents with them. They were all they had now, and while they'd only known each another for a few hours, they'd become a kind of family, and Oliver didn't want to abandon them.

If he was a being of pure thought in this place, maybe he could *think* his way out. He concentrated on Qwik-Mart, tried to recreate every detail in his mind, and then he imagined himself standing in front of the store, just as he had been before Delia had brought him here. He imagined the cold air on his skin, the solidity of concrete beneath his bare feet, his naked body shivering inside the jacket Julie had loaned him. Nothing happened, though, and he continued drifting in the gray mist, feeling more helpless than ever. Maybe Delia *was* his only way out. If he called to her, gave her what she wanted, *submitted* to her, this would end. He wasn't sure what would happen after that. Would the two of them merge as they'd done before, only this time stay that way? Would they then join with the Monad and lose all sense of their individual identities? That sounded like a kind of death in itself, but was it any worse than spending eternity trapped inside the Monad without ever being part of it?

An idea occurred to him then. If he could summon Delia, could he contact other spirits, maybe ones that hadn't been fully absorbed into the Monad yet? Spirits like his mother and father. Feeling hope for the first time since finding himself in this place, Oliver concentrated. There was a framed photo of his parents sitting on the mantel of their fireplace at home, a picture taken on their wedding day. They were in the process of cutting the cake and feeding each other pieces. Oliver's mother – scarcely much older than Oliver himself was now – had jammed her piece into her new husband's mouth, and both of them were laughing. It was a moment of absolute joy, captured forever, and it was Oliver's favorite image of them. He focused on that image now, and called out to his parents.

Mom...Dad.... Are you here?

He listened, hoping, praying for a response. But there was none.

Maybe they'd already been absorbed by the Monad – but Delia had died long before either of them, and she was still separate, still herself. It didn't make sense. But then nothing had since the moment his mother had torn out her own eyes, so why should it now? Whatever the reason, he couldn't reach his parents, so he'd just have to think of something else. It had to be Delia, he decided. She was the only one who he'd been in contact with in this place, and even though she had left him, he doubted she'd gone far. She was most likely nearby, watching and listening, waiting for him to surrender himself to her. So that's what he would do.

You're right, Delia. We're meant to be together. When we were joined it was like I was truly home for the first time in my life, like I'd finally become whole. Without you, I'm incomplete. Worse than that – I'm nothing. I love you. Please come back to me.

He drew on the love he and Delia had shared when she'd been alive, infused his thoughts with it, broadcast it out into the ether with his words. And then he waited.

He didn't know how long it took, minutes, hours, or days – time meant nothing in this place – but eventually he sensed Delia's presence. She had returned.

I'm so glad you came to your senses, love. Joining with the Monad, becoming part of something so much greater than yourself, is beyond anything you can imagine. It's like becoming God.

I can't wait, Oliver said. *Come to me now.*

Delia did. She flowed over, into, and through him, their essences intertwining, blending, merging, until it was impossible to say where one began and the other ended. They were One, even more so than before when Delia had demonstrated what joining their souls could be like, because now Oliver had given himself over completely to her. And now that she was part of him, *was* him, he let her experience everything that had happened to him today from his perspective, giving her access to all the thoughts and emotions he'd had from her first appearance on his laptop screen until this very moment. She knew his pain and fear, felt them as if they were her own, and she knew that she had been the cause of the worst of it, that she had done this to the man she claimed to love. She saw what she had become – a selfish, greedy, grasping *thing* – and the knowledge sickened her.

No, she said. *I'd never do those things! I'd never hurt you like that! No, no, no, NO!*

Oliver a felt a sudden lurching sensation, and bright light flooded his vision. He felt heavy, weighed down, and it was all he could do to remain upright.

"Hey, are you all right?"

He felt a touch on his arm, and he realized he had a body again. He blinked to clear his vision, and after a moment, he could make out Faizan's worried face.

He smiled. "I am now."

★   ★   ★

Julie still gripped the corkscrew, but she knew it would be useless against a creature like Randall. Her gaze darted to the red-covered book on the sink counter. She didn't know if it controlled Randall and the faceless girls – the Sisters of the Blade – but she'd seen how Jerome had wielded the book at New Life, and the damn thing definitely had some kind of freaky power. If she could get hold of it, maybe she could use that power to protect herself against these ghosts.

But before she could make a move toward the book, Randall reached over and snatched it off the counter.

Sorry, he said. *But this isn't for you. This, however, is.*

He held his free hand up to his mouth and bit hard into the soft flesh of his palm. Blood flowed from the wound, and when he lowered his hand, the blood coalesced and hardened into the shape of a knife. When the blade was finished, he curled his fingers around the handle and gripped it tight while blood continued to drip from his wound and patter onto the restroom's tiled floor.

Jerome was supposed to be the one to kill you, but considering he was too goddamn stupid to look for you in the men's room, I'd say he's forfeited that privilege. Any last words before I gut you like a fucking fish and cut off your face?

"Yeah," Julie said, pointing at the Sisters of the Blade. "What's wrong with them?"

Randall frowned and turned to look at the faceless girls. Their bodies had become hazy, like pictures gone out of focus, and they overlapped one another, as if they were merging. Their forms lost all definition and flowed together, becoming gray mist, threads of bright energy flashing through it like miniature lightning.

No! Not yet! Randall cried. *I'm not finished!*

Tendrils emerged from the mist and streaked toward Randall, wrapping around his neck, wrists, ankles, and pulling him inward. He disappeared into the mist, and it grew larger, taking on a roughly spherical form. The book had entered the mist with Randall, and it was gone as well. The mist ball floated above the restroom floor for several seconds as if it were regarding her. A small tendril emerged from it, stretched toward the blood that Randall had dripped onto the tile, and absorbed it. The tendril then lifted from the floor and slowly extended toward her.

Time to go, Julie thought.

She turned to the restroom door, unlocked it, threw it open, and hauled ass out of there.

★   ★   ★

Jerome sat on the floor in a corner of Qwik-Mart, legs drawn up to his chest, arms wrapped around them. For the first time in hours, he didn't have *The Book* in his hands, and he felt lost. Worse, he felt as if one of his limbs had been cut off, as if a vital part of him had been torn away, lessening him, rendering him empty, hollow, barren. Julie was to have been his first pure kill, the first he would do with his own hands, the way it was *supposed* to be done. She had been his chance to learn at last what it was like to be someone like Randall Beck, someone who held the power of life and death in his hands and who wasn't afraid to wield that power to satisfy his desires. Someone who wasn't weak and worthless like Jerome.

He'd grown up as the youngest of five boys in a household where a man's worth was measured by his physical strength, where cars, sports, and girls were the only things worthy of attention, where men ruled and women did what they were told – or else. Being a bookish boy in such a family made him an anomaly. Neither of his parents nor his siblings read. They wouldn't touch a book unless a gun was put to their heads, and maybe not even then. He was a mystery and a disappointment to his father, who'd played high school football and worked in the tire plant. He was an object of derision and ridicule to his older brothers, and they never passed up an opportunity to tease and bully him. His parents tolerated, even encouraged this behavior. *Maybe it'll make a man out of him,* was his father's attitude. But all it had done was make him miserable.

Books had been his best – and only – friends growing up, and it had remained that way throughout school, and led to him eventually getting his master's in library science. But during his senior year of high school, when Randall had killed his three victims and cut off their faces, Jerome acquired a second equally strong interest – more of an obsession, really – with the Skintaker's murders, and he'd carried it with him into adulthood. Randall was strong, Randall was fierce, Randall didn't let anyone tell him what he could or couldn't do. If he wanted something, he took it. If he wanted to do something, he did it. If he wanted to kill a girl, he killed her. Randall was more of a real man than Jerome's father and brothers could ever be.

When Randall had appeared to him in the library that morning, it had been like a visit from his own personal deity. Randall had given him the opportunity to unleash the urges and desires he'd been suppressing since he'd been a teenager. He'd given him a chance to finally, truly *live*. And what had Jerome done with that opportunity? He'd let it slip through his hands like the weak-ass little bitch that his family had always believed he was. Not only had he failed to kill Julie, he didn't even know where she was – and worst of all, she'd stolen *The Book*. He'd gone outside and looked around for her, but when he saw no sign of her, he'd returned to the store, seeing no point in going anywhere else. He wasn't worthy of Randall and the Sisters of the Blade, wasn't worthy of continued existence. He'd just sit here until the Homecoming was finished, and let the Monad take him with all the others – assuming the Monad would even have him.

He heard one of the restroom doors slam open, and an instant later, he saw Julie come running out of the short hallway. The first thing he noticed was that she wasn't carrying *The Book*. The second thing he noticed was that she held the corkscrew gripped in her right hand, and he thought she planned to attack him. Good. Let her kill him. It was only what he deserved.

But when she saw him, she didn't come toward him, brandishing her weapon and howling for his blood. Instead, she stopped and said, "Give me the keys to the Mercedes. *Now.*"

Jerome looked at her for a moment, uncomprehending. Then he shrugged.

"Why the fuck not?"

He stood, fished the keys out of his pants pocket, and tossed them to her. She caught them, dropped the corkscrew to the ground, and started toward the door.

"Is *The Book* in the restroom?" Jerome asked. Maybe if he could retrieve *The Book*, Randall might forgive him, even give him a chance to redeem himself.

"No," Julie said over her shoulder as she ran. "That goddamn thing ate it."

Jerome didn't know what she was talking about, but then he saw what looked like a small storm cloud emerge from the hallway, electric threads of energy sparking and crackling in its substance. The cloud rushed toward him, tentacles extended from the main mass of its form, and as they reached for him, he had time for a final thought.

I am so fucked....

CHAPTER TWENTY-FIVE

Karen was strapped into one of the pilot seats, and Bennie stood next to her, holding her hand. His grip was too tight and it hurt – just the way Karen liked it. As a ghost, Bennie wasn't affected by the plane's downward trajectory, nor by the way turbulence tossed the aircraft around like a damn toy. He could've been standing safe and secure on the ground for all the effect the bumpy ride had on him. Not Karen. She was jerked and bounced around in her seat, and she sincerely regretted stuffing her belly with some of the snacks she'd salvaged from Qwik-Mart.

Watching the world below grow larger as they descended was hypnotic. At first there were green and brown patches of land separated by hair-thin lines that she knew were roads. As the lines got bigger, tiny squares became visible. *Those are houses*, she thought. She wondered how many people who inhabited those homes were still alive. Not many, she guessed. The Homecoming was almost done, and those few who yet lived would soon be harvested.

The roads grew larger, and she could now see small specks gliding along them. Vehicles, although far fewer than she would've expected. People desperately searching for someplace safe where they could ride out what was happening. *Fucking morons.* The buildings became larger, more numerous, closer together, and she began to make out their details. Then they reached the west edge of town, and the Steiner Tire and Rubber plant came into view – Echo Springs's largest employer, and its parking lot was nearly deserted in the middle of the day. *The end of the world's definitely a good reason to cut out of work early*, she thought.

We'll be there soon, Bennie said. He turned to her and smiled. *And when we get there, I'll have a surprise for you.*

The plane's engines were screaming so loud now that if Bennie had spoken with a physical voice instead of with his mind, she wouldn't have been able to hear him. She wondered what sort of *surprise* he was talking about. Whatever it was, she doubted it was going to be pleasant. In fact, she was counting on it.

The ground continued coming up to meet them, and now Karen could read the text on billboards and business signs. The roads were deserted, and she saw no people on the sidewalks or in parking lots. Echo Springs might not be dead yet, but it was damn close.

And then there it was – *Qwik Mart*. She could see Faizan, Julie, and Oliver outside the store, rushing toward the Mercedes. But not Mari. Had the Black bitch not made it? Too bad. She was going to miss out on a spectacular death, one better than she – or the others – deserved, to be honest. It was thoughtful of Bennie to ensure that she had a perfect view of her 'friends' as the plane crushed them into paste. He'd always been good to her like that.

★ ★ ★

Only a few more moments now....

Ready for your surprise?

Before she could respond, Bennie placed a hand on top of her head. She didn't feel anything at first, but then the engines' shriek began to lower in pitch, rapidly descending into a low, grinding moan. Julie, Oliver, and Faizan were no longer coming closer. They remained where they were, tiny dolls that stood frozen in the act of running toward Jerome's Mercedes.

"What did you do? Don't tell me you stopped time so that I'm going to have to sit here forever and never get to see those fuckers die!"

That would be too cruel, even for me. I've merely slowed your perception of time. Events are still progressing, but at a rate so slow they're almost imperceptible. The plane will crash, but to you it will seem to take decades to do so. You will experience every agonizing sensation as intensely as you would if time were flowing normally, but the pain of each cut, contusion, splintered bone, and pierced organ will continue on and on....

Karen understood then the trap that Bennie had caught her in – a personal hell tailor-made just for her.

"You fucking bastard," she said.

She started laughing then, and Bennie joined her. They laughed and laughed and laughed, but after a time – a *long* time – Karen's laughter turned to screams.

And those screams continued for many years.

★   ★   ★

When Julie burst out of the store, she almost collided with Oliver and Faizan. She wanted to ask them if they were okay, if they knew where Mari and Karen were, but there wasn't time. The mist ball thing was coming, and they—

Screaming came from inside Qwik-Mart, accompanied by the sound of snapping bones. The screaming trailed off to a gurgling moan before ending, and an instant later Jerome's body flew through the store's broken window. It hit the parking lot's asphalt with a dull thud and slid several feet before coming to a stop. Blood ran from Jerome's mouth, and his arms and legs looked like a rag doll's, as if he were a sack of skin filled with soft stuffing.

"What the actual *fuck*?" Oliver said.

Faizan turned to look at the window and his eyes widened.

"I saw something like that on the news this morning," he said. "It was killing people in Japan!"

"Well, now Echo Springs has one of its very own," Julie said. "Come on, we have to get out of here before—"

She was cut off again, this time by the sound of jet engines. They all looked up to see a large aircraft heading straight for them like the judgment of a wrathful and capricious god.

"You've got to be shitting me," Julie said softly. She stood with Faizan and Oliver for a second, transfixed by the sight of several thousand pounds of metal hurtling toward them. She shook her head to clear it – which, given her concussion, was an extremely poor choice – and then she grabbed

Oliver's and Faizan's arms and started dragging them toward the Mercedes. They allowed her to lead them, but neither could take their eyes off the incoming aircraft.

Once they reached the car, Faizan and Oliver returned to their senses, and they were able to run to the passenger side to let themselves in. Julie slid behind the driver's side, turned on the car, put it in gear, and jammed the gas pedal to the floor. Tires squealed and the back end fishtailed, but then the car straightened and shot toward the road. Julie accidentally struck a person who had been turned into a sphere by the ghost kid and sent him or her rolling across the parking lot. Her stomach twisted with nausea, but she fought the sensation down, kept the pedal to the floor, and drove like she'd never driven before.

★   ★   ★

Despite the massive injuries Jerome's body had suffered to both his skeletal and muscular systems, not to mention his internal organs, he wasn't quite dead yet. He lay on the asphalt outside Qwik-Mart, breathing shallowly through his broken and bloody nose, dazed and unsure what had happened to him or where he was. The last thing he remembered was seeing Julie come out from where the restrooms were located, and only now did he realize that she must've been hiding in the men's room all along. It hadn't even occurred to him to look in there. After all, it was the *men's* room. *I'm a fucking idiot.* Then he remembered seeing the mini storm cloud, or whatever it was, coming at him, reaching out with tendrils that extruded from its main mass. Those tendrils wrapped around him and then…then…. He was dead, he knew that. His brain just hadn't gotten the message yet.

He heard a sound then, loud, grating, and at first he couldn't place it, but then he realized what it was: a plane. A big one, from the sound of it, low and close. Was he at an airport? That didn't make sense. He was at Qwik-Mart, wasn't he? He struggled to turn his head, just a little, enough so that he could see the plane and confirm for himself just where the hell he was. If a man was going to die, he should at least know the goddamn site of his death. His broken body was a symphony of pain, and he could barely manage to raise his head an inch off the asphalt, angle it, and then let it fall back. He barely felt his skull crack against the hard ground – he was in too much agony for a love tap like that to register – but his maneuver had succeeded. His head was now angled slightly toward the sky, enough so he could see what was coming toward him.

It was indeed a fucking airplane. A goddamn jet, actually, a *big* one, and it looked like it was heading straight toward him, almost as if the thing were a guided missile sent to destroy him specifically. He wondered if he would pass out from his injuries in the last few seconds before the plane slammed into the ground, or if he'd remain conscious just long enough to experience the crash's full impact. It didn't matter, he supposed. Either way, his life was going to be over soon. Then his spirit could join the Monad, and he would dwell in the house of the Lord forever.

He watched the plane come closer…closer…. The engines' shriek stabbed into his ears like hot pokers and vibrated the asphalt beneath him, making it seem as if the ground were shivering in anticipation of what was to come. And then the plane just…stopped. It froze in midair, its nose less than fifty feet from where Jerome lay. He heard a voice in his head.

My wife thought it would be nice if you joined her, so I expanded my temporal extension field to include you. Hope you're comfortable down there. You're going to be in that position for a very long time.

Jerome continued looking up at the plane – not that he had any choice now – his body screaming its agony to the universe.

* * *

Julie didn't know how far away they needed to get from the crash site in order to be in the clear, but she figured they were about to find out. She was right.

Behind them came a sound like a thousand claps of thunder, followed by a loud *whoosh*. Bright light flared in the Mercedes's rearview mirror, and Julie averted her eyes. *Shit,* she thought. It wasn't just the jet fuel going up, as bad as that was – it was also the gas in the tanks that fed Qwik-Mart's pumps.

"Hold on!" she shouted, just as the shock wave hit them.

Hot wind blasted the back of the Mercedes, and Julie fought the steering wheel in an attempt to keep the vehicle under control. She was bounced around in her seat, as were Faizan and Oliver. Oliver sat directly next to her, and he was slammed back and forth between Julie and Faizan like a pinball. Julie cursed herself for being in such a hurry that she hadn't told them to put on their seatbelts, but if she had, they might not have gotten away from Qwik-Mart in time. As it was, there was still an excellent chance that they weren't going to make it.

Objects began pelting the Mercedes, small ones that made metallic pings on the roof, larger ones that sounded like birds falling out of the sky. She tried not to imagine a huge, jagged chunk of jet fuselage arcing through the sky toward them, and failed utterly. *Just concentrate on keeping this fucker on the road,* she told herself, and she did. Several larger objects struck the Mercedes – one hitting the trunk so hard that the Mercedes was nearly knocked off the road – but nothing as bad as a big chunk of airplane. The air inside the car became warm, then hot. Faizan reached for the control to lower the passenger-side window, and Julie warned him not to.

"We don't know what kind of chemical fumes are in the air," she said.

He nodded, looking chastened.

Julie kept their speed up for several more minutes, but no other objects, large or small, pelted the vehicle, and a quick glance at the rearview showed a massive inferno blazing where Qwik-Mart had been, black smoke billowing into the sky. But it was far enough behind them now that she thought they were good. All three of them were drenched with sweat, some of it due to heat, some of it undoubtedly due to sheer terror.

"Okay, we can open the windows," Julie said, "but just a little at first, until we make sure the air's all right."

Faizan and Julie both lowered their windows several inches. Cold February air rushed in, and Julie thought she'd never felt anything so good on her skin. There was a slight chemical tang to the air, but it was probably harmless enough – most likely the stink clinging to the outside of the Mercedes – and she decided they could keep the windows down like this.

They were on Orchard Street, heading for Route 2, the most direct

236 • TIM WAGGONER

way out of town from here. The road was empty of traffic except for their vehicle, and the buildings they passed appeared deserted. Julie wondered if there was anyone left alive in Echo Springs besides them, and she wasn't sure whether to hope there was or not, given how bad things had gotten. She had no idea if the countryside beyond town was safe, as that half-crazed guy on the radio had said earlier, but it was the only plan they had, and she figured they should stick to it until a better one came along.

"Did either of you see Mari or Karen?" she asked.

"No, but I got back after Faizan," Oliver said.

"I didn't see them either," Faizan said. "Do you think they were still in Qwik-Mart when...." He trailed off, unable to make himself finish the thought.

"Maybe they're still stuck in whatever place they got sucked into," Oliver said.

"God, I hope not," Faizan said. "That would be awful!"

Julie wasn't sure what the two of them were talking about. Get back from *where*? But she decided she didn't want to know, at least not right now. She had another question on her mind, one she thought far more important.

"Jerome spoke of something called the Monad," she said. "What the hell *is* it?"

"Delia showed me," Oliver said. "She took me there, into its mind."

Oliver went on to tell Julie and Faizan what Delia had revealed to him, about how the Monad was the consciousness created from the spirits of all the humans who'd ever died throughout history.

"We don't go to heaven when we die," he said. "We go to the Monad."

Julie was having a hard time wrapping her brain around this concept.

"If this is true, then everyone eventually becomes part of the Monad, right?"

Oliver nodded. "We will too, when our time comes. There's nothing we can do to stop it. All we can do is postpone it for as long as we can."

That's a cheery thought. "So then why did the Monad want to harvest the human race now?" Julie asked. "Why have the Homecoming at all?"

"When I was inside its mind, I was separate from it," Oliver said. "But to escape, I had to join my spirit to Delia's completely, make us one. When that happened, Delia understood everything she'd done to me today, how it had made me feel – especially about her. That knowledge was too much for her to bear, so she kicked me out of the Monad and back into the real world. But I learned some things while we were joined. I know why the Monad decided to stage the Homecoming today. After tens and thousands of years, it had finally absorbed enough spirits to become a fully sentient individual in its own right. It didn't need to wait for the rest of humanity to die naturally. The job was mostly done. It just wanted to finish the last little bit, kind of like topping off a drink."

"What are those weird orbs?" Faizan said. "The gray things that look like they have little lightning storms inside."

"Once a person dies, their spirit is released from their body. It can remain separate for a time, but eventually it's drawn to other spirits, and them to it. They merge, becoming small-scale versions of the Monad. They're sweeping around the world right now, killing people and collecting their souls, growing larger and larger. Eventually they'll gather together, merge, and then join with the Monad. When that happens, the Homecoming will truly be over."

"Where *is* the Monad?" Julie asked.

Oliver shrugged. "Everywhere. Nowhere. It's hard to explain. But it's here, and it always has been, at least as long as people have."

"What I don't get," Faizan said, "is why the Monad would need to send…I don't know what you'd call them. Emissaries? Separate spirits like the ones that came after us. Delia, my father, that creepy guy who was with Jerome—"

"And those women without any faces," Oliver said, and shuddered.

Faizan continued. "The Monad would have to purposely separate them from itself. Maybe even recreate them somehow if they no longer existed as themselves. Why go to all that trouble? Why send them to torment us before killing us?"

"That's easy to explain," Oliver said. "The Monad is made of human spirits, and humans are petty, selfish, and vindictive. It wanted revenge on everyone who was still alive for all the slights – real, perceived, or simply imagined – suffered by the souls that formed its essence."

"So there's a world-mind," Julie said, "a kind of god, really, and you're telling me it's an asshole because people are assholes."

"That pretty much sums it up," Oliver said.

"And that's what we get to look forward to being part of one day," Julie said. "Fan-fucking-tastic."

"Maybe the Monad isn't all bad," Faizan said. "Your brother's ghost came to help you, didn't he? And Oliver's mother appeared in the kitchen of her home and told Mari to go save Oliver."

Julie sighed. "I hope you're right. Because I *hate* the idea of spending the rest of eternity as part of…a…." She trailed off as she caught sight of an object in the rearview mirror approaching swiftly. It was a small-scale Monad, one about the size of a house, multiple tendrils whipping the air, energy coruscating within its gray misty form as well as across its surface, making it resemble a living thunderstorm. It floated several feet above the road, and as fast as it was rushing toward them, she knew it would be upon them in moments. If they couldn't outrun the goddamn thing, they would end up joining it much sooner than any of them would like.

Julie floored the gas pedal once more, but this time she said, "Buckle up."

The Mercedes's engine roared, the car leaped forward, and the chase was on.

CHAPTER TWENTY-SIX

Julie knew she shouldn't keep looking at the rearview mirror to monitor the Lesser Monad's progress – doing so could only distract her when she needed her full focus to be on driving – but she couldn't help herself. Each time she was heartened to see they'd put a little more distance between themselves and the mist ball, but it was clear they weren't going to be able to outrun the thing. Plus, the car's rear end had started to shimmy a bit, and she was afraid that whatever large object had struck the trunk had done something to mess up the back tires. Whatever the reason, the car began to shake violently when it got close to ninety, so she was forced to keep their speed around eighty-five. Fast, but not fast enough.

Faizan and Oliver had half-turned in their seats so they could look out the rear window, and they observed the Lesser Monad with a mixture of wonderment and terror.

"Are those...faces?" Oliver asked.

"I think so," Faizan said. "It's hard to tell, they come and go so fast."

Julie glanced at the rearview mirror again, trying to see what her companions were talking about. Shapes moved on the surface of the Lesser Monad, and yes, they did look like faces – huge ones that emerged from the mist, then quickly submerged as others took their place. All of the faces shared one thing: their features were twisted into masks of fury, brows furrowed, eyes blazing with anger, mouths open as if they were screaming in rage, although no sound came out. Bolts of energy were now shooting off the Lesser Monad, and its tentacles thrashed the air so wildly they were little more than blurs. She thought she recognized some of the faces as belonging to those patients who had haunted her, the ones she'd failed to save. But she wasn't the only one to recognize the faces of the Lesser Monad.

"That's Delia!" Oliver said. "And Randall, and those faceless women!"

"And my father!" Faizan said. "And that one – isn't that...."

Julie recognized this latest face. After all, she'd last seen it only a short time ago.

"It's Jerome," she said. The next face belonged to a squalling baby. *Mari's daughter?* Julie wondered. Maybe. The faces continued alternating, switching so swiftly that it was hard to keep track of them.

"Please tell me we're close to Route 2," Oliver said. He looked forward, as if intending to gauge their progress, but then shouted, "Look out!"

Julie tore her gaze away from the rearview and saw a man standing in the middle of the road directly in front of them. She jammed her foot on the brake, and the Mercedes's tires shrieked in protest. She fought to keep the car from spinning out, but she feared that despite her efforts, they were either going to hit the man or roll the vehicle. But neither of these things happened. The Mercedes came to a stop less than three yards from where the man stood. He hadn't moved so much as an inch the entire time the car had been coming at him.

Now that they were close, Julie could see that the man was Brian. Her brother was in even worse shape than the last time she'd seen him. His flesh was a mottled gray, ragged and torn, his clothes little more than tattered shreds of cloth, his eyes dead and staring. Despite his appearance, Julie was thrilled by his arrival. He'd come to her aid before. Perhaps he was doing so again.

Faizan had continued keeping an eye on the Lesser Monad, and now he said, "It's still coming – fast."

Julie put the car in park, lowered the driver's-side window all the way down, and leaned her head out.

"Brian! Help us, please!"

Brian's dead gaze fixed on her as he started to walk forward.

You're mine, he said.

Julie remembered him saying the same thing in Oliver's basement, when he'd saved her from Delia. It had seemed slightly sinister then, but it was much more so now.

"I don't understand," she said.

Brian continued looking at her as he came closer.

Do you know what it was like being the firstborn in our family? The expectations Mother and Father had of me? The pressure they put on me to achieve? Nothing I ever did was good enough for them. Even when I was accepted to med school, it wasn't the best one, and while I graduated third in my class, it wasn't first. They never had such high expectations of you, though. You were the secondborn, and a girl, at that. All you had to do to gain their approval was be pretty and obedient and not fuck up too badly. You had it so goddamn easy! I hated you for that. And when the Homecoming began, I was determined to make sure no one else got to kill you but me. That's why I protected you — to keep you for myself. But time's run out, sis, and if I don't kill you now, I'll lose my chance. He had almost reached the Mercedes, and his gaze flicked to Faizan and Oliver. *And I'll kill your friends too, just for the hell of it — and there isn't a goddamn thing you can do to stop me.*

His mouth stretched into a wide grin, displaying broken, yellowed teeth.

Faizan was still looking through the back window.

"It's almost here!" he shouted.

Brian dashed toward Julie, hands held out, fingers curled like claws, face a mask of absolute hatred. Julie could only sit there and watch her brother come for her. The entire time she'd been growing up, she'd had no idea how her brother truly felt about her. He'd always treated her with love. But was it love that prompted his actions, or the responsibility their parents had put on him to be a 'good' brother? He might've harbored certain resentments when he'd been alive — what sibling doesn't? — but had he really hated her this much, or had his time as part of the Monad intensified his darker emotions, turning him into this vengeful creature intent on killing her? She supposed once she was dead and part of the Monad herself, she'd know.

"I'm sorry," she said as he came at her.

But when his hands were mere inches from her throat, one of the Lesser Monad's tentacles caught him around the waist and lifted him off the ground. She leaned farther out the window so she could see what was happening. The Lesser Monad, large as a three-story building now, had caught up to them and floated directly behind the Mercedes. The energy bolts surging across its form sizzled and cracked, filling the air with the acrid scent of ozone. Jerome's face was on its surface right now, and the tentacle held Brian in front of Jerome's eyes, as if the Lesser Monad wanted to examine him.

They are ours, the Lesser Monad said in Jerome's thought-voice. *As are you.*

Brian raised his hands to unleash a torrent of stingers at the Lesser Monad, but before he could, Jerome's mouth opened wide and the tentacle tossed Brian inside. Jerome's mouth snapped shut, he chewed for several seconds, then smiled.

Delicious.

It was Jerome's voice, but it boomed in the humans' minds like artillery fire, and they winced with each word he spoke.

Surprised to see me? You shouldn't be. A little thing like a plane crash and a resulting inferno can't do any lasting damage to a being like me. Slowed me down a little, I'll admit, but we're all together now, here at the end, and that's what counts.

Oliver was looking through the rear window now too, and Julie leaned over to put her arm around both him and Faizan. They might die in the next few moments, but she wanted to make sure none of them died alone.

Do you know what it was like for me? Jerome said. *I was still alive when the three of you drove off, if only barely. My perception of time was slowed to a crawl, each second seeming to last for days, weeks, months. For me, it took decades for the crash to happen, and I was in agony the entire time. Can you imagine what that does to a person's sanity?*

Jerome's face melted away and Karen's replaced it.

She gave them a cruel smile. *It was glorious.*

Jerome's face returned, his features rapidly obscuring hers, irritated that she'd wrested control of the Lesser Monad from him.

I'm going to kill you now, Julie. You were promised to me. You belong to me. And after you're dead, I will gather your spirit into me, and we will be together for all time. Doesn't that sound lovely?

Julie gritted her teeth. "I don't belong to anyone but myself. Not to Brian, and sure as shit not to you!"

It's adorable you believe that, Jerome said, and stretched a gray mist tentacle toward her.

Light flooded through the Mercedes's windshield. Julie, Oliver, and Faizan turned to see where it was coming from, and saw a glowing white orb the size of their car hovering in the air in front of them. The light was so intense that it was difficult to look at the thing, but then the illumination dimmed a bit, and they were able to see it better. Like the Lesser Monad, a series of faces manifested on its surface. Oliver's mother and father, her partner Nick, a woman she didn't recognize....

"That's my mom!" Faizan said.

Then there was another woman, one who looked like Karen, except her face was far kinder. Her face was followed by that of a younger woman who Julie thought resembled her. The woman's daughter, maybe? Then there was a man's face, and although Julie didn't know it, she sensed that this was Lewis, Mari's husband. And then his face gave way and Mari herself appeared. She smiled at the three of them, and they could feel warmth like that of a summer sun radiate from the orb.

Go, Mari said. *We kept ourselves apart for this moment, and we'll hold him off as long as we can.*

Her face receded into the orb, leaving its surface smooth and featureless once more. Then the glowing orb rose into the air and streaked toward the Lesser Monad. As it struck the giant mist ball, Jerome's psychic cry of pain and anger tore through their minds. The orb pressed against the Lesser Monad, as if trying to push it back, and the Lesser Monad's tentacles slapped at the orb, trying to get a purchase on its smooth surface and failing.

"We need to go," Oliver said.

"Yes, we do," Julie agreed.

She put the Mercedes in gear and hit the gas.

CHAPTER TWENTY-SEVEN

They soon reached Route 2, took it, and continued driving for the next thirty minutes. They were well outside of town now, surrounded by farmhouses and empty fields. Julie supposed those fields would remain empty come spring, and likely for every spring thereafter. Even if any of the farmers had survived to plant crops, who would buy their harvest? It was a nearly empty world now, and it was only going to get emptier.

Her head still throbbed like a motherfucker and eventually she needed to stop and rest. She pulled halfway into a ditch and parked the Mercedes. Before she turned off the engine, she checked the gas gauge. They had less than a quarter of a tank left. Despite the cold, they all got out to stretch their legs. Julie was dizzy and she leaned back against the car and closed her eyes.

"Would one of you mind driving for a while?" she asked. "My head's killing me."

"Sure," Faizan said. "I will."

They stood in silence for several moments, until Oliver said, "I've got to get back into the car. My feet are freezing!"

Julie had forgotten the boy didn't have any shoes – or pants, for that matter. They'd have to see about getting him some clothes somewhere. They needed food and water as well. And they could use a decent first aid kit.

She opened her eyes and did her best to smile. "Let's go."

They got back in the car, Faizan behind the wheel, Oliver next to him, Julie by the passenger window. What she really wanted to do was lie down in the back seat, close her eyes, and sleep for a couple weeks, but she didn't want to leave Oliver and Faizan alone right now, not after everything they'd been through.

Faizan turned on the car's engine, but he didn't put the vehicle in drive right away.

"What do you think happened to them?" he asked. "Our friends and family, I mean."

"I assume they were eventually absorbed into the Monad, like all the other spirits," Julie said. "But I don't really know."

"It gives me hope," Oliver said.

"What does?" Julie asked.

"That some of us remain good after we die. If there are enough good people within the Monad, maybe being part of it won't be so bad."

And what exactly constitutes 'enough'? Julie thought. She didn't say this aloud, though.

"There are other small Monads out there," Faizan said. "A lot of them. And they're going to join together and keep getting bigger. Eventually they'll find us. *All* of us."

Julie understood what he meant. The Homecoming might be over, but there were likely other survivors left. Maybe not a lot, but some. Faizan was suggesting that the Monad wouldn't stop harvesting souls until it had claimed every last human life on the planet. And then it would…what? Sit around and contemplate its own existence for eternity? She couldn't possibly guess what goals such a being might have, and even if she could somehow know, she didn't think she wanted to.

"Oliver, you said the Monad behaved like a human because it was made up of human spirits," Julie said.

"Yeah," Oliver confirmed.

"Then maybe the damn thing will get tired, decide it's done enough work for the time being, and wait for the rest of us to die on our own." Julie supposed this wasn't much in the way of comfort, but it was all she had to offer.

"Do you really think that will happen?" Oliver asked, a note of hope in his voice.

"After the day we've been through, I'd say anything was possible." Julie looked at Faizan. "Let's hit the road."

"Um, where are we going?" he asked.

"I have no idea," she admitted. "Just start driving. We'll figure out the rest as we go."

Faizan nodded. He put the car in drive, pulled onto the road, and the next leg of their journey began. They all knew where it would end – with their spirits absorbed by the Monad – but anything could happen between now and then. Anything at all.

ACKNOWLEDGEMENTS

Thanks to my amazing agent, the unstoppable Cherry Weiner, and thanks to editor extraordinaire Don D'Auria for his unwavering faith in my work all these years. Special thanks to Mariam Naeem, who read a draft of the manuscript and provided valuable feedback. Thanks also to Michael Valsted, Dan Coxon and Josie Karani for helping to give the book a final polish. And of course, thanks to my wife, Christine Avery. I couldn't do it without you, my love.

FLAME TREE PRESS
FICTION WITHOUT FRONTIERS
Award-Winning Authors & Original Voices

Flame Tree Press is the trade fiction imprint of Flame Tree
Publishing, focusing on excellent writing in horror and the
supernatural, crime and mystery, science fiction and fantasy.
Our aim is to explore beyond the boundaries of the everyday,
with tales from both award-winning authors and original voices.

•

Other titles available by Tim Waggoner:
The Mouth of the Dark
They Kill
The Forever House
Your Turn to Suffer

Other horror and suspense titles available include:
Snowball by Gregory Bastianelli
Thirteen Days by Sunset Beach by Ramsey Campbell
Think Yourself Lucky by Ramsey Campbell
The Hungry Moon by Ramsey Campbell
The Influence by Ramsey Campbell
The Wise Friend by Ramsey Campbell
The Haunting of Henderson Close by Catherine Cavendish
The Garden of Bewitchment by Catherine Cavendish
The House by the Cemetery by John Everson
The Devil's Equinox by John Everson
Hellrider by JG Faherty
The Toy Thief by D.W. Gillespie
One By One by D.W. Gillespie
Black Wings by Megan Hart
The Playing Card Killer by Russell James
The Sorrows by Jonathan Janz
Will Haunt You by Brian Kirk
We Are Monsters by Brian Kirk
Hearthstone Cottage by Frazer Lee
Those Who Came Before by J.H. Moncrieff
Stoker's Wilde by Steven Hopstaken & Melissa Prusi
Creature by Hunter Shea
Ghost Mine by Hunter Shea
Slash by Hunter Shea

•

Join our mailing list for free short stories, new release details,
news about our authors and special promotions:

flametreepress.com